CATCH A FALLING STAR

A BLINGWOOD BILLIONAIRES NOVEL

BOOK THREE

EMILY JAMES

ALSO BY EMILY JAMES:

The Blingwood Billionaires series

Book 1—Sorry. Not Sorry

Book 2 – Chasing the Wrong Bride

Book 3 – Catch a Falling Star

The Love in Short series

Book 1—Operation My Fake Girlfriend

Book 2—Sexy With Attitude Too

Book 3—You Only Love Once

Book 4—Leaving Out Love

The Power of Ten series

Book 1—Ten Dates

Book 2—Ten Dares

Book 3—Ten Lies

CHAPTER 1

JESSIE

*T*his was the part of parenting that really chapped my ass; waking up at the butt-crack of dawn to feed, wash, and dress a willful toddler—who just wants to sleep in like any other normal person—to race across town to day care and then huff it all the way back for another dazzlingly cheerful day at work.

If the mad dash to the bus stop on this particular day—which has me forgetting Macy's favorite stuffed animal—wasn't enough to send me into a spiral, then the canceled bus that cost me the last of my pay check on an Uber, very nearly sent me over the edge.

By the time we reach the squeaky, bright yellow gate that marks the entrance to Sunny Starts Day Care, little Macy is clinging to me, so I softly coo and kiss her temple as I remind her that Lisa is going to take really good care of her while Momma goes to work.

With her vivacious dark curls that are the exact same as

her father's, Macy couldn't look less like me. My almost white-blonde hair is down to my waist, thanks to a lack of time and money to get a trim—forget a style; those days are long gone.

Being a single mom at twenty-three isn't how I'd imagined my life would go, but I love my daughter fiercely and wouldn't change a thing. Our lives are a stark contrast to that of the baby daddy, a jet-setting, Hollywood superstar who'd rather party than be involved in his daughter's life. That bastard is probably sipping champagne for breakfast while I am about to start a ten-hour shift as a maid manager.

Last I heard Tate Blingwood had an entourage of personal assistants so big they have to travel on separate planes—which is unsurprising since his ego probably takes up most of the first plane.

Urgh. I HATE Tate Blingwood and I'm reminded just how much I hate him multiple times a day. He is literally *everywhere* I go. Okay, so not in the physical sense. He doesn't sully himself by showing up at the mini-mart or the little pancake place by the ocean that Macy loves. You wouldn't see him dead in a laundromat with a pile of puke-covered bedding and a half-asleep toddler, but still, he is every-damn-where—like on the bus sign that's advertising his latest movie. It only makes me feel marginally better that *someone* graffitied black teeth on his sickly smile and the slogan *Triptastic Tate* beneath the part where some reviewer called his latest pukefest the "hottest movie of the year."

Triptastic Tate.

I smirk.

I'm proud of his nickname. It came about after a member of the public captured him acting like a fool in a bar. He was juggling—probably drunk—and entertaining a bunch of people, when he slipped and took out an entire table of drinks. Then "someone" took that original video, trimmed it, edited it and BabyMomma4You posted it on social media. It went viral and racked up over six million views. Now, I'm not saying it was me who made that incredibly funny, viral meme—which would, after all, be a matter for the lawyers—but if it were proven to be me, I'd definitely deserve a high-five and a bottle of champagne for bringing that smug bastard down a peg or two.

At the door to the day-care center, Macy pins me with a stare that screams, don't you dare leave me here, and my heart starts to break. I distract her by letting her press the doorbell and Macy's smile lights up when the bell *ding dongs* seven times.

"Macy!" Lisa sings as she opens the door. "Where's happy Macy?" Then she makes a show of looking around and Macy's smile widens a fraction. "We're going to have so much fun today, aren't we, pumpkin?" She holds out her arms to take Macy from me, but I cling onto her a moment longer, wrapping her in an enormous hug and promising Momma will be back just as soon as she can.

I kiss Macy's pudgy cheeks three times before I release her into Lisa's waiting arms and am relieved when she nuzzles into her. "Bye-bye," she says and my chest starts to pull inward, crushing my heart a millimeter at a time. I wonder if leaving your kid at day care ever gets easier, but since Macy's been coming here for two years now, and the pain is still the same, I doubt it.

Moms have to go to work.

She's just the same as the other kids.

Macy's not suffering because I'm a young single mom.

It's the same stuff I tell myself every day. It's also the stuff that keeps me awake at night worrying. Am I giving her the best life I can? Sure, money is tight—so tight it's borderline strangulation. But Macy is loved. So damn loved.

And not to mention, I was raised by a single mother and I turned out okay.

I'm doing my best.

That's enough, isn't it?

I smooth Macy's curls away from her eyes and kiss the tip of her nose, then check my watch. I have exactly eleven minutes to dash across town before I need to start my shift as the newly promoted maid manager at the Blingwood Resort. And even though I will definitely be late, I give Macy one more kiss before I turn and get ready to sprint.

"Before you go," Lisa says, handing Macy to one of the other day-care workers and holding out her hand in a no-nonsense gesture designed to stop me.

"I'm in a hurry," I reply, focusing my attention on a loose thread on my pink maid shirt.

"It's about the outstanding fees."

"Outstanding fees? I'm up to date with all my payments," I insist.

"Have you received my emails?"

"Emails?" I check; I haven't had any emails from day care. "Let me double check later when I have more time. I've got to get to work, and paying day-care fees will be impossible if I get fired from my job," I add a little sarcastically, but it sounds strangled.

"The new admin girl made a mistake." Lisa shrugs like it's no big deal as she continues, "She's only been billing you for part-time, not full, and your balance is now over two thousand. You really need to check your email."

My stomach plummets into the soles of my shoes while Lisa has the audacity to laugh like a few thousand dollars is peanuts.

"We're going to need you to settle up ASAP. It'd be a shame for Macy to lose her spot here now that she's settled."

We both glance over to where Macy is pushing a toy stroller across the carpet and my heart melts.

"You're joking?" I say even though Lisa's expression has turned deadly serious. "I settle up in full and on time every month. How can this be happening?"

"An oversight. By you and us, it seems. How did you not notice that the monthly fee was half of what it should be?" Lisa's stare is accusatory and anger spikes up my back.

"The monthly fee is more than half my salary, so, no, it never feels too little," I bite back.

She switches tactics. "Having a child is expensive. Can't you ask the father for help?"

I'd rather die than go to that bastard for money.

"No, I can't ask the father. This is your mistake. Surely you can't expect—"

"Are you refusing to pay?" Lisa is now the no-nonsense owner of a business, not the sweet, lovable caretaker of children, whom she claims to adore. "If so, we can call the lawyer to start proceedings, but we much prefer things don't go that far…. Not to mention we'll be forced to give Macy's spot to the next child on the waiting list."

"This isn't fair! I thought I was paying the right amount. You can't revoke Macy's spot until I cough up a few thousand —which is your bookkeeper's fault. How am I supposed to work and pay back the balance without day care?"

She waits a beat, looks over at Macy who is giggling and toddling across the floor, holding hands with one of the day care ladies. "Look, since Macy is such a sweet girl, and we'd hate to lose her, I'll offer you a payment plan. The outstanding fees, repayable over six months. How does that sound?"

Like I'm about to barf.

Lisa grins like she's being generous by offering me the choice of food *or* diapers.

"Send me the details in writing," I call over my shoulder. "I have to get to work." And I'm running away from the scene of the crime before I can think too closely about where I'm going to find all this extra money.

When I make it to the bus stop and join the line of people, the bus driver tells me the vehicle is full and closes the doors.

Great!

This day cannot get any worse.

AT WORK, before I've even had the chance to get my morning coffee, I'm met with a series of problems. Two maids called in sick, so I have a bunch of staff to reroute to make sure the rooms still get serviced. Then one of our industrial washing machines breaks down and floods the laundry, so now I have a major shortage of towels and a heavy case of wishing it was my day off.

The day seems to swing from crap to shit and by 11 a.m., I am so dehydrated I take my water bottle to the bathroom and go hide for five minutes.

My phone, that I keep in the pouch of my apron in case there is a problem with Macy, buzzes with a notification and I sit on the toilet lid and take it out. Perspiration has my skin slick so I wipe my hands on the skirt of my entirely pink, ridiculous uniform, and swipe it to life only to be met by a headline from the celebrity gossip site I follow that reads: "Tate Blingwood: naked capers." I skim the article that explains how my one-time lover, forever shirking bastard baby daddy, and Hollywood heartthrob got caught yesterday running naked through LA. The comments are wild, from people swearing his schlong broke the Guinness record for thickest and longest penis ever, to others who are convinced they can see his ballsack if you pause the video at just the right moment. I pause the video where they say but they're full of shit. There's a nice view of his perky ass but no swinging ballsack action. And his penis? Yeah, it's thick and long and potentially a record breaker, but his personality? Small, shallow, and pathetic.

Tate Blingwood.

I sigh.

It was supposed to be one sex-filled night of no-strings action. My body flushes and heat fills me as I remember just how lust-fueled our encounter was. I was on spring break. Hot and horny and faced with the most beautiful-looking man I had ever laid eyes on.

Tate wasn't nearly as famous back then, just a guy trying to get his really big break and I liked that about him. He was humble, unsure of himself. A tryer. Down to earth and funny. He'd told me about the movie work he'd done to date, but he was waiting for that really big hit to push him to the next level of his career. We'd talked all day and night about our hopes and dreams, his wanting to secure the lead spot in the drama he auditioned for and me wanting to finish up my degree and get a job working as an ad exec. But the next morning, after what I thought was the beginning of my forever with this incredible man, he was gone, and all that remained was a note on his pillow telling me "thanks for an unforgettable night... give me a call" and a hundred bucks on the nightstand.

I saw red.

I threw his number in the trash. There was no way I was going to chase down a man who couldn't be bothered to wait around and kiss me good morning, and who thought so little of me that he left money after we'd spent the night together. That was a punch to the gut, considering we'd spent the entire day together and had—what I thought—was an unde-niable and immediate connection. It wasn't until a month and two little lines later on a pregnancy stick, I wished I'd kept that number. That was three years ago but it feels like yesterday.

Unforgettable!

What a joke.

Tate Blingwood breaks the internet on a daily basis. He's pictured on the covers of magazines, often with runway models and movie stars from London to New York. He's rich and entitled, spoiled and selfish. There are always reports in the media that he spent fifty grand on a dinner, ten on a bottle of fancy champagne, a few million on a penthouse and then another couple because he decided he wanted the one beside it. Okay so he does some stuff for charity. He rebuilt a homeless shelter with his brother after it was destroyed by wild fires, and most recently he was part of a clean-up diving crew picking up litter from the ocean to save the turtles, but I bet he just does that stuff as a PR stunt.

Fame turned Tate Blingwood into an egotistical, big-headed bastard who is too high and mighty to meet and take care of his own daughter. He's probably got a trail of baby-mommas and kids all chasing him like he's the Pied Piper of LA.

Not that I care.

Macy and I don't need a douchebag in our lives.

We. Are. Fine. On. Our. Own.

"Jessie, you in here?" I hear Skyla call.

"Yep, coming!" I slide my phone back into my apron and push the flush lever, then I walk out into the staff bathroom and wash my hands.

"I had an emergency job come in and you're the only person who can deal with it," Skyla says apologetically.

"What is it?" I ask cautiously. As the head of housekeep-ing, there are plenty of tasks that apparently only *I* can deal with, and not all of them are glamorous. Like when a guest left a particularly large present in the toilet and no one could make it flush—it took me almost twenty minutes to saw that damn thing up.

"Logan called," she starts and I smile. Logan is my boss. His assistant Layla texted me yesterday to say that he flew to her mother's house in Oregon, got down on one knee and proposed. Of course, I knew those two were falling in love way before they did, and I was thrilled to hear they're making things official and getting married. They're currently at his lake house getting reacquainted. "He and Layla are going to be gone at least a week on business." She winks filthily and we both know there's not going to be any business getting done unless it is of the naked variety. "But there's a task that Logan says he only trusts you with."

"Oh?" I grin. It's nice that my boss trusts me with his most important tasks and not just the shit ones. It makes me feel valued. I love my job here. Long ago, I'd had dreams of finishing college and getting my media degree, but then I had Macy and became a single mom and fate threw me a different hand—not that I'd change any of it. My life has turned out fine, even if Tate Blingwood left me knocked-up and then went on to become an international movie star.

"It's Tate Blingwood," she announces and I feel the contents of my stomach turn watery. "He's here."

"Here? What is he doing here? How did he find me? What does he want?" I sound stricken. I'm on the brink of throwing up, fainting and having a hissy fit.

"He's here because of the media storm. He was videoed naked running through town and it blew up the internet. Now there are reports that Dinky, the world's biggest family entertainment and media company, is dropping him from a franchise movie deal he's scheduled to shoot. He could wind up penniless and washed up." Skyla stops talking and examines my expression curiously. "Are you okay?"

"What? I'm fine. Of course, he's not here for me." I laugh loudly and try to breathe. Why would he be here looking for the baby momma his people accused of being a stalker? No, he denied all knowledge of me and doesn't know I work here —which is probably a good thing since he'd probably have me fired. "So, why's he here? I mean, I know his brother owns this place and no one is going to turn down a free room at a fancy hotel, but his mother lives close by. Why would he stay here at the resort, and what's that got to do with me, anyway? Nothing, if you ask me." I finally stop speaking to take a breath, but the room feels like it's shrinking so fast the walls are going to asphyxiate me.

"There's a ton of paparazzi at his mom's. They are at mine and Drew's place too. Drew told them he's in Alaska, and his PR person is backing up that claim by tagging him at a retreat there but they're a suspicious bunch, and they're looking for the money shot of him. Apparently, there's a finder's fee to rat Tate out so the press can get the first scoop on whether Dinky has dropped him from the franchise, which would be catastrophic for Tate's career. He's sched- uled to shoot three movies, and Drew says once one produc- tion company drops you, others will too. There are people walking the streets of LA as we speak looking for a naked Tate. It's insane how bloodthirsty and crazy people are for him. Anyway, the media want the scoop on why he was naked running through town and he's here, laying low until the fuss dies down."

"He's here," I repeat, unable to process all that she just told me. "Tate Blingwood is here… in the hotel?"

"Yep. He's in Penthouse 2. But no one can know except you and me. Logan said to warn you not to let the other maids go into that penthouse. This place will fill up with journalists and paparazzi if they find out he's here and well, we still have a resort to run. Logan wants you to go and introduce yourself to Tate and bring him anything he wants. For the next two weeks at least, you are his personal maid— no task is too small. He's the boss's brother after all."

"Me?" My tone is strangled. "Oh no. He doesn't want me. What about you?" I ask, clutching at straws.

Skyla's brows crinkle and she chuckles. "What use is the HR manager to him?"

"Oh. Yeah. I see. Okay, so not you. What about Sally?"

Skyla looks at me as if I've gone half crazy. "Umm, she's a receptionist and the biggest gossip in the resort?!"

"Hannah, then? I'll ask Hannah to stop throwing up at once and come in to look after him. He'll be in good hands," I say.

Skyla's hand lands on mine and she studies me carefully. "Logan asked for *you*. You're the only person he trusts not to sell his brother out. The tabloids are offering a ton of money for his whereabouts. That's why no one can know. Tate's PR people are trying to smooth things over with Dinky Media Corp but he's a grown-ass adult, naked, and on the screen of every phone in America. Even as hot as he is, his reputation is getting ruined. He could lose every- thing he's worked for. We have to help him. Logan said he'll give you a thousand-dollar bonus if you take care of him."

"A thousand bucks?!" My eyes light up. It could pay some of my outstanding day care expenses. Still, I'm reluctant. When I found out I was pregnant, I reached out to his people. I sent emails, I made phone calls, I even reached out through the Tate Blingwood Official Fan Club and they made out like I was some deluded fan and threatened me with a restraining order. It was the most humiliating experience of my entire life and I've never told a soul about it. Nearly three years later, I bet Tate Blingwood doesn't even remember the girl from spring break who beat him in a mud-wrestling competition, much less the multiple phone calls to let him know of his prodigy.

"Fine, I'll do it," I huff. "But he better not give me any shit. I'm not pandering to a stuck-up star. That bastard is already skating on thin ice."

"That's my girl!" Skyla sings then laughs at my reaction. "What's he done to piss you off, anyway? Tate's really nice when you get to know him."

I swish cold water onto my wrists and feign indifference. "You have to say that since he's your brother-in-law." I don't mean to roll my eyes but I can't help it. Skyla is normally a good judge of character, but falling in love with Tate's eldest brother has definitely clouded her judgment of *Triptastic Tate*. "He's fake. His whole online demeanor is false: clearing ocean waste in the Maldives and then flashing his ass around town. It's disgusting. What sort of role model is he anyway!" I hiss.

All these years later and I'm still furious with him. But if Tate Blingwood doesn't want to be a father to the most amazing child on earth, then screw him. I'll put up with him for a thousand bucks and then he can fuck off back to LaLa land and leave me and Macy the hell alone.

CHAPTER 2

TATE

"*T*ripod are saying the naked video of you is still trending and people are more interested in your naked butt than they are in the movie you just shot. Also, the merchandise sales through your fan club have dropped 50% —apparently people don't want to buy T-shirts with pictures of your face when they can look at your ass for free," Gaynor, my PR manager, says from one side of the three-way Zoom call.

Tripod is the production company for the movie I just finished filming. They're a small, independent film company, who cast me to elevate their reputation—so it's little wonder they are annoyed that my latest incident has tanked their advertising endeavors.

"They're unlikely to cast you again if this negative press keeps up," Jason, my agent, says. "I'm sorry, Tate, but this is bad. There's no sugarcoating it. You were on the cusp of signing a lucrative franchise deal with Dinky, the biggest family media corporation in the world. They haven't confirmed it yet, but there's talk about them dropping you. That deal alone is worth seventy million. Tell me again, how did you find yourself naked on the streets of LA?" Jason hisses, pissed that his 15 percent is at risk.

I throw my hands up, angry that I'm having to defend myself. "One minute I'm having a drink while I get changed for the promo photoshoot, the next, some asshole has whipped away my clothes, shoved me out the back door of the studio and locked it. Twenty paps were waiting and chasing me down the street. This isn't my fault!" I fume. Some fucker must have staged all of this to make a quick buck.

"Maybe if you weren't drinking at 2 p.m. on a Tuesday, then you would have been more aware of what was going on!" Jason says and my gut twists. He's old enough to be my father and admonishes me like one too—if he hadn't been with me since the start of my fame, and one of the few people who hasn't sold me out, then I'd fire his ass. But as it stands, Jason is one of only a handful of people whom I can trust and I need him on my side, so I try to explain my latest fuck-up with as much calmness as I can muster.

"Jason, you know I hate photoshoots. I drink because they're so goddamned boring. All the waiting around and assistants fawning over me. You know I hate that part of the business and a small drink helps calm my nerves." Okay, so it was several small drinks that the team kept pouring for me, but in my defense, I never drink on movie sets. I love acting but being a "star" has turned out to be a lot harder than I thought it'd be. When I'm getting interviewed and photographed, sometimes the impostor syndrome over-whelms me and anxiety has me saying and doing stupid shit that always bites me in the ass later. A slug of vodka here and there helps take the edge off.

Jason's face screws up like he's both unimpressed with my excuses and watching his cut of my income shrink in real time. "If Dinky drops you from the franchise, every director and casting exec. in Hollywood are going to start wondering if you're old news. People will think your career is on a downward trajectory when you've only just got to the top the past two years! We have to save the Dinky deal—"

Gaynor interrupts Jason. "Screw Dinky! We'll take Tate elsewhere. There's been speculation of deals for a show on YouTube—"

"What?! You cannot be serious—"

"His online presence needs to increase—"

"Both of you. Stop! Just stop," I hiss. "My cell is lit up with comments from people who swear they can see my ballsack. The trolls are having a fucking party at my expense and I want to know who took my fucking clothes from the photo-shoot and tipped off the paparazzi that I'd be standing there naked! Those fuckers chased me through LA. I had to hide behind a dumpster!"

Jason and Gaynor stop quarreling long enough to stare at me through the screen and I begin to think I'm getting some-where. "This could end my career."

Gaynor shakes her head. "It'll blow over. We'll get you handing out candy in Walmart. The kids will lap it up—"

"It'll take more than a cheap PR stunt," Jason interrupts.

"I don't get it. You guys are supposed to handle this stuff. Jason, where was my security detail?"

Jason holds his head in his hands then says, "Tate, you told them all to take the day off." He sighs and gives me a look of sheer disappointment through the screen of my phone. "I can't be with you every minute of the day—"

Knowing I've disappointed one of the people I look up to hits me like a fist.

"How do I fix it?"

Gaynor's finger taps her chin. "We've got to clean up your image. Dinky serves the family market. Getting wasted and naked might send the music business into a frenzy but it does more harm than good in the movie biz. You need to be seen as honest, decent and reliable. A role model. Someone kids look up to, fathers want to emulate, and mothers want to marry."

"I have to appeal to everyone. No pressure then?" I joke.

Gaynor nods. "A company like Dinky wants America's next dear little sweetheart. With the right image correction, we could pull this back. Cut back on the drinking and behave in a wholesome manner."

Jason frowns like he knows this won't be easy for me. "Just for a while until the Dinky deal is signed. Right now, you look like a spoiled playboy. You're out at parties, and that video of you juggling and crashing into a table full of drinks is still going viral…. If you want the Dinky deal, you've got to work hard to repair your image."

He may have a point. Lately my online presence is mostly me acting like a fool because I love to make people laugh. But it's overshadowing the honest-to-god passion in my life which is acting. My image probably could use an adjustment but I resent being called a playboy. I haven't played around since… since that night during spring break when I got roped into mud wrestling the hottest woman I have ever laid eyes on.

It's been three years, but that time with Jessie will stay with me my whole life. I still wonder if I hadn't had to rush off the next morning, if things might have been different. That morning when I woke, I had no less than thirty texts from Jason the day before. I was too wrapped up in Jessie to even pay attention to my phone. But the moment I opened my phone and saw I'd landed the part and it was mine for the taking, I'd hauled ass to the studio and signed the contract for my very first lead role. It was the perfect movie and exactly the right role that catapulted me to fame and stardom. My life has been a whirlwind ever since. I'd left her a note with my phone number and a hundred bucks on the nightstand to pay for the room, but she never called.

One night when I visited Drew in New York, I'd been waxing on about that day with her and how real it'd felt. While my fame is incredible, it's the one aspect Hollywood seems to lack—being real. Drew teased me about looking for her and posting for a missing Jessie on social media; he said she's probably kicking herself for never calling. I thought about doing it, but it came down to this: if she didn't want me when I was just a working actor, a nobody, then if she showed up now it'd be just for my money and fame. Not to mention the hordes of women who would respond to a plea like that. I'd be inundated with crazies and look like a desperate loser.

No. Jessie from spring break was a fun transgression but there's no way I could trust her now. Not when 80 percent of the people I meet try to sell me out.

Not worth the risk.

Gaynor pulls out her tablet in front of my screen and begins tapping. "A steady relationship would help you appear more wholesome. Romantic dinners, walks along the beach. We could set up some paps to chance upon you at the movies… doing normal things like a normal person. It'd help you appear relatable."

"Hey—I am relatable!"

Jason stares at me boldly. "Tate, I'm sorry to give you this reality check, but a ten grand bottle of champagne on a Tuesday afternoon does not make you even close to relatable."

Maybe I do need to dial my drinking back. But a relationship? That sounds way too risky.

17

"I don't like the sound of this, Jason," I complain.

"It may not be what you want, but it could be what you need. You stand to lose seventy million dollars and end your career if this deal falls through."

"You're making me feel like a prostitute."

"Everyone in this business is selling something, Tate. And right now, your job is to sell your charm to the masses by appearing to be just like them. I'm sure there'll be plenty of women up for the job. A model or reality star, perhaps?"

"There must be another way."

"Not that I can think of. If Dinky drops you from the franchise and Tripod decide they're no longer casting you, the work will dry up. You'll end up shooting yogurt commercials in Montana. Is that really a risk you want to take? It's certainly not going to afford the lifestyle you've suddenly grown accustomed to. Private planes, luxury resorts, multiple personal assistants... shall I continue?" Jason's sporting a devious smile like he knows he's got me by the balls.

"Then you won't get your 15 percent," I shoot back, even though getting dropped from Dinky would break me. While I've enjoyed the lifestyle, at the heart of it, all I have ever wanted to do is act. When I feel like I'm not enough, when I feel uncomfortable in my own skin, acting has been my escape to and from myself. But would I be happy on a stage in a nothing town, performing in front of twenty people after feeling the level of success I've gotten used to? I doubt it.

"Tate, you can have everything. A fake relationship is just another role. You're an actor. Act," he tells me.

"I'll clean up my image, lay low for a bit at my brother's resort, just like you want, but I am not pretending to be in love. I draw the line at fucking with people's feelings."

"You don't have to fuck with people's feelings. I'll look out for someone trustworthy who wants in on the pretense. You won't even have to kiss her. Just give your custom wink—and the paps and the public will eat that shit up," Jason says, like it's that easy. And I suppose it is easy, *for him*. He's not the one pretending to have a fake girlfriend!

"I'll think it over. When will my assistant get here? I'm starving," I say, deliberately changing the subject.

"I've given your team the next two weeks off—you won't need them at your brother's resort. They'll be on standby for the premiere of the Tripod movie. For now, lay low, eat room service, and for God's sake, don't do anything else to draw attention to yourself until we can figure this mess out. Baby-Momma4You already posted a comeback meme to the naked run through town. I'm sending it to you now."

BabyMomma4You has become my online nemesis. She or he is always there, waiting in the wings ready to rip into me. Some of the stuff she comes up with is pretty funny—even though it irks the shit out of me. The photoshopped images and quick remarks have become both the annoyance and sometimes highlight of my day. I can't reply or comment, my PR manager has me firmly on lockdown when it comes to responding to trolls—it does more harm than good, she tells me. But boy, would I like to give them a piece of my mind.

My phone instantly alights with a text and I click the link Jason sent. In record time, BabyMomma4You has created a reinvented edition of my paparazzi video, but in it I'm wearing a diaper and there's a caption beneath it asking, "Will Tate Blingwood ever grow up?"

"He's trying," I mutter to no one in particular.

"Take no notice," Jason says, shaking his head. "It's just another crazy fan, like the hundreds of crazy fans we deal with for you on a day-to-day basis. Honestly, the claims the team are handling get more elaborate by the week—everything from you promised to pay a woman's college tuition if she sent you intimate photos, to women claiming they're having your babies. Last week I had a woman from Denver send in court documents for alimony—she provided actual proof that you and she were married—"

"Actual proof?" I question, knowing there's no way I married any woman—no matter how drunk I was. Ever.

"Oh, her proof was indisputable." Jason chuckles and his mood lightens. "A marriage license tattooed on her thigh clearly citing your name and hers. She's legally changed her name to Blingwood and sent us the papers and the photographs of her leg to prove it."

I can't even bring myself to laugh. The lengths some people will go to freaks me the fuck out.

"You're a man in demand," Jason adds. "You have at least three kids a week getting born. There's even a fan site where people vote whose kid looks the most like you," Jason laughs.

I guess it's funny, when it's not happening to you.

"But you need a family image. Moving forward, if it's not clean and wholesome, we swerve it. We can't afford to lose the Dinky deal. Got it?"

I nod.

"Let's reconvene in a few days. Meanwhile, Gaynor can schedule some positive publicity leading up to the premiere of the Galactic Futures movie. How do you feel about donating to the shelter? We can spin it as a random act of kindness—that you gave your Louis Vuitton suit and Calvin Kleins to a homeless guy. In fact, I'll send one of our assistants downtown and find a guy who'll go on record and say as much."

I have no choice but to go along with the plan. At least this way, a homeless guy might have the money to make a down payment on a rental or buy a hotel room for a few months. Anything that will make this go away and outshine the interest of my naked butt on social media so my mother and niece aren't constantly reminded of it sounds like a bargain.

"Trust me and do as I say, and all this negative press will go away and you'll be back in favor," Gaynor promises.

"I'll scout for a woman you can date and liaise with the director at Dinky," Jason says. "They've already started hyping you as the lead for the franchise so they'd be chucking a ton of money away recasting it now. We might still manage to save this, if you don't do anything else to fuck this up!"

"Cool," I reply and end the call. But it's not cool. I'm stuck in a penthouse prison for two weeks while all this goes on. Okay, so it's a very nice prison with a big screen TV and a view of the ocean but it still sucks.

I flip on the TV and scroll some channels but I only seem to find the ones that are covering my story. They've also picked up on a trending video by BabyMomma4You who posted a feature by a reporter on the street showing my butt, but she's cut out their real comments and switched them with stock footage of old ladies commenting stuff like, "that boy won't ever grow up," and "known him since he was in diapers and he's always been trouble." The way they've cut the clips and staged the voice-overs would be pretty funny— if I wasn't the butt of the joke.

I switch off the TV and pick up the room service menu. I haven't eaten since yesterday and so I call down to order. "A burger, two turkey sandwiches and a large fries for Penthouse 2, please."

The person on the receiving end huffs throatily, sounding royally pissed off. I guess it is quite a lot of food but since I won't be leaving this room, I decide to enjoy the perks. "Anything else, your majesty?"

I wonder if Logan told whoever it is that answered that there's top secret royalty in the penthouse, and so I let her comment slide. Logan assured me that no one would spill that I'm here. He's arranged for the maid manager he trusts to bring me whatever I need but he's warned me she only works from 8 until 6. Mom and Drew will take care of anything I need outside those hours. I trust Logan completely so if he says this maid manager will take care of me, I don't doubt that she'll be the best person for the job.

"Have you got any cheesecake? Ice cream? Oh, and if you could find me some of those little chocolate-covered peanuts, that'd be great," I reply. Now I've decided I'm hungry, I'm famished.

"A burger, two turkey sandwiches, large fries, cheesecake, ice cream, and some of those little chocolate-covered peanuts. Would you like me to get the doctor on standby for your pending cardiac arrest, too?" The woman, probably in her twenties, hisses and I smile at the sound of her voice. I don't know who the hell put a stick up her ass today but I try to keep my reply polite.

"Nope. Just the food." I imagine the expression on her face when she delivers my food and sees it's *the* Tate Bling-wood that she's feeding and I smile. She'll regret being so pissy with me then—not that I'd sleep with a fan. At least I haven't once yet in the three years I've been famous. An image of the woman from spring break pops into my head, covered in mud and so determined to beat me that I almost let her… and then she beat me fair and square by pinning my arm behind my back and sticking my face in a puddle and, just like that, I was a goner. She was the girl for me.

I often wonder if I hadn't got the call to say that I'd been cast as the lead in the movie that shot me to fame the morning after the hottest night of my life, if things might have worked out between me and her.

Who am I kidding?

Apart from my immediate friends and family, I can't trust people.

Pretty much everyone has sold a story on me. From my mother's neighbor, to my high school sweethearts. Even the janitor from my gym sold a story on how much weight I lift. People see a quick buck and they take it, no matter the cost. Even if all the stories have been sensationalized lies.

No, I wouldn't have been able to trust the woman from spring break. The price of fame and the career I love is isolation and loneliness, and I need to get used to it.

The woman from room service tells me I'll get the food once she's got time because, "You're not the only guest here," and then she hangs up, so I hit the mini bar. It's been a helluva week and I need to kick back and relax.

CHAPTER 3

JESSIE

"*I*f Penthouse 2 rings that damn bell for service one more time, I swear I'm going to—" I fume, but then smirk as I imagine Tate up in the penthouse two hours after he placed his order for half the menu. He'll be getting dizzy with fury by now. I bet he's so hungry, he's seeing stars in front of his eyes.

I nearly laugh.

"Jessie, that food's sitting on the counter going cold, are you ever going to take it up?" the head chef, Fernando, asks as he brushes past me carrying a bowl of tomatoes. I reach out and take one, then sit on the counter, staring at Tate's food as it spoils on the heating plate.

"Oh, he said he doesn't want it yet," I say, innocently. "He told me he likes it cold and stale like his heart."

Fernando looks at me like I'm a little crazy but begins chopping the tomatoes at the speed of light. He's in his late fifties and moves about the kitchen with flair like a salsa dancer in the international finals with salad as his partner.

The room service line rings again and I answer since I'm doing nothing.

"Hey, I know you're probably really busy down there. It's peak season and you guys all work really hard, but I ordered some lunch quite a while ago. Will it be here soon? I'm in Penthouse 2." His voice is soft like velvet and it takes me right back to that night. All he had to do was smile and I was putty in his hands. Of course, I've learned a lesson or two since then so I am immune to such flattery.

"I already said it was coming," I bite back, hoping he doesn't tell Logan I'm being a bitch but also not managing to dig deep enough to find kindness for the guy who ditched a pregnant and scared young woman like she was nothing.

"I know, I know," he says then hiccups. "It's just, I'm on my third whiskey and I should probably eat. What's your name, anyway?"

My heart comes to a complete stop. That's the exact line he used on me when I had him face down in the mud with his arm pulled up tight behind his back in our wrestling match. He smiled up at me, all pearly white teeth and cute-as-fuck dimples and said, "I guess I can't lie and say I let you win. What's your name, anyway?" And I gave him my name and blushed like I was his number one fan, even though he wasn't even famous yet.

"My name is maid," I grit. "I'm bringing your food. It won't be long. Perhaps you should hold your breath."

"Oh, thanks um maid. I'll see you in a minute, then?" he replies, sounding confused by my lack of formalities.

"Yeah, you will," I reply and hang up. *Right after I've done my laundry.*

* * *

25

I TAKE my time washing my and Macy's laundry during my break. I have my lunch in the staff cafeteria and then I sit on the bench outside the penthouse and eat chocolate-covered nuts while I stare up at the balcony of Penthouse 2.

That's when I set eyes on him for the first time.

Tate Blingwood looks every bit as good as the man on the billboards. He keeps his head down to hide his identity and his dark curls fan across his face when the wind hits them from exactly the right angle. He's staring at his phone and I blush as I remember that night. Fast and frantic at first, then sensual like we were savoring every part of it. He told me he was waiting to find out if he'd been cast for his first lead role in a movie that was set to make his career.

Tossing his number in the trash the next morning because I was a little hungover and my feelings were a lot hurt was the right thing to do. The papers reported that he moved on pretty darn quickly—he's been pictured with more than a dozen women since our night together. There are always rumors circulating about who he is dating and it changes every week.

Not that I care.

Tate Blingwood is a dirty dog and Macy and I are better off without him.

I stand and dust chocolate crumbs from my pink maid uniform and prepare to go face him. Trepidation—not how he looks as he sways as he watches the ocean—has my knees weakening. The sun hits the highlights in his dark hair and he sips whiskey from a glass that probably costs more than my entire year's salary.

We're so different, yet we made something so perfect.

Macy.

She's incredible. And she deserves a father who worships her.

Tate stumbles a little as he turns to head back inside and I pull myself up straight. He doesn't want her and we don't want him.

Look at him, day drinking from the balcony of his brother's penthouse. Laying low like a coward. It was probably a good thing he didn't want us; Macy doesn't need an asshole father in her life. It's just so surprising because his family is so good, kindhearted people with care and compassion. Tate may have been those things when I met him, but once fame hit, he's certainly unrecognizable to the man I thought I'd instantly known. But then again, it was only a day, and my luck in having decent men in my life is zilch.

I march into the kitchen, grab Tate's spoiled lunch—pulling out the turkey and leaving him with a few salad leaves in between the now hardening bread—and then I march up to that son of a bitch's penthouse, ready to give him a piece of my mind if he so much as blinks at me the wrong way.

But when I walk inside the expanse of the penthouse, with its marble floors and open-plan living and kitchen area, he's not there. Only the scent of expensive whiskey and deep, dark musky cologne hangs in the air.

I drop the plate on the counter and investigate further. A hotel jacket is thrown over a chair. The bifold doors that open up to the balcony are still wide open and a gentle ocean breeze chills my arms. The TV remotes are strewn on the coffee table, not in their usual holders. He's only been here a few hours and already the place is untidy.

The maid in me wants to set to putting this place back together, but I pause when I see him lying on the sofa, still fully dressed with shoes on. An empty glass is sideways on his lap. The buttons on his shirt are mismatched and he has a three-day stubble on his handsome face as he peacefully snuffles, fast asleep. He's gorgeous, even with a face that looks exhausted with his mouth wide open.

I take longer to admire him than I approve of. I hate this man. He let Macy down. He let me down. We deserved better. He and his people treated us worse than dirt. I screw my face up as I take in all the luxury around him. Then I check my watch. It's not long until I finish my shift and I have to get the bus to collect Macy, who will be exhausted after an eleven-hour day at day care.

Life could have been better. Easier. If we had two wages, she could spend more time with me. If she had a father who paid his way, she could have brand new clothes and not hand-me downs. Macy's never had a vacation and she thinks the bus is fun; little does she understand it's because we can't afford a car. Whereas Tate Blingwood's life is so damn comfortable.

The idea is a lightning bolt and just as dangerous.

Perhaps karma demands I make his life a little *less* comfortable.

Maybe my plan will even make me feel *so much* better.

Driven by impulse and annoyance, I set to work. Once I'm done making him less comfortable, I skip out the door, leaving him sleeping, and my smile carries me all the way across town on the bus.

They say revenge is a dish best served cold, but I prefer it freezing.

CHAPTER 4

TATE

I shiver and reach for the comforter that was artfully draped on the sofa when I closed my eyes but it's not there. Goosebumps prickle my arms. It's freezing, and if I didn't know I was in Santa Barbara, California at my brother's luxury resort, then I'd swear I was in an igloo somewhere in Antarctica.

The sky outside is pitch black and I stretch and blink a few times until my eyes adjust to the scarcity of light. The air conditioning is blasting out on full power. It seems to believe it's powering one of those walk-in freezers you get in commercial kitchens. In fact, as soon as I register how cold it is, my body reacts and uncontrollable shivers rack through my body and my teeth start to chatter. I'm so cold even the pit of my stomach feels frozen, which reminds me of my late lunch order. Scanning the dimly lit room, I see a loaded tray of food on the counter and I figure the maid must have brought it in while I was sleeping, so I get up to go switch the air off—guessing it wasn't reset after the last guest set it to some kind of ice therapy timer—and get my food. I take one step before my leg abruptly stops, and I topple forward.

The coffee table that I swear was there earlier is now across the room next to the door, and time slows as I freefall while desperately flailing my arms in a futile attempt to regain my balance. My stomach lurches and a strangled sound forces its way past my lips as I careen toward the floor and face plant the ornamental rug.

"Fuck!" I hiss, even though I am alone. "That hurt!"

I'm probably going to have a fucking carpet burn on my cheek and my temple pounds like a mother— "What the fuck?" When I try to stand, my feet barely move, like they're tied together. I look down to inspect what the hell is going on, assuming I'm still asleep and my dream has warped into a nightmare—which, after the shitshow of the last few days could be my subconscious reacting—but when I look at my feet, a deep sense of shock falls over me.

My laces are tied together.

They're not just tied, they're in some kind of specialist army knot that won't come undone no matter how much I wrestle with the lace with my now frozen fingers. It's so fucking tight I have to get up and hop to the kitchen to cut the fuckers off.

Once I've finished my escape-artist routine, I switch on the lights and turn the air conditioner off, hoping the feeling in my fingers returns.

I was pissed after my conversation with Jason and Gaynor, and definitely feeling the effects of the whiskey I drank before I passed out with hunger, but I wasn't suicidal enough to tie my own damn laces together.

"This is fucked up," I say and look around the place, wondering if some crazy fan has gotten in and is going to drug and torture me like that chick did in that Stephen King film. I look around and thoroughly check the suite, even go so far as to check under the bed but I'm definitely alone.

It's so rare to be this alone that I even ponder what might have happened if I hit my head. If I died here, my mom and my siblings would be the only ones upset at my funeral. Sure, the newspapers would cover it, and perhaps a few fans might cry, Jason might even take a month to find his next big client, but I have no one to truly mourn me.

It's a sobering thought that I shake away by focusing on who was trying to kill me in the first place. First someone takes my clothes, forcing me to sprint across town naked, and now, someone is getting into my hotel room.

No one is supposed to know I'm in here apart from my immediate family, including Skyla, Drew's wife and Layla, Logan's new fiancée. I wouldn't put it past one of my brothers to pull this shit but I wasn't expecting to see Drew until tonight and Logan is out of town with Layla. Hell, maybe one of them came up here, found me asleep and fucked with me. I wouldn't put it past them.

I list who else knows I'm here: my agent, Jason; my PR woman, Gaynor; the maid Logan put in charge of my care, and—right as I think of her, the doors to the elevator that open directly into the penthouse whoosh and there she stands.

"Mom!"

"Tatey, baby! I brought you some clothes," she says walking right in and dropping one of my old high school backpacks on the floor. She's also carrying a pooch in her purse draped over her shoulder. Since my mom opened a rescue center, she's always got a dog with her.

Mom's wearing sweats and one of her signature slogan T Shirt's that reads: *I woof you.* Her white, curly hair has escaped from the hair tie and she looks like she's windswept from rushing all the way over here. "What have you done to

31

your face?" She's in front of me in a nanosecond, stroking my red cheek that stings like a bitch. Then she looks down. "Why don't you have any laces in your shoes?" Her face becomes pained by concern. "Baby, things aren't so bad…" Her lips tremble and I shake my head.

"I wasn't about to turn them into a noose, Mom. Either Drew or Logan were in here while I was sleeping and the fuckers tied my laces together."

Mom hides her relieved smile beneath her hand and replies, "It must have been Drew. Logan is with Layla at the lake house. They just announced their engagement!" Her smile widens and her voice goes up by at least twenty octaves as she sings the words. Her happiness at this revelation is unsurprising; my mother is a romantic fool who thinks love alone powers the world to orbit the sun. And, judging by the way her smile slips as she refocuses her thoughts on me, she's not impressed by the mere star before her. "But let's deal with you. CNN is speculating your career is over because Dinky doesn't want a drunk, naked fool at the helm of their latest franchise. What are we going to do with you, Tatey?"

"Mom, stop calling me that. I'm a thirty-year old grown-ass man!"

"I spent fifteen hours pushing you out of my hoo-ha, I earned the right to call you whatever the hell I want. And quit your cussing, you've got an image to revive." She shakes her head and I find myself nodding. "Now, have you eaten? You don't look like you have? And why is it so cold in here?" She reaches into her purse and grabs the dog, wrapping it in her sweater to keep it warm. "You're both going to catch colds at this rate."

"I've got a sandwich and some food over there." I thumb toward the food even though it's probably partially frozen. "I'll probably order a pizza."

Mom stares at me pointedly. "You can't order in. No one

can know you're here. Logan told the guy downstairs on security that I'm having some work done at the house and that I'll be in and out of this penthouse so it wouldn't raise suspicions. Everyone knows I'd never order a pizza—I'm gluten free since last May. Logan's been kind enough to let you borrow this place, and since you come with a media frenzy, the least you can do is lay low. Jason called me as well, and we're all going to work together to keep you safe until the trolls and ogres subside. Eat your food." She nods at the plate and it takes me right back to when I was twelve.

We sit at the counter and mom watches me eat the frigid, stale food that tastes like shit and then she says, "You look like you could use a shower. Don't forget to wash behind your ears."

I hug Mom and then I see her to the elevator. "I wish you'd find someone nice to take care of you, son. Like your brothers did. Look how happy they are."

I shake my head. "You know it's impossible to find people I can trust." Right as I say it, an image of the girl from three years ago pops into my head.

"She's out there," Mom replies. "Not everyone will sell you out to the press. You've just been unlucky, is all. Your leading lady is just waiting to pop into your life."

I nod, wishing she were right. I'm sick of being lonely. The parties, travel and money can get boring when you've got no one to enjoy them with.

"Oh, before I forget, Drew said he'd come by later. Maybe you can speak to him about safety. Tying shoe laces together," Mom tuts, "what's next?" She shakes her head and I shrug.

"At least he moved the table." I nod my head to the glass coffee table that got moved and would have hurt like a bitch.

Mom grins. "Yes, that was thoughtful of him. I'll come back to visit tomorrow. Text me if you need anything."

* * *

"IF IT WASN'T YOU, then this place is fucking haunted," I tell Drew two hours later. "It's not just the shoe laces. The shower was set to freezing, there was toothpaste in the hotel facewash, and there are no towels."

Drew, the fucker, smirks as he shrugs. "How the mighty Hollywood superstar has fallen. No towels? Did you have to dry your famous ballsack on the curtains?"

"No! I used my shirt." I sigh, not sure if I'm more pissed off about the calamity in the hotel room or that I'm forced to be here in the first place. "Just tell me. It was you, wasn't it?" Drew shakes his head and I don't believe him for a second. "I feel like I'm in a reality TV show and somebody booby-trapped the place."

I pick up the remote control and lean back into the couch and press the On button for the TV but nothing happens. I do it twice more and then slide the back off the control. "There's no fucking batteries in the damn thing." I press the button again like by some miracle the fancy-ass TV Logan has installed in his penthouse might have controls that work without batteries and am unsurprised when nothing happens. "Don't suppose you have any?" I ask Drew and he laughs.

"Let me just check my pocket." I wait, watching him before he shakes his head and says, "Of course I don't have batteries, dick!"

I sigh and use my finger and thumb to massage my temple and my new bruise smarts.

"I've only been in here a day and I feel like I'm going fucking crazy."

Drew lightly punches me on the arm. "It'll all blow over. You eaten?"

I nod. Cold, shit, stale food. "Yes, I've eaten. There's some left but I wouldn't recommend it. You want some leftover meatless sandwich?"

Drew holds up his hand in a no gesture. "Skyla's making her famous ricotta tortellini and it's fucking amazing."

"Any chance of some leftovers later?" I ask, my mouth watering.

Drew shakes his head. "Callie and I always fight over the leftovers. Callie usually wins." He shrugs and I cross my arms at the sheer unfairness. It's not like I can fight my niece for the food, even if I could get my ass over there.

I fiddle with the remote, not sure who or what to be pissed off at.

"I'll bring you some batteries next time I come over. You've only got to put up with being in this place for two weeks," Drew reminds me, "and besides, Jessie will be here during her shifts to take care of you."

"What did you just say?"

"It's only for two weeks—"

"No, not that. The name. What did you say?"

"The maid. She'll be here to take—"

"The name, Drew. What name did you say?" I hiss and the urgency in my voice makes me sound unhinged.

"Jessie. She's a maid here. Logan's got her all prepped to take care of you. You'll like her. Everyone here does."

"You got a picture of her?"

Drew looks at me like I am indeed unhinged. "No, I don't got a fucking picture. What the fuck is up with you? Jessie is Skyla's friend, so don't fuck around with her just because you're bored."

"What else do you know about her?"

"She won't rat you out. She's Skyla's buddy and she saved Logan from marrying Dana—she's the woman who discovered Dana was lying about the pregnancy." Drew studies my face and his expression becomes concerned. "You getting paranoid? Don't sweat it, no one knows you're here. You just got to lie low and you're going to be fine."

"Jessie," I roll the name over in my mouth, liking how it tastes. It can't be *my* Jessie working as a maid. Jessie was so smart she's probably finished college and working at the White House in charge of their media campaigns. She was so quick-witted and in control, she could even be running a country somewhere, and she's probably never even given me a second thought. No way it's the same Jessie. There must be more than a million Jessies in America.

I sigh.

Wishful thinking, asshole.

"I'll come over with some batteries and watch the Monday night game with you, how's that?"

I nod. "Thanks, man. You're a fucker who ties shoelaces together, but I love ya!"

Drew chuckles and then shakes his head like I'm the crazy one. "It wasn't me. Try to stay sane, okay?"

"I'll do my best," I reply and wonder how the hell I'm going to keep myself occupied. At least tomorrow the maid will be in and out to give me some company. Maybe she'll even be a Tate Blingwood fan. A friendly face to pass the time with would sure be nice.

CHAPTER 5

JESSIE

*T*he first text I receive from my friend Layla has me grinning my damn face off:

I'm engaged!

The second, not so much:

I hope you don't mind, but I sent Tate Blingwood your phone number. See you soon. Love, the-soon-to-be Mrs. Blingwood (it's going to take me awhile to get used to calling myself that!).

Great!

Tate-mother-fucking-Blingwood.

As if thinking of him hasn't kept me awake all night, now he is infiltrating all of my day and my phone too.

Right as I swipe Layla's text away, I get another from a number I don't recognize.

> Hi. Can you bring me up some breakfast please? Just some bacon and eggs will do. Maybe a little avocado, sourdough—4 slices should be enough, sausage, some maple syrup—sugar free if you can get it, and apples and bananas—but not green ones. Also, if they have chips can you grab them too—salted will do just fine, unless they have parmesan. And, did they not have any chocolate-covered peanuts yesterday? They weren't on the tray. Can you bring batteries too? I think my damn brother took the last ones. Thanks!

The entitled arrogance of his text message has me immediately deleting it but another one pings right after it.

> I hate to be a pain, but could I also get some toilet paper, toothpaste, towels, and some Le Bio facewash. You might need to go to the store to find it as I doubt the hotel stocks it. Also, could you find me the instructions for the microwave? My brother just dropped off some leftovers but I can't seem to find the On button. You're a star. Thanks!

Then another text follows that one immediately:

> My assistant would normally do all this for me but my agent gave her two weeks off since the paparazzi know if they find her, they'll find me.

Then he adds a winky face. *The sheer arrogance of this man...*

I google the facewash and almost spew at the cost.

$180 for facewash!

Urgh. That's a month's worth of formula, diapers, and fruit for most people.

Tate Blingwood is a spoiled, rich, entitled bastard! He can fuck off if he thinks I'm hauling my ass all the way across town during rush hour for facewash.

Until my phone rings and I know he's got me by the flaps.

"Hi, Logan. How are you?" I ask my boss, who is also Tate Blingwood's older brother.

"I'm great. Truly, great," he replies and I can hear the happiness oozing from his voice. "I thought I better call and apologize for dropping my brother on you. Honestly, you and Skyla are the only people I trust with this information. The press will go nuts if they find out he's at the resort and well, I know Tate can be a little high maintenance, but he needs you."

"High maintenance? I'm on speed dial for a diva! Tate seems to think I'm his personal assistant, private Uber Eats driver and cosmetics dealer. He can't even operate the microwave without technical support."

Logan laughs like I'm kidding. "He's used to having an assistant do all this stuff for him. It's only for two weeks, Jessie. Of course, I'll drop an extra thousand bucks in your pay to compensate you, unless you don't think you can handle it, in which case I'll find someone else. I know I'm asking a lot." The sincerity in Logan's voice isn't enough to stop my rant.

"Handle it? I can handle him just fine," I reply curtly. I just hoped I'd never have to see him again, never mind handle him. "It's fine. I can babysit your brother, no problem," I reply and Logan chuckles deeply.

"Is there any chance you could work some later shifts? I'm worried about him, and knowing you can attend to him is easing my guilt. Of course, I'll pay you double for any extra hours you work."

I need the money too badly to object so I reply, "Sure. So long as Betty and my mom can take care of Macy, it should be fine." I wonder if I should mention that I know his brother, but since I am probably just one in a long line of baby mommas, I'm banking on Tate having forgotten all about me long ago.

"Great! Layla, she agreed! I told you it'd be fine," he calls out and I picture the happy couple in a beautiful lake house, *hammering* out the terms of their new relationship.

"Logan," I say, my tone deceptively mild, bringing him back to our conversation.

"Yeah?"

"You break Layla's heart and I will kill you."

The line goes silent and I wonder if I overstepped. Layla is one of my besties now, but Logan is still my boss and some people think murder threats in the workplace are inappropriate. My anxiety lifts when he lets out a booming laugh and replies, "I love how much you care for your friends, Jessie. I owe you a debt. If you hadn't enlightened me as to Dana's plan to trap me with a fake baby and the ensuing marriage, I would never have found Layla. I'm the happiest I have ever been and in part, that's all thanks to you. I'm not going to mess this up."

"Good," I reply, feeling stronger and I decide, while my boss is in his happy place, I'll push the terms of our agreement. "Does your gratitude mean you won't ever fire me?"

He laughs again. "Why would I ever fire you? You're one of my best workers."

I nod. He's right. I am one of his best workers, but that was before I had to deal with Tate.

"Would you mind putting that in an email to me?" I ask, wishing I'd had the foresight to record his promise not to fire me. "Just a quick, 'I Logan Blingwood won't ever fire Jessie Yates, no matter the circumstances.'"

"Um, sure, I can do that," he says with an air of confusion.

"Great. I better go. Your brother wants facewash."

"Good luck," he says before cackling and telling Layla, "Stop tickling me." When he hangs up and my puke at their cuteness has been swallowed down, I start arranging childcare.

* * *

"I KNOW YOU'RE BUSY, MOM," I tell her. Mom has six kids and two part-time jobs, it's not like I ask her to mind her grand-baby lightly. "But I could really use the extra cash. Lisa from day care is emailing me about the fees and I'm worried Macy will lose her place if I don't find the extra money."

Mom yells at one of my sisters to stop eating all the Cap'N Crunch straight from the box and then answers, "I can do Wednesday and Thursday nights. I might be able to do Sunday but it depends if Jake is working. He doesn't get his hours 'til Friday."

"Jake?" I ask innocently. My mother has been single for just three weeks and I was afraid she'd jump straight into something new.

"Jake. He's a caller at bingo. Jessie, he's so nice. You're going to love him!"

My mom says this about all the guys she meets. It's little wonder my sisters and I nearly all have different dads and my mom's dating history reads like a who's-who of dead-beats. So much so that since my twin sisters' dad walked out, I've refused to learn or use any of her boyfriends' names.

"Mom, are you sure you're ready to date again? You only just got rid of what's-his-name."

"His name was John. Jake will be different. I can feel it. And, don't think I haven't noticed that you call all my boyfriends what's his name. You really need to get better at learning their names."

"And you really need to get better at selecting guys."

Mom sighs and I feel bad for hurting her. It's not like she doesn't try to find love. Mom loves hard, but she loves instantly and it's bitten her on the ass so many times I've lost count. "I know, honey, but Jake will be different, you'll see."

"Okay, if you say so, but Mom, are you still taking the pill? And do you still have that box of condoms I bought you?" I don't suppose many daughters have to have the safe-sex talk with their moms, I honestly wish I didn't but after six kids, it's necessary.

"Oh, yes darling. I take it every day and haven't been a day late since the twins were born."

"Keep taking it, Mom. But use the condoms as well. With how fertile you are, you'll be birthing daughters right into your eighties if we're not careful!"

"Wouldn't that be wonderful!" Mom says but I interrupt her with a yell.

"NO! It wouldn't be wonderful. I'm twenty-three. I don't want to have baby siblings anymore. Please, just take the pill and use the condoms and stop introducing your boyfriends to us."

The line goes silent and I use the opportunity to work on my breathing. I'm probably taking the stress of having to work with Tate out on my mom, but I also worry about her. She has a part-time job selling sex toys on the internet and at parties, and she's the cleaner for the bingo hall. Mom doesn't have two cents to rub together, and I worry how she'll fair as she ages. Being the oldest daughter is hard when you have to be the mother too.

"Lecture over?" Mom asks and it's my turn to sigh.

"Let me know when what's-his-name gets his shifts so I know if I can work. And Mom…"

"Yes, sweetie."

"Thanks. I love you."

"I love you too. And Jessie?"

"Yeah?"

"Don't be so hard on Jake when you meet him. I know your father let you down, but not all men are like he is."

An image of my father dressed in his police uniform—a so-called fine, upstanding member of the community—flashes in front of my eyes and I feel my muscles stiffen.

He wasn't fine or upstanding.

I still remember being seven years old and turning up at the police station with a Best-Dad-in-the-World cup and asking for Chuck Peters, then proudly announcing that I was his daughter.

I'd convinced myself that he had somehow missed the message that I was his daughter. I was sure once he knew he was my dad, he'd scoop me up like I was in some kind of Hallmark movie and we'd go get ice cream, but it didn't go down like that. The guys at the station laughed booming, painful cackles. A guy hollered, "Hey, Chuck, you better start saving for college," and that's when I saw my dad's expression sour. I had never felt so small and insignificant. He told me, "Hey kid, I'm not your dad, your momma is a two-bit-whore who's slept with every guy at the station," and then gave me fifty cents and told me never to come back.

So I used one of those two quarters to scratch the word *dik* on the hood of his car. I should have etched the word asshole, but in my defense I was a late bloomer with reading and my vision was blurred by tears.

* * *

EMILY JAMES

"ARen't you supposed to be at the beck and call of the celebrity in Penthouse 2?" Skyla whispers as I make my way out of the staff cafeteria.

"Who says I'm not? I just raced across town and used the last of my credit to spend almost 200 bucks on facewash for that asshole," I huff.

Skyla takes me by my arm and guides me to the side of the cafeteria where we won't be heard. "Are you okay? I was only joking. I know you'll take care of him and..." She studies me carefully, her eyes probing like she's suddenly become an honorary member of the FBI. "You look gorgeous today. Are you wearing makeup?"

"No," I cut her off immediately, grabbing an unused napkin someone left behind on one of the Formica tables and rubbing off the fancy cherry lip gloss I tried on at the cosmetics store. "I had to wait while at the check-out," I say pointing at the box of Tate's facewash. "I was bored, that's all. I don't give two figs what Tate Blingwood thinks of my appearance. If he doesn't like it, he can just..."

Skyla chuckles warily. "I was only saying you look nice. Are you sure you're okay? Is it too much, working with Tate? Do you want me to talk to Logan? Maybe we can find someone else to run around after him if he's being a diva."

"I'm fine." I shake my head but from the way Skyla looks at me, she knows I'm lying so I admit. "I saw the baby daddy. I'm fine, but I'm also freaked out."

"Where did you see him? Did he say anything?" Her face crinkles with concern and I bat it away.

"He hasn't said shit." I keep my comment vague since Skyla is married to Tate's eldest brother, Drew. Telling her Tate is the baby daddy would put her in a difficult position. The last thing I want is Tate's family—who are some of the nicest people I know—guilting him into doing the right thing. Tate and his team made it clear; he is not interested in becoming a father and that's fine by me. Macy and I don't need him. I decided long ago there's no point in telling anyone who Macy's father is—not that people would believe me anyway.

Skyla waits for me to continue but after a moment's silence, she realizes my lips are buttoned and insists, "We'll have lunch when Layla is back. Just the three of us. I probably haven't been around as much as I used to be since I married Drew, but I'm here for you. If ever you want to talk, I'm here. Okay?"

I nod. Suddenly it feels like my throat is swelling up and, since I can't afford to get emotional before I have to face Tate, I lock everything down tight and smile. "I'm fine, babe. I'm happy for you and Drew. Don't worry about me, I am fine. Absolutely fine," I add to emphasize just how fine I am.

Skyla doesn't look convinced but she lets go of my arm and takes a step back as though she is willing to pretend for my sake and I'm grateful.

"I'm on my way to the penthouse," I tell her. "Wish me luck."

Skyla laughs and replies, "You won't need it. Tate's a pussy cat."

MY CLEANING CART is loaded down with cleaning supplies, fresh sheets, towels and balanced precariously on top is a tray with Tate's (now cold) breakfast items. Still, I stand outside the elevator to Tate's penthouse in my pink maid uniform for a full fifteen minutes before I pluck up the courage to press the button, enter the code, and walk inside.

It's no big deal, I tell myself as the elevator journeys upward.

He's nothing more than a guy. He's like any other guy, I

insist, forcing myself to breathe.

He's just a Hollywood star and the baby daddy.

Seeing him, face to face, really isn't a big deal.

I bite back any emotions I am feeling and, as the doors swoosh open, I shove the cart and waltz inside. I'm here to do my job and get outta here. So I shouldn't be relieved that I don't immediately see him, but I am.

Maybe he put on a hat to disguise his big famous head and went out to seek food.

A smile creeps on my face and I start unloading the towels that I decided he could have. I don't want him stinking up the place if I have to come here, so it's better he can wash and dry himself for both our sakes.

I'm so grateful he went out, I'm humming a tune and working fast, unloading his tray of food onto the counter, noticing he left quite a lot of the food I brought him yesterday. I place his damn facewash beside his food tray and set to work.

The air is set to a comfortable 70 degrees and I picture Tate shivering as he woke yesterday. The coffee table I moved is set to its former position and I wonder if he managed to untie the double-sheet bend knot that one of my step-dads taught me on a camping trip years ago.

I'm carrying towels to the bathroom, wondering if I should call the day care center and check on Macy, when the door swings open and I face-plant smooth, hard skin that has a faint minty scent. Water droplets glisten on his sculpted chest and I lick my lip to remove the ones that transferred to me. Then I catch myself and immediately step back.

Tate Blingwood stands one step away from me, mouth agape.

I close my own mouth.

He's even more gorgeous than I remember, all glossy ebony hair, still wet from the shower. His grin is dimpled and sexy and my knees immediately weaken. I can't help but freeze, my eyes as big and round as his pecs. His eyes are wide like his shoulders and his knowing smile is so disarming my heart starts racing. I want to swoon, but I won't. Not for him.

So I look down instead, which is a major mistake.

I thought I was being funny, removing the towels from his bathroom on my last visit, but the sight before me is anything but funny. It's HUGELY serious. Scratch that, it was a massive, enormous, colossal… mistake!

His cock is just like I remember it. Smooth and long and thick and capable… I clamp my eyes and my legs shut.

"Sorry, I've been air drying since there are no towels," he says apologetically.

"Towels!" I snarl and thrust the pile at him, still not daring to open my eyes.

I turn my back to him and open my eyes as I rush to the safety of my cart, planning to get the hell out of dodge.

"Jessie?" His voice is pure silk and my vagina replies with a purr.

I shake my head and begin rooting through my cart, wishing I had thought to bring a disguise.

"Jessie. It's you, isn't it?"

I turn to face him, slowly, like he's holding a bomb and it might go off. When I take him in, my mouth dries. His body is perfectly tan. He shows off all his thick, corded muscles like he's waiting for a photographer to show up at any moment. At least he's wrapped one of the hotel towels around his waist, but still a sadness, that I'll never get to see his penis again, washes over me.

"I can't believe it," he says, grinning widely and proudly showing off his perfect white teeth. He closes the gap between us. His smile is huge like he's pleased to see me. It takes me by surprise and has my blood pressure rocketing.

"It's really you. I never thought I'd see you again." The fond look he's giving me is knee weakening and at total odds with the way things went down when his team told me to back off. He looks so happy that it's making it difficult to remain angry with him.

Difficult, but not impossible.

"Hoped you'd never see me again, you mean," I say under my breath in a cold, mirthless tone. "Your food is on the counter. I'm here to service the room, and I'd prefer it if you were wearing clothes while I do it." The disgusted glare I give him as I look him up and down completely contradicts the tantalizing view before me, but I don't care. Anger mixes with something else and, unable to bear looking at his face a moment longer, I turn my back, grab random items from the cart. Then I speak as I take long strides to hastily make space between us. "I'll start with the bathroom. It should give you time to dress and get out of the bedroom before I go change the sheets."

I'm on the verge of a panic attack as I lock myself in the bathroom that still has the steamy scent of Tate Blingwood.

I sit on the floor as my heart beats uncontrollably.

It's not like I didn't know seeing him would be hard. But I didn't expect it to feel like we'd never been apart. Like he didn't take my heart and wipe his ass with it. He made me feel—No, I let him make me feel like I was nothing. And I swore to myself, after the way my dad treated me, I would never allow another man to have that kind of power over my emotions.

It stops now.

So I pick up the oven cleaner I mistakenly picked out of the cart and begin scrubbing the toilet like I'm being paid to do. I'll finish cleaning the bathroom then the rest of the penthouse, and I won't so much as even make eye contact with Tate fucking Blingwood!

CHAPTER 6

I throw on sweats and a clean tee and settle myself on the couch as I wait for Jessie to surface from the bathroom.

I can't believe it's her. The spitfire from spring break. I'm so excited to see her again, I can't wait for her to come out, so I wind up pacing the room.

It wasn't the reunion I occasionally let myself imagine, but that's understandable. Jessie's probably in shock. Since I went A list, even people I've known my whole life get flustered around me. Take my Auntie Sue, I have to sign an autograph for her each time I see her even though she spent numerous summers changing my diapers and putting me in time outs. Shock. That's all it is. Jessie'll come around when she realizes I'm still the same Tate from spring break and maybe having her around for a bit will liven up my time in prison.

The door opens so quietly I barely notice her in her

adorable little pink maid uniform that is now my new favorite kink.

She's still really fucking hot.

Hotter than I remember.

Jessie turns her head, scowls at me, and then walks right into the bedroom.

I follow, trying not to be disheartened.

"I haven't seen you since spring break. It must be what, three years?"

Jessie doesn't so much as look in my direction as she angrily strips the sheets from the bed. Had I known Jessie, my Jessie, was the maid sent to look after me, I would have asked her to bring up a bottle of champagne.

"I still remember you," I tell her, in case she thinks I forgot about her. "Vividly," I add, throwing her my signature Blingwood smile that all my fans go crazy for. But it's like she doesn't notice I'm standing beside her, and so, to get her attention I begin helping her by pulling the pillow cases off. She doesn't make eye contact and it starts to feel really weird so I say, "Do you know who I am?"

Jessie immediately stops what she is doing and glares at me, her expression incensed. I suddenly realize that a celebrity saying, "Do you know who I am?" sounds arrogant and egotistical. I drop the pillow and instead fluff my hair. "I didn't mean. This isn't going like I planned—"

"Do I know who you are? Do. I. Know. Who. You. Are? HA!"

"Okay, so you know who I am. I didn't mean—"

"I know exactly who you are, Tate fucking Blingwood."

She's glaring at me like she wants to hurt me but it's also sexy as fuck—or at least it would be if I wasn't nervous she might actually hurt me.

"You don't look pleased to see me," I say, stating the obvious. Since I became famous, I've never been met with such hostility. People generally love me. "Is something wrong? I know I left in a hurry that morning but I got the call I'd been waiting for and... I had to leave immediately to sign the contract for the film. My agent, Jason, he said they needed to start shooting in Europe right away, but I left my phone number on the pillow. You didn't call."

She blinks three times then shakes her head. "You left without a goodbye. Oh, but you were sure to leave me a hundred spot. Thanks for that, by the way." She laughs bitterly and I take a step toward her, holding out my hands in case I need to protect myself. "Let's not pretend like you're suddenly interested in me, Tate. The only reason you're even talking to me is because you're stuck in this room and you're bored senseless. Your lies aren't necessary. You forgot about me the second you walked out the hotel room three years ago, just like I did you."

Shit. That stung. I didn't expect her to have forgotten me. Our time together was unforgettable. At least, I thought it was. I never forgot about her. But something in the way she's wringing the sheets in her hands has me certain that if I told her, she'd probably fashion them into a noose for my neck.

Just like that, her walls go back up and she goes back to dealing with the bed, forgetting that I exist, and it irks me.

"Hey. I'm talking to you—"

"And I'm working," she hisses. "I'm not one of your harpy fans you can throw your sexy smile at and have them fall to their knees. I'm a grown-ass woman with responsibilities and a job to do. So, let me to do my job."

But instead, I yank the sheet she is wrestling with forward and she stumbles toward me.

"Why are you so pissed?" The indignation in my voice slices through the air and she lifts her delicate, heart-shaped face to me. Her gaze starts as vulnerable, hurt even, but it quickly turns angry.

"Because I hate you and everything men like you stand for."

I wasn't expecting this version of my Jessie but even when she's standing before me, glaring at me, I don't believe she hates me. What I did to piss her off… leaving the morning after we met and never saying goodbye… I left her a note and money to pay the hotel bill. Not that I'm expecting a thank you, but her hostility is unwarranted. No one has ever hated me this much, except maybe some of the online trolls, but I'm pretty sure they hate everyone.

"Really? You hate me?" I ask disbelievingly.

She nods but the way she's looking at me, like she doesn't know whether to fight me or fuck me has me torn between anger and arousal.

My arms fold against my chest, righteously. "And what exactly do 'men like me' stand for?"

Jessie throws down the sheet and her hands rest on her teeny little waist. At only a little above five feet, she shouldn't look as fierce as she does. It's unbelievably sexy. "Hmm. Let me see, selfish, arrogant, sure of himself, and full of—"

I step forward and close the distance between us. If she wants to call me out on all my flaws, then she can do it up close. Her vanilla scent has me lightheaded. Staring in her perfectly blue eyes renders me dizzy.

Still, she doesn't back down and huffs as she crosses her arms over her chest and angles her face up at me. Even though her lips are pursed and pouting, she's got the sweetest mouth I've ever seen. Her teeth bite down into her lower lip and she suddenly doesn't look so sure she hates me.

"Those are some pretty strong allegations. But I don't think you hate me at all." The tension between us is electric. It pulsates right through my body and I know she can feel it too. "I remember how good it was between us and I know you do too."

Jessie's mouth parts seductively. Her tongue darts out and sweeps her lower lip like she lost control of its sharpness, and I'm glad of it. I lower my head. Now that she's in front of me, the memories of our time come flooding back and it seems criminal not to take the chance and kiss her. So, I do. I press my lips against hers and the second we touch, I'm a goner. My fingers dive into her long, blonde hair, reveling in its silkiness. I pull her closer so I can dip my tongue in to taste her, and even though I'm not entirely convinced she won't bite me, I'm delighted when she opens up and lets me in.

Our eyes stay open and untrusting as we taste and tease one another, but I know I'm winning as her arms unfold and her hands move to my ass where her fingers knead my flesh. It's everything but also not nearly enough. I'm tall and she's tiny so the height difference has us both leaning at awkward angles. When she lets out a soft moan, it's all the encouragement I need to swoop down and lift her by her ass until she wraps her legs around me.

"I've been thinking about fucking you non-stop," I tell her, breaking our kiss to taste her neck. It's not entirely a lie. Over the past three years, in those quiet moments when I have a chance to really be by myself, my mind always went back to thoughts of her.

"I still hate you," she insists, arching her back to give me better access.

I trail kisses to the apex of her breasts and begin undoing the buttons of her maid uniform.

No way she fucking hates me.

"Say it again," I say, pulling her bra cup aside and covering her tight little bud with my mouth.

"I still hate you," she replies breathlessly, pushing her body against mine. "This changes nothing."

I lower her down on the bed and continue undoing the

buttons that make her little pink dress open up like a present at Christmas. She can pretend to hate me if that turns her on but she's not immune to my charms. I know she wants me like I want her. I also know, she's going to love me soon enough.

Splayed out before me, white cotton underwear askew, my balls are already threatening to explode when her hand reaches out, tugs down my sweats, and she palms my cock. A bead of precum instantly releases and she hums her appreciation as she works me.

I pay equal attention to her breasts and then pull her arms above her head because if she keeps sliding her hands up and down my cock, our reunion is not going to last nearly as long as I want it to. "I've missed these perky tits," I tell her, then kiss a trail down to her naval. Her skin is softer than I remember, rounder, more creped beneath her naval, but it's still fucking perfect. Every part of her is like coming home. I dip my head down and slide her panties down. My finger traces the slickness of her folds and she writhes beneath my touch. Laid out like this, vulnerable and so reactive to my touch, I feel utterly honored. "You're so fucking wet for me," I say, circling my finger against her tender spot. Looking up at her beautifully splayed out and flawless, her expression turns almost annoyed with herself. But I push the thought aside since she's definitely into it and I can't wait to taste her. I lower my head already licking my lips as if readying for a feast but before my tongue can reach what it craves, Jessie flips me over in what can only be described as some kind of *WWE* move and she straddles me.

"Whoa there, princess, I was looking forward to that," I tell her as she pushes me against the mattress. When I try to lean up, she has me pinned.

"Ah-ah," she replies, shaking her head. "You're not fucking me this time, Blingwood. If we're doing this, I'm in control."

I'm inclined to object but then she pulls a condom out of the breast pocket of her uniform and slides it down on me.

"You came prepared?" I say, remembering how neither of us had one last time and I had to run across the motel parking lot to buy the last one out of the vending machine.

"I'm never not prepared anymore," she replies and I'm about to ask what she means when she distracts me by pushing herself all the way down on my length, angrily milking my cock like I did her dirty.

It feels so fucking good I almost blow my load but I hold back because I need to see her come apart for me.

Jessie's fingers dig into my shoulders, holding me down as she pumps, sliding her clit against me as she lands her stroke and then powering back up so my entire length feels the friction. Her expression is lustful, bordering on fury as she brings us both higher and, while I've palmed myself to pleasure numerous times, it's been so long since I came during sex, that I can feel my climax nearing.

"Jessie, fuck. Baby…"

"Stop talking and let me fuck you," she orders and her hand moves to my throat, pinning me to the bed. It's so damn powerful and sexy, I'm desperate to come but I hold back, waiting for her first. Her maid uniform, completely undone, hangs off her slender shoulders. Her tits, almost free of her bra, bounce as she drives herself up and down on my cock. She is completely in control, but I've never felt more power than this thing between us or saw anyone more beautiful.

"If you keep… fuck! I'm going to…" I'm struggling to hold on but Jessie's hips quicken and her core tightens—and if I couldn't tell by her tightening grip, I can tell from the way guttural cusses escape from her lips. She's so fucking close. I drive my hips up and we stare in each other's eyes, caught in a moment of total and utter primal need and then, right as her gaze softens and her mouth opens, she lets out a mewling gasp. I watch her face contort with blissful ecstasy and feel a moment of total and utter joy. My own release fires off like a rocket, and I pull her close to me, imagining we are one.

"That was… fuck, Jessie."

I kiss all the way up her neck and she relaxes in my arms. The moment is perfection and I'm so blissed out that I lay her down beside me and pull out, wrapping my arms around her so we can spoon. A half a second later she gets up.

"I've got work to do," she says and suddenly she's off the bed, slipping her underwear back into place and buttoning up her dress.

"Come back to bed." I try to catch hold of her wrist but she pulls it away.

Then she checks her watch. "Fuck! I'm going to be late." She rushes from the room and, still naked, I chase after her. "Wait! When will I see you again?" I ask.

"Unfortunately, tomorrow," she replies and pushes her cart into the waiting elevator, flattening the creases in her dress with her palms.

"What do you mean, unfortunately?"

But the doors close before she can explain and I'm wondering why the hell she said, "Unfortunately."

CHAPTER 7

JESSIE

"*H*ow was your shift?" Skyla asks as I walk into the locker room.

I've been trying hard to stop swearing since Macy started picking up words but there are moments when only a fuck will do. Today is one of those days.

"I fucked the baby daddy. I fucked him and I liked it," I say, falling down onto my knees to get my purse from the bottom of the cabinet. But once I'm down there, I can't get back up.

"Wait. Slow down. The baby daddy. How? You've been working in pentho—" Skyla loses control of her tongue. She's suddenly frozen and has joined me in a state of shock. "You… you hate him. You say it all the time. Tate. No. Tate. No. I don't believe it. It can't be. You—"

"It's Tate," I admit.

Skyla drops down beside me on the tiled floor and takes my hand.

"How?" she asks.

"Well, his peepee went in my vajayjay—"

"I know how babies are made. I mean, how did you meet? And how have you kept this to yourself for so long? Why has he never mentioned he's a father? And how did you end up sleeping with him anyway?"

I shrug, having no idea where to start. "Three years ago, spring break," I say simply, like it's obvious. "I was on vacation with a group of girls from college. We were all drinking and having fun and then they announced the mud-wrestling competition in the resort and you know how I like a challenge."

Skyla laughs. "I know you never lose."

I nod. "I beat that bastard. And then I went and fucked him to celebrate. It was before he was famous. He was just some dude—"

"Some hot, tall, gorgeous dude—"

I cut her off with a glare. "Some hot, tall, gorgeous emotionally unavailable guy who ditched me the morning after the greatest sex of my life." I don't tell her it was the best night of my life, and the first time I'd ever made a real connection with a man. At least I'd thought that... but Tate is no better to Macy than my father was to me.

"So, he was gone in the morning and you never saw him again? Then you found out you were having Macy? But you went after him, right? He does know he's Macy's father?" she checks, her mouth lopsided with confusion.

"Yes, I told his people." That's the one thing I never understood. None of Tate's family know he's a father, or at least they never mentioned it to me, which makes sense I guess. If he didn't want to admit it then, he wouldn't tell his family. In TV interviews, Tate talks about *one day* becoming a father and having a huge family, but I guess that's just acting —telling the people what they want to hear. "When his people told him about me, Tate told them he didn't know who I was."

My fists ball. I can't believe I gave in so easily and fucked him. But I couldn't stop myself. The second I saw him, I wanted him.

"So, you guys just..."

"It was a mistake," I say. "He was bored, holed up in a penthouse hiding from the press and he's used to women throwing themselves at him. No wonder he was so smooth, so assured. It's like he knows no mortal woman can resist him. He wanted to get laid and I just rolled over and let him —okay, so I climbed on top of him and screwed him, but I didn't put up a fight or even make him work for it. When it came down to it, I wanted his dick as much as he wanted to give it to me."

"He is very good-looking," Skyla replies, concentrating on me intently. "You're only human."

"He's not good-looking. He's a trip hazard and I just fell right down onto his dick. Fuck!" I hiss. "What was I thinking?!"

"So, what did he say about Macy?"

"He didn't even mention her. He gave me some half-hearted excuse for running out on me the morning after and... I never said any of the things I've wanted to all these years."

"Well, what did he tell you back when you told him you were pregnant?"

"When I found out I was expecting, I reached out to him —well, to his people. I sent emails, made phone calls, I even joined his official fan club and wrote to them. All I got in return was a copy and paste email that said, 'Welcome to the club. Subscribe for only $19.99 a month and you'll get this cool, free T shirt.'" A hollow chuckle escapes my lips. "Like I want a T-shirt with his stupid damn face on it," I say sarcasti-

59

cally, screwing up my nose. I can barely even admit to myself that I subscribed and that I keep his T-shirt in the bottom drawer of the dresser.

"I don't believe he doesn't want to be in Macy's life. I've met Tate more than a dozen times now. Granted, I'm still getting to know him, but he loves kids. He's amazing with Callie."

"Yeah, I've heard he's good with Callie, but that's because she's his niece. He doesn't actually have any responsibility, does he?"

"I guess not," Skyla replies. "But he does stuff with her. The two of them are close. They both have this ongoing joke where they buy inappropriate T-shirts for Cassandra and she wears them and pretends not to get the joke."

I let out a, "Hmph." I've noticed Cassandra's T-shirts and they are pretty funny.

"Callie and Tate are sweet together—sweeter than most uncles and nieces are. They're always texting and video-calling. Tate would be a great father. It doesn't make sense." She shakes her head and ponders, then comes back with another question, "So how did you end up having sex today, if you hate him so much?"

"We…. I…" I blow out a long breath, unsure exactly how it happened or what triggered it. "He turned on his damn Blingwood charm."

Skyla nods knowingly. Since she's married to the eldest Blingwood brother, she knows exactly how powerful their damn charm can be.

"I started strong. I was sure I was going to be able to clean his crap and serve him food without even having to talk to him but…"

"But?" Skyla asks, hanging off my every word.

"I'm weak. He got up in my grill and I caved. I hate him, but he's really fucking tall, and built, and good-looking."

Skyla smirks, watching my hands carve shapes as I animatedly describe him. "He is good-looking. All the Blingwood men are. Bastards."

"My resolve broke and we were naked, well, the essential parts were naked and then…"

"You banged a Blingwood. And now you regret it?"

I nod then shake my head. "I don't regret it. I wanted it, Skyla. Like, I really fucking wanted him." My skin still tingles from his touch. "But no good can come from this. I need to protect Macy. I can't be weak, I don't want to make the same mistakes my mom made, jumping from one deadbeat guy who doesn't want a kid to the next. I promised Macy at the moment of her birth that we wouldn't be like my mom and me. If it's not solid, secure, and lasting then I'm out. I swore to her." I shake my head again, feeling so torn that anything that feels so good can be so bad. And then I realize, as much as I try not to be like my mom, I am like her. My recent behavior proves it. "No more, Sky. I'm done. It was a one-time thing. Well, technically a two-time thing but there will not be a third time," I insist.

She sighs heavily. "I can't believe he doesn't want to be in Macy's life. If he just met her, he'd fall in love with her in an instant—"

"No!" I stand and pace. "Fuck him! Macy won't ever beg anyone to be in her life. She deserves people begging her to spend time with *her* because she's amazing. Besides, he obviously has other kids. He didn't even remember I was one of the baby mommas. He came onto me in the penthouse and I…" I kick myself, hard. "I melted right into him. I'm so angry I didn't have better restraint. I've imagined running into Tate so many times, fantasized about it, but each and every time, I punched him right in the face."

"What are you going to do? At the very least you should hit him for child support—it's not like he can't afford it, he's loaded. He should pay! And Cassandra, she's a grandmother. Drew and Logan, they're uncles. That makes me Macy's aunt now." Her watery grin takes over her face as she hugs her chest.

"You've been Macy's aunt since forever," I tell her. But she's right about the others. Logan, Drew, their sister Tabitha, and their mother Cassandra—they're awesome people. They've met Macy at various times during my time here, and they've always been kind. If Tate is too coward to tell them he's got a daughter and they want to get to know Macy and have a relationship with her, they should have the chance. "I'm going to have to speak to him. I don't want his money but one day when Macy is older, she might want to find out for herself why she never knew him—I know I did, and Tate'll owe her that conversation." The clock on the wall chimes. "I better go. Can you keep this to yourself for now? I know I'm asking a huge favor for you not to tell Drew, but I need to think how I'm going to approach this, and I don't want the Blingwood family to be mad at me for not telling them who Macy is. When I got the job here and it was obvious they had no idea who I or Macy were, I kept my mouth shut. I wanted to tell them, but it's not an easy conversation to broach with the baby daddy's family, especially when I didn't know if I'd be believed, quite frankly they still may not."

Skyla stands and pulls me into a hug. "Nonsense. We're all family now, and they're going to be glad to have you—even if Tate Blingwood is too much of a big dope to realize."

I pull away, and reply, "I hope so."

* * *

BY THE TIME Macy and I are home eating dinner, Tate has texted me three times and called me twice. I don't answer.

The more I stare at Macy, the more I feel like a traitor for jumping into bed with the father who rejected her.

"Mommy loves you so much," I tell Macy, sweeping her beautiful dark unruly curls back behind her ears. "You're precious. I'll love you enough for the whole damn world."

"Swing. Swing. Swing," Macy says, completely ignoring my declaration and staring at the TV that's showing a commercial for an outside playset, and I feel bad we don't have a backyard, and on my wage there's fat chance of us ever having one. But that doesn't mean she'll miss out.

"Does Macy want to go to the park and swing?" I ask, even though dusk will be setting in soon.

"Swing, swing, swing," Macy says, her pudgy cheeks lifting up.

"Come on then, kiddo. Just for a half an hour, though. You need to take a bath and go bubbies soon."

I grab my phone and then notice another missed call from Tate, so I put it down on the counter and Macy and I count the steps that lead from our apartment down to the sidewalk. Then I take her hand and we walk to the park, both of us wearing sun dresses and simple sandals.

It's a beautiful, mild evening and the sky is a perfect shade of crimson. As soon as the park is in view, Macy gets more excited and for the first time today I manage to breathe like we're free. On a night as perfect as this, it'd be easy for me to think with Tate Blingwood out of sight, he's out of mind.

I still have to face him tomorrow, but this time, I definitely won't be sleeping with him.

CHAPTER 8

TATE

"*W*hat about Stella Brimworth?" Jason says on the video call. "She was your co-star on your last movie and already suggested something might have happened between you guys."

I remember the comment Jason's talking about. Awhile back, Stella started her own skincare line and mentioned my name multiple times when she was promoting the heck out of it. It pissed me off at the time and I told her to stop dropping my name. She eventually apologized and I let it go since we still need to work together to promote the Tripod movie we filmed together.

"No. Stella's not my type," I reply.

"Okay, well that's four women who are up to the job and you've said no to every one of them. What do you want to do, Tate?"

"My number one goal is to save my career, Jason." *And to find out why Jessie hates me so much.* I've been scrolling and moping since she left. Scrolling because I've been waiting for Jessie to call me back and apologize for running out on me, and moping because she's treating me like she hates me even though I've done nothing wrong. Okay, so maybe I should have stuck around that day three years ago, but I left a note and she didn't call. That's on her! "The public loved me just a few days ago, now it's like they hate me. My chiropractor just sold an interview telling everyone I'm always late and I once farted on the PT table. I have *never* farted on a PT table!"

"It's the lemming effect. One bad piece of press turns into two, then three more come out the woodwork and before you know it, everyone is following suit. If we're not careful, it's going to become uncool to like you."

I cover my eyes and ask, "Is my ass still trending?"

"It is," Jason chuckles. "We're on a limited timeframe here to get you the good press you need to go forward with the franchise and solidify this deal that you desperately need with Dinky. Now, who's going to be your leading lady?"

A vision of Jessie in her pink maid uniform, scowling at me, flashes in front of my eyes. Then I shake my head because that chick is crazy. The angry sex was hot, but it was a one-time thing. I'm not getting tangled up with her, no matter how much I want to. There's too much at stake.

Jason, bored of waiting for my decision, pushes, "Dinky is playing hard to get and I heard a rumor that one of the execs met with Tom Dordan."

Tom Dordan is a guy my age famous for sitcom work. He's talented, sure, and he cleaned up at the sitcom awards but he's not Tate Blingwood.

"We need something serious. Something concrete that's going to get the public on our side. If we don't do something to improve your image soon, Tom Dordan is going to get the Dinky franchise."

"Jason, that was supposed to be mine. How can they just go and give it away?"

"Tate, we hadn't signed the deal. You needed time off after filming and we scheduled to sign at the end of the month. None of us could have anticipated you'd end up running through LA naked and Dinky would withhold the deal. Not to mention earlier today an online rumor popped up that you're in a multi relationship with three women from Hamburg! God only knows where they find this stuff." Jason sighs, his voice sounding loaded down with stress that I immediately feel responsible for. "False rumors are commonplace in Hollywood, after all, we spin plenty of our own fake news but if the media can't find material, they'll make shit up—and when they do that, it's always bad. That's why we have two options, date Stella or someone else and show up to events as your most wholesome self, or lose the deal."

I suddenly feel sick.

The Dinky franchise is career elevating. A huge deal like that would make me unstoppable and set me apart from all the other male actors I'm competing with, not to mention the part is perfect for me and excites me more than all other scripts. It's a film I can proudly show my niece, who is usually too young to watch my work. But there's no way I can fake-date Stella. I wouldn't want to do it anyway, but after what happened with me and Jessie, I can't bring myself to even think about being with anyone else.

"Give me some time," I tell Jason and he warns me not to take too long. Then I hang up, unable to properly focus on deals and media campaigns when all I can think about is Jessie and what went down earlier and how much I want to pin her against the wall and show her I'm not the asshole she thinks I am.

I'm so confused. I pace into the bedroom and look at the

bed I not-slept with Jessie on. The sheets are still unmade and the smell of her skin still hangs in the air.

"Fuck it!" I need to go out. I grab my baseball cap and a scarf and cover up as much of my face as I can. I need some air.

* * *

THERE'S a security guy at the bottom of the elevator when I get out, but I keep my head down and ignore him as I walk through the foyer with the single purpose of reaching the ocean.

I walk along the sand, kicking shells and feeling an over-whelming sense of loneliness. The sky is a perfect shade of red and the moon is low in the sky. Dusk is falling into night. Being a star wasn't supposed to be like this. Apart from my family, I don't know who to trust. I just want to act.

As I get farther along the beach, I reach a park up ahead and see a little kid getting pushed by her mom on the swing and I slow my pace. The kid is hollering out with the sheer joy of being free and her mom is cooing her.

It's cute to watch and I hang back far enough that I don't look like a pedophile and watch for a moment.

Then I notice who the woman is.

Jessie.

She's wearing some kind of light sundress that flaps around in the breeze and her blonde hair almost covers her face as it's blown in every direction but I'd know her anywhere.

I enter the park through the gate, knowing I should be turning right back around, having promised myself not a half an hour ago that I wasn't going to pursue anything with her, but I can't help myself. The kid has dark curls and is so free and wild, she doesn't hold the rope. No, instead she puts her hands in the air and screams to go faster.

"I didn't know you had a kid," I start and my voice startles Jessie. I slide off my hat and the scarf that covers my lower face, but I can tell from the way her eyes widen that she knows it's me.

"What are you—what are you doing here?" she stutters like she's angry or maybe it's just shock, as she looks from me to the kid.

The swing goes back and forth, slowing down as Jessie forgets to push.

"I needed some air," I meet her tone just as coolly.

Jessie stares directly at the kid.

"Is she your kid?" I ask, but she's staring at her with such a protective fierceness that I already know the answer. "What's her name?" I ask when she doesn't reply to my first question.

Jessie shakes her head and then lurches forward and pulls the child from the swing, balancing her on her hip like she's done it a million times. The kid protests, then her mouth stretches open with a huge yawn that displays an impressive amount of baby teeth.

"How old is she?" I ask.

"Two," she says and her mouth immediately closes.

"Two? You must have gotten pregnant right after we—"

"I have to go," she blurts, squeezing her eyes shut like she's in pain.

Jessie turns and dashes away and I step after her. "Wait!" I call but Jessie doesn't wait. She breaks into a sprint while the cute little kid stares back at me, her dark curls bouncing in the wind... *just like my own do.*

And that's when I realize, I am in deep, deep shit.

CHAPTER 9

JESSIE

Tate: We need to talk.

I'm not sure if I've been staring at his text message for an hour or five, but it was still light when I came and sat on the sofa after putting Macy to bed and now the sky is pitch black.

I was sure facing him, whenever that time came, would be simple, but now here I am, no closer to getting the answers I need *and* I made matters worse by sleeping with him.

There's a knock at the door that pulls me from the deep, dark place inside my head and I haul myself off the couch and trudge to the door, wondering if maybe it's my friend Betty with a casserole or home-baked something or other.

Through the glass pane in the door, I can tell immediately it isn't Betty.

"How did you find me?" I ask, pulling open the door. He's so big he almost completely fills the doorway.

He grins and says, "My mom knows the location of every person in this resort. At this point, I'm pretty sure she secretly works for the government."

I step aside and gesture with my hand. "Do you want to come in?"

His gaze pauses on mine. Serious but not unfriendly. "Yes, please." He walks inside my apartment and the space shrinks.

"There's not much room. Just two little bedrooms, a bathroom and a small kitchen/living area but it's enough space for me and Macy," I say, kneeling down on the carpet and putting the building bricks Macy was playing with earlier back in the basket.

"Macy," he repeats like the word is a foreign language he's trying to learn. "Macy." He nods his head like he approves.

"Do you want a drink or a..." I shrug. "I have coffee and orange juice. Or water. I haven't had chance to buy groceries."

He shakes his head and gestures to the sofa that's filled with soft toys. "You mind if I sit?"

"Sure," I reply and he carefully moves some of Macy's toys out of the way so there is enough room for us to sit, but I don't move. I stay kneeling on the carpet so there is space between us.

Tate glances around the room, his eyes darting from photographs and a painting by Macy that I taped to the door, to the underwear I hand-washed yesterday that's long since dried but still hanging on my little collapsible drying rack. He hasn't said anything derogatory, and his expression isn't judgmental but he continues to take the place in, and a defensive current vibrates up my back.

My small apartment that comes with my job. The scant, well used furniture. The few secondhand toys strewn about the place. I can see how it must look to someone like him, someone with his kind of means, like I'm barely surviving and my pride takes a hit.

"Did you want something?" I ask more curtly than I mean. "I still have to clean up and I'm hoping to squeeze some sleep in before I have to get up and take Macy to day care."

"Macy," he says her name again and it makes my heart feel heavier. "She goes to day care?"

"Like most two year olds," I say as though it's obvious, taking a deep breath. "Look, I don't know why you came here but I'm not down for a repeat of earlier. It was a mistake and honestly, I don't know what—"

"Is she mine? Is Macy my daughter?" Tate asks slowly, his expression is a mix of confusion and curiosity, but it quickly turns serious as he waits for my answer.

"Yes, she's yours—biologically at least, but let's not pretend you didn't already know that."

"She's mine?" Shock falls over Tate's features making him look years younger. His gaze doesn't budge from mine as he waits and it's pinning me to the spot.

"Yes, she's yours. I don't sleep around, if that's what you're implying, which you basically did a few years ago. Thanks for the hundred, by the way, but it's taken far more than that to raise her. When I slept with you, it'd been four months since I'd been with any other guys. There's no question she's yours." His mouth pops open like he's going to speak and then he closes it again. "Look, I offered to do the DNA test and your people told me it wasn't necessary—"

"DNA test?"

"Yes. A fucking DNA test. I told them I'd prove it, and they told me I was deluded. That you'd denied ever knowing me."

He leans forward onto his knees, trying to fit the puzzle pieces together. "Who is they?"

"Your people. I contacted your management company, your fan club, your PR firm. I reached out to your security contractors, Tate. Essentially, I humiliated myself over and over again and they either ignored me or they told me that there was a mistake. Tate Blingwood is far too high and mighty to impregnate a mere mortal. Who did I think I was? Maybe I was drunk and mistook some other dude for *the* Tate Blingwood. Eventually they told me they had checked, and there was absolutely no way Tate Blingwood was in Santa Barbra during spring break."

He scrunches his nose. "But I was there."

"Ya think!" I hiss back at him. "I know you were fucking there. You know you were there, but do you think anyone would believe me?" I pinch my eyes closed for a second and push away the memories of feeling like a desperate loser who'd lie about an encounter to bag a celebrity, so I bring the conversation back to the here and now. "Look, I don't want you or your money. Macy and I are just fine without you. If the rest of your family want a relationship with Macy, then we can arrange something but mostly I just want her to be able to one day speak to you if she wants to. She might want answers eventually. Like why you never saw her or whatever. She deserves answers, if she decides she wants them—"

"What do you mean, 'if she wants to know why she never saw me?' She's going to see me. I'm her father. She's my daughter. Of course, she's going to see me."

It's my turn to be confused. "You don't want a relationship with her. You told your people I was lying."

His eyes sear into mine so sincerely that I have to remind myself he's an asshole just to stop myself from leaning into him. "Jessie, no. I didn't tell anyone you were lying. This is the first I've heard of it." He shakes his head and his stare turns angry, offended even. "So that's why you were so furious with me yesterday? You think I'm the kind of guy who would leave his kid to fend for itself?"

"Excuse me?! Fend for herself? No. Luckily for Macy, I've been taking care of her and doing a pretty good job of it!"

"I'm not saying you aren't! But why didn't you call me? I left you my cell number. You could have called me directly."

Outraged that he is even accusing me of doing anything wrong, I blast him, "For the record, Tate, you left without waking me to even tell me your fabulous news that you got the lead, you left $100 bucks on the table, making me feel like I was charging you for sex, so yeah... I threw your number in the trash, only to find out a month later —Surprise!"

My face must be red with anger, so I'm thankful the bedroom door is shut and Macy can't see me upset or hear us arguing.

Tate's hands reach into his hair and he tugs his dark locks at the root. "The money was to pay you for the room. You were a college student and you'd already paid for the room ahead of time. I was covering your costs not paying for your services!"

"Yeah, well that definitely wasn't how it made me feel."

He looks shocked, remorseful even. "Fuck. I'm sorry. I'm going to get to the bottom of this." He pulls out his cell phone and presses speed dial, then puts it on loud speaker.

"Hey, Tate. How—"

"Have you ever heard from a Jessie?" Tate's voice is booming. Angry.

"Jessie? Salvadore? She's in Budapest shooting an action movie, I think. Do you think she'd be a good person for the fake relationship?"

I scrunch my face at Tate. I've heard of Jessie Salvadore. She's a celebrity. Of course, she's the Jessie they think of and not a little nobody maid manager. But the mention of a fake relationship has me screwing my face harder. This is the life he leads, where everything is fake and contrived.

"No. Not her. Jessie...." He looks at me and mouths, "What's your surname?"

"Yates," I hiss back.

"Jessie Yates. She's been trying to get in contact with me. You heard of her?"

"Can't say I have. Who is she?" the guy on the other end of the phone asks.

"The woman from spring break," Tate says like that might prompt him. "The woman I just discovered had my baby."

Though it's not directed at me, Tate's voice is mean. His anger makes his story more believable and mirrors how I'm feeling. For a moment it's like we're on the same side. That maybe he really didn't get the memo. But where does that leave us?

"What are you talking about, Tate? A baby? Are you kidding me, an illegitimate child is the last thing we need."

"My daughter is not an inconvenience." I huff out an angry growl and Tate at least has the decency to look apologetic.

He blinks a long, slow blink and holds his hand out steady. "No. She's not."

I hadn't considered the scenario that he never got any of my messages. I tried so many times to contact him, often when I was tired and angry, that it seemed obvious he knew and was deliberately avoiding stepping up.

"So, you're saying that this Jessie has turned up and she's saying she had your baby?" Jason asks but rolls into his next sentence without leaving Tate the chance to answer. "Is it actually feasible and not just another allegation from a crazy fan?"

"It's feasible. Jason, she looks just like me," he says, his eyes fixing on the framed photograph on the table beside him.

"Well, I hope you haven't gone on record with this. You'll need to make her take a DNA test—"

"Shut up, Jason. I never slept with any of those women, but this one I did. She's genuine and I want to know how this news never got to me. What the fuck, man. I'm a father!"

"Tate, *if* we received word like this and *if* it seemed genuine, we would have brought it to you. It's probably all bullshi—"

"Don't you dare fucking say it. I have lost years with my daughter."

The line goes quiet and I watch Tate silently fume. He seems genuine, which throws me. All this time, I thought he didn't want to be saddled with a kid while his career was taking off, but if his surprise is real and not some kind of early midlife crisis, then now I feel a sense of loss, for him and Macy.

"I wouldn't keep anything like this from you, Tate, but we get a dozen such letters a week. It's the nature of the business. How many stalkers have you had?"

"Like, six?"

"Exactly. We need to protect you in this, if Dinky discovers you've got a secret child, well… we're going to have to spin this carefully if it turns out to be true." Tate runs his hands through his glossy curls, and I can see turmoil in his eyes. "We'll arrange a DNA test. I'll have the legal team put something together for the woman to sign—"

"Jason. I don't give a damn if word gets out. I have a daughter!"

"Let's make sure she's actually yours first, then we'll deal with how everyone else finds out," Jason replies and Tate initially nods, then shakes his head like he doesn't know which way is up.

Tate hangs up and sits in silence for a full two minutes before his gaze turns back to the photograph beside him. It's one of me and Macy at the beach and he picks it up and holds it in his hands.

"It was taken on my birthday. Skyla and Layla organized a picnic and... it was a fun day. Macy adores digging in the sand, paddling in the sea. She just loves the ocean."

He strokes his finger across the glass. "I can't believe I missed two years because of my team's arrogance. And for the record, Jessie, please believe me. I left you that money to pay you back for the hotel; it was never meant to slander you."

My eyes start to sting and I let out a deep sigh at our time wasted. "I guess it's like Jason said, you get hundreds of claims."

Tate's floppy curls fall over his eyes and he strokes them back so he can lock his gaze on mine. The familiar pull of attraction reels me in and he's looking at me like he feels it too. It'd be so easy to lean forward, lift my chin, and wait and see if he moves to kiss me. I feel like he would, like he'd pin me down right here and take me if I gave him the signal, but to what end?

He's gorgeous. Mesmerizing. But there's no way I can get involved with a spoiled star with endless means. What would happen when the relationship blew up? Tate says he wants to be involved in Macy's life now, but that might just be because he's in between films, down on his luck, and bored. Will he be so interested in getting to know Macy at 2 a.m. when she's spiking a fever? Or what if he likes being a father so much that he decides he wants her full-time. Tate can give Macy a life I could never dream of. And he could probably afford lawyers that can spin some lies and take her away from me.

No. No matter which way I look at it, I'm unbreakably tied to Tate Blingwood forever. A relationship between us, no matter how good I know it would be physically, could destroy both Macy and me emotionally. My mom had a custody battle with one of my sister's dad's and it got crazy and mean. It'd be dancing with madness. It'd never work out, we're too different, and Macy's happiness is too important to jeopardize.

"Can I see her? Can I see Macy?" he asks, seemingly vulnerable.

"Just for a moment." I stand, then lead him through to her bedroom where she is fast asleep.

Tate creeps up to the bed so quietly, I'm not even sure he's breathing. "Beautiful," he whispers, not taking his eyes off her. "Does she always sleep like this? One leg in, one leg out of the covers?"

"Yeah, she takes up the whole bed," I reply fondly.

Tate lets out a hushed chuckle. In his eyes is sheer adoration and it has my throat aching. "I sleep like that. She's like her old man." A grin takes over his face.

"In the mornings, she climbs into my bed, and even though she's small, she pushes me right out to the edge."

He fixes me with a stare so lovely my legs weaken. "I'd love to see that."

Sharing information about my daughter is a double-edged sword. The nuances of raising her have been solely my privilege up until now. They feel private, like they're mine. Yet on the other hand, I've never had anyone to intimately confide with. Sharing with Tate and watching him marvel over details that might seem mundane to anyone else feels so big that swallowing suddenly becomes difficult.

"We should leave Macy to sleep. She has day care in the morning and she's cranky when she's tired."

"She gets that from me," he says, following me out, and I stop suddenly in the entranceway. I turn to him slowly, trying to find a way to explain my torn-up emotions.

"I feel out of control. I don't know if I can trust you with her yet. It's been just me and Macy for so long, I don't know how to navigate this situation. Whatever happens next, we have to do what's best for Macy."

He grabs my wrist and even though his clasp is light, electricity pulses through my body. "You can trust me. I won't ever do a thing to hurt that little girl in there. And we're agreed. Macy comes first. Always."

"She's only two. We have to go slow with this. Give her time to adjust."

"I'll go as slow as you like."

"We can't screw this up. Which means we can't screw around like we did yesterday. It's out of our systems now and so there'll be no repeats."

Tate's mouth opens like he's about to object then it closes and he takes a step back, his gaze never leaving mine. "Whatever you want." His thumb rubs circles against my wrist. "I promise, I'm going to be a good father to Macy."

Every fiber of me wants to believe him, but I've been burned before. My mom had many boyfriends with big promises and huge gestures. But over time, their commitments always waned.

"Macy deserves someone who is going to show up for her. Someone she can rely on. Tate, when I first saw you in the penthouse, you were sleeping off nearly a half a bottle of whiskey. Are you sure you're ready for this?"

His jaw tenses with frustration. "I'd had a rough day and... I didn't know about Macy. She changes everything. Everything. I won't even miss the drinking. You won't believe this but I woke up after that and Drew had tied my damn laces together and fucked with my place and all I could think was, I could've hit my head and died and I left nothing of any value behind. Now, well shit, I'm a father."

He watches my lips tip up into a smirk. "Maybe it wasn't Drew," I reply.

"Yeah. You think I tied my own laces?"

"Or..." My teeth clamp down on my lip and his eyes widen with realization.

"You? You tied my laces and screwed with my facewash?"

"Yes. And if you hadn't got yourself in a mess, then I wouldn't have had the opportunity. What if you got in that state around Macy. She could get hurt or—"

"I would never get drunk around her."

"Really?"

"Yes! What do you take me for?"

I shrug. "I'm just saying, you hurt her or put her at risk in any way, you're gone."

"I get it, okay! You think I'm not capable, but I'm going to prove you wrong. And you owe me some batteries."

"And you owe me almost two hundred bucks for fancy facewash," I counter.

He pulls out his wallet and hands me a bunch of twenties.

"So, when can I meet her?"

"I don't know. I need some time to prepare both her and myself."

"But you'll let me see her?"

I nod, knowing that unless he proves himself unsafe to be around her, I can't stand in the way of Macy knowing her father. "You made her too. She looks more like you than she does me."

"I can't believe it. I feel like I need to scream it out loud to make it real."

"It's going to feel pretty real when she has a level ten meltdown on the floor of Walmart," I joke then shut up. Like Tate Blingwood is ever going to wind up in Walmart. There's so much to navigate, so much to discuss, I'm overwhelmed and exhausted. "You'd better go. I have to be up early and..."

79

He nods but doesn't move. He smells so damn good that it's muddying my thoughts. "I guess you have my number now. So, we can..."

"We can. And I'll see you tomorrow. I'm still your maid for a while yet."

Macy lets out a light cough and it startles Tate.

"What was that? Is she okay? Should we call a doctor?" Tate asks.

I use the distraction to step back to clear my nostrils of his cologne. "Just a cough. She's fine. You better go," I say even though part of me wants him to stay. "I have an early start."

He takes a step toward the door and stops, picking up the cup I keep on the shelf.

"What's this?" he asks, turning it over in his hands and running his fingers along the text that reads: *World's Best Dad*.

It's the one I bought for my own dad. I'm not sure why I've kept it all these years except as a reminder not to delude myself with wishful thinking.

I take the cup from him and put it back on the shelf. "It's none of your business. Look, you might be Macy's father and we might have to figure this out somehow for her sake, but let's get this straight, Macy means more to me than anyone else in the whole world, and so if you're just some chump on an ego trip, then move along because we don't need you messing with her head. I will protect her at all costs and if you want a relationship with her, you better not mess this up."

His smile fades. "Some chump on an ego trip?"

I nod. I didn't mean to offend him, but it's better I'm clear about the boundaries now than have him think I'll tolerate him picking Macy up and setting her aside as the mood strikes.

"I have no intention of messing this up."

CATCH A FALLING STAR

"Good," I say.

"Good," he counters. "So, I'll see you tomorrow?" He looks as pissed off with me as I am with him.

"You will."

He takes a step toward the door and then stiffens, his fists balling. "You need me to do anything before I go?"

I laugh. "What would I need you to do at—" I glance at the clock on the wall "—almost 10 p.m.?"

"I don't know, put up a shelf or go to the grocery store?"

I laugh again. "We should probably build up to the dad duties."

"Okay, well if you or Macy need anything, anything at all, you just call me." He pulls his cell from his pocket and points. "I'll be waiting."

"I'll try to think of some things," I tell him and steer him to the door. Then I remember his hat and scarf and grab them from the sofa. "Here, in case anyone sees you."

"Oh yeah," he says, putting his hat on and pulling his scarf across his face. "I've got to clean up my image, I'm a father now."

"Yes, you are," I reply and see him out.

A part of me longs to trust Tate, and after tonight I think he has good intentions, but I've also learned the hard way that good intentions don't always equate to meaningful actions.

81

CHAPTER 10

TATE

*T*he resort is quiet on the way back to the penthouse, just a few revelers at the beach bar who are too drunk to notice there's a guy walking around, looking ridiculous with a scarf over his face in the middle of August in California.

I'm certain the guy on security recognizes me, but he doesn't say anything and lets me punch in the private code in the elevator to take me straight to the top. My thoughts are whirling and in other circumstances, I would crack open a bottle of something to celebrate or call one of my brother's or my sister, Tab's, to bend their ears on what the fuck I should do—but since Jessie hasn't agreed that I can tell anyone yet, I keep myself locked down. I don't want to screw this up.

I sit down on the couch and stare out the window. This is the biggest thing that's ever happened to me. Bigger than landing that lead three years ago, which took me away from them. I can't honestly say I regret taking that opportunity, but I do wish I'd done things differently. Had I just woken Jessie that morning and shared the news, she and I could have been a part of raising Macy from the start and shared the success I've found. I probably wouldn't be in the mess that I'm in, sensationalized actor who's on his way to obscurity because of his behavior. One thing I do know is that I have to get that Dinky deal, work with the franchise, and secure our daughter's financial future. While I've done well, I've only been in the business for three years and that's hardly the level of wealth I need to support my new family. One thing I do know is that as of tonight, I'm a changed man.

* * *

My head is so full of emotions that I barely sleep, but in the morning I make a start by calling Gaynor.

"Hello, Daddy," she says seductively.

"Cut it out, Gaynor." I'm in no mood for joking. She's probably already conspired with Jason how to spin the story for the maximum effect, but I'm not calling her to discuss my career. "Did you know she was trying to reach me?"

"The girl? Babe, we get a ton of those emails a week. Some even write letters with lipstick kisses. We don't respond to them. If I entertained every crazy bitch who deluded themselves into thinking they had 'one special night' with you, then I'd never get any work done. Besides, Kelly goes through the fan mail and she only keeps what we can use for promoting you—"

"You throw my fan mail in the trash?"

"Yeah, of course. Why would we keep them? They're mostly just a list of what they'd like to do to you, an occasional letter begging for money, and requests for child support. And your fans are persistent motherfuckers, some write six times a week—at least they take Sundays off. But they're crazy. You saw them outside the Golden Globes."

The night of the Golden Globes was bad. I had a wardrobe malfunction during the live TV broadcast. One of the models who escorted me on stage accidentally tripped. She tried to hold onto me for support but ended up ripping my already stylishly ripped T-shirt right off my body. It was on every news channel worldwide, me doing the Golden Globes shirtless. By the time the award show was over, swathes of women stormed the building screaming my name. My security detail had to sneak me out, and the news channels covered it for weeks—though Gaynor insisted it was fabulous publicity since the movie I was promoting shot to the number one spot and my fan club subscriptions doubled. It was insane and not something I ever want to go through again.

"Jessie isn't like those fans, and in the future, if people are taking the time to write me, I think I should read them."

There's a noticeable pause before she replies, "Sure. You want to waste hours of your life reading your fan mail, who am I to stop you? You want to read the stuff trashing you too? 'Cuz there's plenty of that."

I never really considered it before but then I decide, "Yeah. I want a balanced view. I need a reality check. I've already got a posse of people who constantly feed my ego."

When I'm not imprisoned in the penthouse, I've got two stylists, a small army of security detail, Jason, Gaynor, my business manager, my driver, PA, not to mention regular visits from the masseuse, hair stylist, and a team of cleaning staff at each of my properties. I'm rarely alone, yet I feel lonely most of the time. And to top it off, they all shower me with praise even when I fuck up or I'm acting like a jerk.

"Cool. Now, when will we get the results of the DNA test? If the kid's yours, we'll need to decide our game plan."

"The kid is mine, Gaynor. I can feel it."

"Okay, well if you're certain, you have a couple of options. 1) You could hide the kid and not go public with the news, but the press will probably find out anyway so it's better we're in control of the narrative. Or 2) You could sell the interview to the highest bidder, explain how you only just found out and how happy you are... blah, blah, blah. I personally prefer the second option. Being super daddy might make you more appealing to Dinky if we spin the 'family man' image. Oh, and we should dig into Jessie, too. The press will want to know who the mother is and if she's hiding any secrets, then they'll do the cha-cha under the world's spotlight, so you'd better find out if there're any skeletons in Jessie's closet."

"I..." I hadn't thought about the impact of my career and fame on Macy and Jessie. I order Gaynor not to make any announcements until I've spoken to Jessie. She has to be on board with any plans moving forward.

"Don't sweat it. I've got this. Give me her number and I'll call her."

"No, leave it to me. I'm seeing her later and I don't want to scare her off with all this stuff, not when she's still coming to terms with me being around."

The elevator opens and Drew and my niece Callie walk in. Behind them is Skyla and she's giving me a pissed-off stare that suddenly makes sense. I guess she didn't talk to Jessie yet. "I got to go. Talk to you later."

I hang up the call and go greet Drew, Skyla and Callie.

"Brought you something that might give you a little freedom," Drew says placing a bike helmet and a set of keys on the counter.

"You're giving me your Harley? Thanks, brother," I reply, playfully digging my niece in the arm.

"Loaning. I want it back when you're no longer on house

arrest. Wear the helmet. It'll hide your big head and stop Mom from busting my ass for letting her 'baby ride around on something dangerous.'" He rolls his eyes and I throw him a shit-eating grin.

"What'll Mom say when she finds out you let her favorite son ride around town on a motorcycle?" I tease but I'm already excited to get some wind in my hair.

Drew chuckles. "Probably for the best if she doesn't find out."

"Can you take me for a ride?" Callie asks and all three adults in the room respond with a flat, "NO!"

"No fair," Callie huffs and pulls out some batteries from the pocket of her jacket. "Guess you won't want these, then?"

I tackle her immediately, lifting her up onto my shoulder, taking the batteries, and dumping her on the sectional sofa. "You'll have to do better than that!" I tease.

"Skyla brought you some leftover lasagna," Drew tells me and I notice she's still looking at me like she wants to punch me.

Skyla narrows her eyes at me. "I'll put it in the fridge. You'll need to warm it before eating it, if you can manage to work the microwave?"

I thrust the batteries into Drew's hands and tell him to fix the remote, then follow Skyla. "I know you know," I whisper and she slams the fridge.

"Yes. And you're very lucky you still have all your teeth." She smiles scornfully.

"What I mean to say is, I didn't know about Macy. I only just found out about…"

"You didn't know?"

I shake my head. "I swear, if I knew, I'd have been there, for every step." Even as I say it, I'm imagining Macy's first steps and wringing my hands that I missed them. "From now on, I'm going to be there."

Skyla looks me up and down. Her expression softens. "It never made sense to me that you didn't know. You're great with Callie and... You better not screw this up."

"I won't," I immediately reply.

"Good. I guess we'll have to keep it to ourselves until Jessie is ready for everyone else to find out." She nods her head toward Callie and Drew.

"For now, yes. But I can't wait to tell everyone." The grin takes over my face. Family barbeques, weddings, my heart thumps like crazy when I think about Christmas with the whole family. Me with Jessie, watching our daughter opening every toy from the shop. "It's going to be epic, except she fucking hates me."

"I'm sure she doesn't hate you." Skyla squeezes my arm but her expression doesn't even come close to sure. "Jessie's strong and stubborn. She's had to be or else she would never have gotten through some tough years. She'll come around and when she does, it's going to be great."

"You're right," I say. "I've just got to win her over." Skyla measures my face and then hugs me.

"You're a daddy!"

We both hop up and down in silent glee.

"Tate, do you want to put my wife down before or after I rip your arm off and beat you with it?" Drew says cheerfully from behind me and I put Skyla down and step away.

"Sorry," I say sheepishly. "I've had a rough few days and she gives good hugs."

"I know," he deadpans. "That's one of the many reasons I married her."

"Why did you guys elope, anyway? I mean, the only person you invited was Callie." I wonder if they'd had a normal wedding, maybe I would have run into Jessie sooner.

Skyla and Drew share a look so deep and meaningful that it feels depraved to watch, so I step away.

"Once we decided we were forever, we didn't want to waste another moment. Logan wasn't exactly in a good mental space to attend a wedding after he got ditched at the altar, and you were committed to a three-month filming schedule, so we decided to go ahead and do it, just us," Drew answers. "When you know what you want, waiting isn't an option."

Drew has his arms wrapped around Skyla like she's the most precious thing in the entire world and suddenly, the space in my own arms feels empty.

"Maybe you'll stumble upon your special someone soon," Skyla says knowingly and Drew guffaws. "Yeah, Tate. Flick through your rolodex and summon yourself a bride. A wedding will help deter your playboy image and also give Mom something to focus on once Layla and Logan's nuptials are over with."

"Nah, no way! Uncle Tate is way too selfish for marriage. When he babysat me, he made me sign a prenup that I wouldn't eat his share of the pizza when he went to the bathroom. And he took the TV controller with him!" Callie says, poking her tongue out and everyone laughs.

The selfish comment stings and I start to think about all the ways I'm going to need to change. I turn to Callie and narrow my eyes, ready to tease her. "You always steal my food and flick the TV to your ridiculous reality TV shows, I was merely protecting my interests," I reply, dropping on the sofa next to her and tickling her until she declares she's going to pee on me.

At that moment the elevator doors whoosh open and Jessie pushes a cart that's taller than she is into the penthouse.

"What's so funny?" Jessie says, glancing over at us. She's wearing her pink maid uniform and my dick immediately takes notice.

"Nothing. These guys were just leaving," I say.

"No, we weren't," Callie replies, proving she has no intention of going anywhere by kicking off her shoes and sprawling out on the sofa. "We were about to discuss how Uncle Tate needs some good PR to save the Dinky deal but that probably won't happen because he's such an utter pillock."

"Hey, I am not a pillock!" I insist, enunciating the word slowly even though I have no idea what it means. Across the room, Jessie looks amused like she is on Callie's side. I glance back at Callie and ask, "What's a pillock?"

"It's British slang. Me and some of the kids from school are brushing up before our school trip to Europe."

"First of all, it's 'some of the kids and I' and I'm so happy that your expensive education is paying such dividends," Drew drawls, casting Callie with a serious stare, not that she cares. "But we really do have to go. You have to get to said expensive school for camp, and Sky and I have got to get to work. We'll see you later," Drew says to me. "Don't get up to any mischief."

I shrug, not paying attention. Him mentioning school has got my mind whirling through all kinds of scenarios. Like, Macy is smart, she's going to need a great school that can keep up with her. And college, I don't know if she has a fund set up already, but I'll need to make sure it's the biggest, best fund there is, and housing... Callie has a massive room in the house my brother built and it's still bursting at the seams with all her crap.

"Hey, Drew?" I say and he pauses on his way out and turns back to look at me. "You got space in your calendar to design me a house?"

"I'm sure I can squeeze you in but I thought you preferred penthouse living?" he questions, and until recently he was right. I own two penthouses, but they're not exactly kid-friendly, what with their top floor, 360-degree balconies.

"I'm looking for something with more rooms and extra space. And a backyard, near the beach," I reply, thinking of all the things Macy will want and need.

"Give it some thought and we'll schedule an appointment."

Callie puts on her shoes and digs me in the ribs before following Skyla and Drew out. I don't miss the look Skyla gives Jessie before they board the elevator, which is a mix of happiness and excitement, but the one Jessie gives her back is less sure. Nervous even. But I guess that's understandable, this situation is new, uncharted waters.

But I'm determined we'll figure it out.

* * *

"You don't have to help me clean," Jessie tells me.

"And you don't have to clean this place for me, but since you insisted, I'm helping."

She continues wiping out the microwave where the calzone I reheated exploded and oozed out everywhere, and I hold the trash can and look at her. She really is beautiful, even sweaty and cussing from my incompetence in the kitchen.

My Jessie is flawless.

"Besides, I want you to tell me everything. Like, how was the birth? Did you have anyone with you? What was Macy's first word?" My heart sinks as I immediately guess it wasn't daddy.

She pauses and smiles, still staring into the microwave, then she pulls off her gloves, and reaches into the pouch in her apron and pulls out her phone. Swiping it to life, she scrolls up through a million photos like she's starting at the beginning. I scoot closer to her so I can see better and am hit by her sweet scent.

"This is me pregnant at nine months. I was absolutely enormous and my toes got so fat they looked like little sausages dangling from meat patties."

"You're making me hungry," I joke, staring at the picture and feeling amazement that she grew our child in her tiny little body. She looked beautiful pregnant—all soft angles and voluptuous curves. I've heard people say a woman glows when she's pregnant, but Jessie shone.

"You're always hungry," she deadpans and then swipes to the next one which is of Macy. Tiny and blue, she looks barely alive and my hands sweat even though I know she is just fine.

"Was she okay? When she was born, did she come out with any medical issues? Because I have great insurance. I can afford the best health care. If there's anything she needs, anything you need, it's there. I have it and now, so do you both."

Her eyes crinkle as she examines me. "We already have good health care. It's one of the reasons I took this job. Logan's health insurance is top notch and our premiums are ridiculously low."

"Oh, well he'd better," I reply, feeling redundant.

"Macy was born at 4:02 a.m. on Thursday the seventeenth of January, making her a Capricorn."

I never gave a damn about horoscopes but suddenly I'm interested. "A Capricorn." I smile like it's miraculous. "So, it'll be her third birthday in a few months. We'll have to throw her a party. A huge one with cake and a petting zoo and..." I suddenly realize I know next to nothing about kids parties. "I'll hire a party planner."

Jessie laughs. "She'll be three. Give her an empty box and some balloons and she'll be in her element." Jessie scrolls to another photograph. "Macy screamed the whole hospital down. My momma was with me and even though she had six kids of her own, she said she'd never heard a baby scream so loud."

I smile, trying to imagine the relief when Macy announced to the world that she was alive and strong, then I try to remember what I was doing at 4:02 a.m. on Thursday the seventeenth of January that year and feel stricken that I can't remember. I pull out my phone and search through the calendar until I find the date.

"I was in New York," I say, calculating the time zone difference. "I was at a party in the East Village. I remember it because I was jet-lagged and the party was lame and I spent the whole night wishing I was someplace else." I skip forward the next year, to Macy's first birthday. "While Macy was blowing out the candles on her first cake, I was cutting the ribbon on a new children's center in Baltimore." I feel mildly better that at least I was doing something philanthropic, though I'm too ashamed to admit I was only there because Gaynor schedules 10 percent of my personal appearances to appeal to a "wider audience" and also so I don't look like such a spoiled star. "Her second birthday, I was on set in Hawaii."

Jessie smiles a sad smile. "Don't beat yourself up. Maybe if I'd tried harder…"

"You tried hard enough. I should have tried to find you. I always wondered what would have happened between us if Jason called me the next day or week. Maybe we'd have hung out some more."

"No. You did what you could, and I was just some girl you hooked up with—"

"You weren't. I knew it was more, but I couldn't put my finger on why." I lean closer to her. I want to kiss her so badly my lips ache, never mind how badly my balls are reacting with her so close in a tight uniform with a short skirt. "Jessie—"

"No." She shakes her head. "We can't."

"Oh. Yeah, I get it." I don't like it, but I do get why sleeping together might not help us figure out our parenting strategy. I pull away from the magnetism that's drawing me to her and making me desperate to breathe her in until there's a space between us and tell her, "I'm going to make up for lost time, I swear."

"I know you will," she replies almost automatically, and I can tell I'm going to have to prove it to her.

"Can I meet her? You don't have to tell her who I am, but can I come over? Or you could bring her here. Or I could arrange a place, neutral territory."

She puts her index finger to my lips. "You can meet her, just not yet. I have to be sure the timing is right." She takes her finger away and I lean into her, hanging off her every word. "Macy is going to love you."

Six words.

Six simple little words that almost bring me to tears.

"I want her to love me," I admit.

"She will." Jessie's gaze is paused on me and I can feel us getting closer. There's a tension in the air and I know she feels it too, but then she shakes her head, blinking away whatever she was thinking, and then she says, "Right. That's the microwave cleaned. I suppose I ought to think about getting you some lunch. What do you want?"

You.

93

CHAPTER 11

JESSIE

$\mathcal{T}$he days fall into an easy pattern where I show up to work and spend the day hanging out with Tate in his penthouse apartment. He asks about every detail of Macy's life and I revel in filling him in on all the parts he missed. But the nights are the hardest. When Macy is in bed and I'm all alone, except for the back and forth text messages with Tate that cover anything he forgot to ask during the day, and I knew I wouldn't be able to put off them meeting for much longer.

I had hoped there'd be some kind of obvious reason why he couldn't parent Macy. A massive coke habit or displays of reckless anger would make it an easy no. But he's been patient and kind and shown understanding that letting a stranger into Macy's life isn't as easy as rocking up to his place with her overnight bag. He's showing no sign of getting bored, like I anticipated he might. In fact, he seems more eager with every day that passes.

Tate's been sweet, too. He keeps asking for the details of Macy's savings account so he can make a deposit, and he's offered me money. Money my pride won't let me accept right now. I tell him it's all been too sudden but that we'll figure out those details eventually, and he seems content for now to go at my pace. But once he's met Macy, once he starts giving us money, it's going to be harder to put on the brakes or make a U-turn because we'll owe him and Macy will be attached.

Which is how I'm starting to feel. Attached. But also like I want to scoop up my daughter and run far away so I can protect her from anything that might go wrong.

Especially now, standing in the elevator, holding Macy's hand, bringing her to meet her father. Tate's standing there when the elevator opens and he's holding an enormous pink bunny.

"You came!" His eyes light up and a huge smile covers most of his face. Beyond him, the entire room is adorned with the contents of a toy store.

"Hi, Macy," he says adoringly.

"Where did you get all this stuff?" I ask.

"I made a deal with Simon from security. He went to the toy store and got everything he thought a two-year-old would like. I couldn't have my favorite girl show up with no toys to play with," he says to Macy and then his eyes flick to me. "I promise, you're my second favorite."

"Remember, Macy can be shy with strangers and she's not used to men, so it might take her a while," I remind him.

He kneels down to Macy's level and uses the bunny to talk to her. "Hi! My name's Tate. What's yours?"

Macy runs up to the bunny and hugs it, her arms wrapping so tightly that Tate gets the edge of her hug. I watch Tate melt into her as though an overwhelming surge of pride and unfiltered joy has taken him by surprise. His smile is wonderous as he stares at Macy utterly dumbfounded. It's like watching instantaneous, unconditional love wash over a person and the sight makes my throat ache.

"She got over her shyness pretty quickly," he says, casting me a quick glance, and then his gaze returns to Macy—like he's afraid she'll suddenly change her mind about liking him and scream.

"Yes, she likes to prove me wrong, quite often actually."

"Bunny," Macy squeaks with a huge toothy smile and Tate's head snaps to me and then back to Macy in wonder.

"Yes, bunny! You're so clever."

I'm smiling along with them. The beauty of witnessing Tate unravel in the presence of our daughter is an unexpected delight. But the dark side of my soul remains cautious against any premature elation. Like this, on the floor of the penthouse in sweats and a ratty T, smiling at his daughter, it'd be easy to forget that he's an international superstar with leans on his time and attention. The knowledge that his real life is waiting for him tempers the effervescence of my optimism.

Tate is temporarily out of the celebrity circle, but eventually he'll go back to his old life and that might not leave room for Macy. I tell myself I'm being a realist to push away the ache in my chest.

Tate gives Macy a doll and tells her that she can be the princess and then he looks up at me. "Are you going to join us?" He pulls out a random soft toy from the pile and says, "You can be the wicked witch."

I take two steps forward and pull the witch from his hand and Tate's gaze lingers on mine. "The very smartest, most beautiful wicked witch, obviously."

I look at the green soft toy and laugh. "I need to make your snacks, so I'll be over at the counter, chopping carrot sticks and casting spells."

"You already put a spell on me." He waggles his brows and then turns his attention back to Macy. "Quick Macy, run! Mommy's going to make us eat crunchy wands of disappointment!"

Macy cackles a laugh and latches onto his back and Tate scoots on his knees across the living area.

Emotion throttles me. I've never seen Macy take to someone so quickly.

I move to the counter and unload my satchel full of snacks as Tate pretends to be the bunny and tickles Macy until she squeals laughter. I stay on the peripheral, watching, smiling, laughing sometimes. Macy puts the play kitchen chef's hat on Tate's head and they pretend to have a tea party.

"It's like she knows me," he says, looking up from Macy momentarily.

"She kind of does," I reply.

His gaze turns speculative. "How so?"

"Macy. Where's Triptastic Tate?" I say animatedly and Macy's face lights up and she points to Tate.

He looks at me with confusion and I hold up my phone. "Macy's favorite video is of you juggling the lemons. She thinks you're hilarious."

His eyes widen as realization dawns on him. Tate got the nickname Triptastic Tate after he was filmed juggling fruit, tripping in his performance and taking out a table full of drinks. Of course, he doesn't know that I cropped the video that was already online, crowned him with the nickname in the subtitles, dubbed it with humorous music and released it online under my pseudonym BabyMomma4You. "Macy saw me watching the video, and she liked it."

"You stalked me?" he says, his face lighting up gleefully.

"Stalked is a stretch," I coolly reply, my poker face turned on. "That video was everywhere, and besides it was for Macy. She took one look at you and seemed to decide you were interesting—not as interesting as Peppa, but even you can't compete with a talking pig."

"Hmph. A talking pig," he replies and then turns to Macy. "I'm going to be Cal in the new Dinky franchise." He looks amusingly proud of himself for a nanosecond, until Macy accidentally pokes him in the eye with the tip of the teapot.

"Sow wee. Ouchy," Macy says, going back to the play kitchen.

Tate rubs his eye and then says, "You let Macy *meet* me, even though you hated me?" The way he's looking at me is like he's truly touched.

I shrug. "I figured she'd want to know who you were eventually. I know I did and—"

"You didn't know your own dad?"

My stomach drops and I go back to chopping carrot sticks. "That's a long story, for when little ears are not in the room," I say, nodding my head at Macy who is pretending to pour coffee.

Tate nods his understanding and then replies, "I'm going to be different, you know?" He puts the chef's hat on Macy and expertly tucks her hair out the way. "We're going to be different, aren't we?" he says to Macy. "We're going to be perfection."

"Potecton," Macy repeats and Tate shows her how to high five.

* * *

"Same time tomorrow?" Tate asks as I lift an exhausted, sleeping Macy from his arms. His smile is tender and unsure. "Or I could come to you. I like your place better."

"Why do you like my tiny place?" I ask, looking around the flawless expanse of the penthouse. "You could fit my entire living quarters in your kitchen area alone."

His fingers muss his hair, causing his T-shirt to ride up and reveal smooth tanned skin and chiseled abs. "I like your place. The pictures, Macy's artwork. It's lived-in, whereas this place is just a hotel room—a very nice hotel room, but still impersonal. You know?"

I nod my approval. Our place is small and Macy only has a few strategic toys, but we made it our home and it's been a good home with great memories.

"Is it weird that I don't want you both to go? Can't you stay here tonight?" he asks, his hands reaching out, then as though he decided against it, he plunges them deep in his pockets.

I shake my head. "We don't have our stuff here and Macy's used to waking up in her own bed or at Betty's." I already explained to Tate that Betty, who used to be my boss until she recently retired, and my mom mind Macy when I need them to outside of the day care hours.

I reposition Macy who may only be tiny, but is heavy and awkward to carry when she is sleeping deeply like this.

"Let me take her," he says. "I'll carry her back for you. It'll be getting dark soon. I should make sure you both get there safe."

"We'll be fine. You're not supposed to leave the penthouse," I remind him.

"I'm not supposed to do a lot of things," he says mischievously and puts on his hat and scarf. "But rules are made to be broken."

"You're not coming with us. If word gets out, we'll be hounded by all your crazy fans."

"Word won't get out," he replies. "We'll be careful."

"Okay, but keep your head down," I tell him, passing him Macy to hold, and as we're about to get into the elevator, he runs back for the giant bunny.

"That's not inconspicuous at all," I jibe.

"My girl likes her Tate bunny, so he'll be there when she wakes up."

"You say that like it won't be you who has to cart it across town on the bus to day care," I reply only mildly put out.

We get into the elevator and he says, "You take the bus to day care?"

"Yeah," I nod. "Betty loans me her car sometimes but I don't like to take advantage."

He nuzzles Macy, deep in thought and then kisses the top of her head. Side by side, it's impossible to see where his hair ends and Macy's starts. "Did you send for the DNA test or do you want me to do it?" I ask.

He looks straight at me and replies, "I don't need a DNA test, Jessie. She's mine. Any fool can see it."

"I know that, but if you wanted one, just to be certain, we'd do it," I reply, flattered by his absolute faith but also understanding if he needs something concrete. "They just need a hair from her head and some saliva, it doesn't have to be a blood test or anything." I try to move my thoughts away from thinking that it's easier for him to walk away later if he doesn't have proof she's his, but they go there anyway.

"No one is touching a hair on her head. Besides, I have all the proof I need. Did you see the way she was looking at me earlier?" His grin lights up. "I'm not going anywhere, Jessie. I know you think I'm going to disappear but I'm not. I'm here and I'm staying."

The elevator pings open and as we walk through the foyer, we see Simon from security. "Jessie, you're working late tonight and you brought little Macy to your shift?" he asks sweetly, then glances at Tate and whispers, "Don't worry, I haven't told a soul about you being here or the purchases I made for you."

"Thanks, Simon. We're actually in a hurry. Got to get the little one in her own bed," he says.

"Oh, of course. I'll leave you two youngsters to it." I'm walking away before he's finished his sentence and Tate catches up to me.

"He thinks we're dating," I hiss. "Did you tell him that? Did you tell him you're Macy's father?"

"No. I told him you were bringing your kid to work and I wanted her to have some toys to play with."

"You bought half the toy store!"

"Simon wouldn't be the first person to think I have a tendency to overspend. Besides, he seems like a decent guy. He won't snitch, it's fine," Tate replies breezily and even though he's right, Simon is a decent guy and wouldn't rat either of us out, I feel uncomfortable that Tate has this level of power over me. Like he can tell his own narrative and I can't control how it's going to go down. "Are you mad at me?" he asks.

"No."

"You're pissed, tell me why."

I stop and face him. "Don't swear around Macy. She's picking up new words all the time and I don't want those to be the ones she uses."

"Okay," he says slowly. "I won't. Now tell me why you're mad."

"You told Simon I was bringing my daughter to work."

He nods. "I needed to tell him something and he would have seen you walking her in anyway."

"It's unprofessional. He thinks we're dating."

"And that's a problem?"

"It's a huge problem. The people I work with are going to think I'm one of your deluded fans."

"Or they'll think I have exceptionally good taste in women." His smile is so gorgeous I completely forget the counter argument I had prepared.

"Let's just hurry and get you out of sight. Being out in public with you is making me nervous."

We rush the rest of the way, and as I am sticking the key in the door, Betty appears behind us. "I brought my favorite little madam her best supper, Mac 'n cheese!" she sings. "But I wasn't expecting ya'll to have company."

Tate and I both turn at the same time and Betty's expression turns curious.

"A scarf in August. You crazy, man?" she says directly to Tate and he delicately shifts Macy in his arms so he can pull the scarf aside to reveal his face. Betty's mouth pops open and her cheeks rise up with glee. For a second, I think she's going to reach out and touch him but instead she hisses, "Hurry up and open the door, Jessie. I just saw Sally out jogging—well, if you can call it that. Mostly, she's just spying on folk."

Sally works in reception and is the resort gossip. If she sees Tate, word that he's here won't just be out, it'll be on loud speaker.

I open the door and, once we're in side, push it shut and lock it.

"Who's for Mac 'n Cheese?" Betty asks.

"He's just going—"

"I'd love some, thank you," Tate replies, grinning an A-list smile at Betty.

"You two pop Macy to bed and I'll warm up two servings. I'll leave some in the refrigerator for Macy."

* * *

By the time Macy is tucked in bed, Betty has removed my laundry pile from the table, lit candles, and poured two big glasses of wine.

"How did you two meet?" Betty asks and Tate looks to me to answer.

"We're not dating," I tell her. "Tate is, well, he's..." My swallow echoes around the room. "He's Macy's father," I admit and wait for Betty's reaction. I've known Betty two years and I have never mentioned *the* Tate Blingwood is the baby daddy.

"I know he's Macy's father, she looks just like him. I asked how you met, dear? Do you need to clean your ears, Jessie?"

Tate chuckles and I nudge him in the ribs.

"It was a long time ago," I say as Tate replies, "We met during spring break. Jessie was a college student and I was taking the summer off before I started my next job."

"And you both rolled into bed. How lovely." She gleefully rubs her hands together.

"I'm sorry I didn't tell you, Betty. I..."

"I know, love. You thought he did you dirty. And did he?" She pulls her glasses down her nose and studies Tate like she's deciding the best way to incapacitate him.

I shake my head. "It seems like it was a misunderstanding."

Her face colors pink with happiness. "How wonderful. So, you're making up for lost time?"

I shake my head again. "He's getting to know Macy."

"But you're going to give things a go? You can't stay single forever, Jessie. Not when there's a young, handsome, *virile* man beside you."

"No. We're not dating. I'm on Tinder," I blurt wondering why the hell I said that. I joined the platform a few weeks ago under protest from Layla, who swiped a bunch of people on my behalf, but I couldn't bring myself to chat with anyone. When I dare to look his way, Tate has a thick brow raised at me.

"Tinder?"

"Yes. It's the modern way to date, so I hear," I reply unsure why I feel so guilty about it.

"In my day you didn't swipe anything. You threw a pebble at their window and prayed it didn't break the glass and knock him out." Betty takes off her glasses and polishes the lenses, shaking her head as she continues, "It's so much simpler hooking up with the guy who already impregnated you, isn't it?" The question must be rhetorical because she doesn't give me the opportunity to regurgitate all the reasons I have why Tate and I must never get together. She simply says, "It could be the making of you both. But that's just my opinion."

"We're not dating, Betty. We have Macy to think about."

Beside me, Tate's stare burns but I don't dare look his way. He's probably equally uncomfortable with this line of questioning, but Betty has been so good to me, I can't be rude and cut her off so I stay silent and pray the conversation moves on.

Betty's drawn on eyebrows rise up over the rim of her glasses like she thinks I'm the crazy one. "Yes. It'd be awful for Macy if her mother and father were to date. Utterly tragic, in fact. What would people say?"

Tate chokes out a laugh at Betty's abject sarcasm.

"Betty, Tate is a Hollywood star. I imagine they would have quite a lot to say."

"I know he is, dear." She rolls her eyes at me and then smiles at Tate. "I just loved you in *Bellacres Beach*. Will you sign me an autograph?"

"Of course," he replies and pats himself down as though searching for a pen.

"Actually, don't worry about the autograph. Let's have a selfie." She pulls out her cell and he stands beside her. "Do you mind taking your shirt off first. You're shirtless for most of the movie, and Kathy from the bingo won't believe it's you unless she can see the birthmark right above your left peck."

"Betty, he is not taking off his shirt!" I hiss but Tate just smiles and says, "Of course that'd be okay."

I stare at him, wondering if he has gone crazy, but then he takes his shirt off and my mouth falls open. Smooth skin beneath rock hard muscle reveals itself and my mouth waters —even his navel is perfect. Betty grins at me while I take the photo and I swear she knows I'm ogling him too.

"Happy?" Tate asks, putting his shirt back on which returns all sensible thoughts to my head.

"Well, it'd have been better if you were in shorts. Are you wearing boxers?" she asks but I interrupt. "He is not taking off his pants, Betty!"

"Okay. Next time." She winks and then says, "I better go and let you two love birds eat your supper. Have fun!" She nearly skips out of the apartment and shuts the door behind her.

"Macy loves her," I say when she's gone. "So do I, even if she is batshit crazy sometimes."

"She's a smart lady. I think I'm falling in love with her too," Tate replies, and then he pulls out a chair and gestures for me to sit.

"So, you're on Tinder?" he asks casually, leaning back in his chair, satiated from the massive helping of Mac that Betty plated for him. It didn't escape my notice that his portion was almost twice the size of my own, but I decide I won't hold that against him.

I nod my head to my cell that rests on the table between

us. "Layla thought it was time I got back out there and met some guys."

"And have you met some guys?"

I'm tempted to make up some elaborately stylish lifestyle, like I haven't just been working and staying home most nights since having Macy, but the crease between his brows suddenly deepens and pauses me.

"No. I swiped a bunch of guys but I haven't met anyone. Mostly, by the time I've finished my shift and got Macy bathed and tucked into bed, I barely have enough energy to read a chapter of a book before I fall asleep. I'll get to dating eventually, I suppose."

His eyes are sparkly and warm in the candlelight and he's studying me so closely it's making me dizzy.

"You don't believe me?"

"Oh, I believe you, but come on, you're gorgeous. There must have been someone in all this time?"

My nerves zing when he says I'm gorgeous, which is probably due to the enormous glass of wine that I'm halfway through. "There hasn't been anyone. I haven't had time."

"Who are the guys you swiped?"

"None of your business," I reply automatically.

"You're right, I'm sorry." He holds up his palms apologetically.

I thumb my phone to life and press on the app. "I wouldn't let anyone meet Macy until I was absolutely 100 percent certain they were appropriate role models."

I hand him the phone and he takes it with a smile like he's privileged. "You don't have to show me. I'm curious, but it's none of my business. You're so cautious with Macy's care, I'm starting to think anyone within a mile of her has been cleared by the CIA."

I laugh, unprepared to admit that my interest in men since I met him has been zero. I was starting to worry there was something wrong with me until my libido suddenly returned the moment he came back in my life.

He scrolls my phone with rapt interest.

"Be prepared to feel small. There are some pretty great catches on there."

"I doubt that very much," he says. "You're already sitting with greatness. *The* Tate Blingwood, I'll have you know, is *Celebrity Gossip's* hashtag no. 1 best catch two years running. Award winning—"

He stops talking as he gauges my exaggeratedly bored stare and his shoulders drop.

"Okay, so you're not impressed." The humble smile that toys on his lips is loaded with such cuteness that I return his smile. "I'm okay. That doesn't hurt my feelings at all." He holds his chest in mock agony and I bat his arm with my hand and am so unprepared for the electricity that zings up my arm, that I drag my hand away and distract myself by clearing our plates.

"Let's see what *your* fans look like." His thumb scrolls and I watch him intently. "First, your profile picture. You're smiling. That'll never do—you look too eager."

His thumb moves across the screen and I reply from the kitchenette, "I was going for friendly."

He looks up from the phone and grins. "You're way too fierce to be friendly."

"Hey, I can be friendly." Sure, some people mistake my independence and strength for prickliness but it doesn't mean I'm not nice. "I'm friendly to my friends all the time," I say, in my defense.

"Am I your friend now?" Tate asks. "Or do you still hate me?"

I pause at the sink and my throat dries as I try to put a label on what Tate is to me now. I certainly don't hate him. Deep down, I never hated him.

"You're the baby daddy but we can work on being friends," I decide.

I chance a glance at Tate and he's smiling at me with his eyes, which look like warm brandy in the romantically lit room. "I'm going to be a good friend to you," he says, and then he glances down at my phone again. "And I'm going to start by insisting there is no way you're dating this guy. As your friend, I forbid it."

I drop the dishes in the sink and go look. "I thought he was one of the better ones."

"Paul from Pennsylvania. A math teacher with a black belt in 'algebra-fu.'" Tate pulls a sickened face.

"A teacher could be useful when Macy is taking her SATs," I defend, knowing I'll never date Paul anyway.

"I can teach her. I scored a 1350 on the SATs."

"Macy's probably going to be smarter than you by then," I tease, kind of enjoying thinking about life that far down the line.

"Then I'll hire someone. I'll hire the best tutor there is. I'll get someone from Harvard to set up in your kitchen with one of those big whiteboards. It'll be like a scene from *Good Will Hunting*."

I chuckle and it reminds me of when we first met. Tate's ability to make me laugh made me see past his incredible looks. It made me think he was decent and kind.

"I'm subtracting this guy from your search. I mean, who says, 'Come on a date with the mathletics champion of the world and let's calculate the square root of love.'" His puking face is adorable so I play along.

"I thought Paul sounded very nice."

"Paul sounds like a loser. Who's next—"

I snatch my phone out of his hands. "And what about *the* Tate Blingwood? Who's he dating? Rumor has it you and Stella Brimwood had a thing."

He shakes his head and stands, towering over me. "Stella just said that because the illusion of a relationship sells movie tickets and everything else she is affiliating herself with. I've never *been* with her. I've been single since we met the first time."

"Single? No way you've been single all this time," I insist, trying not to sound as though I care either way. Still, hope blooms in my chest. Maybe he isn't the playboy he's made out to be, unless he's lying. But somehow, I know that isn't the case.

"I swear it." Tate puts his hand on his heart. "I've been so busy filming and…" He takes my hand in his. "Jessie, all I care about now is you and my daughter."

I snatch my hand back and tuck away the emotion on my face. "I better do the dishes," I say, but he pulls me back by my waist so he's embracing me from behind and my heart gallops at his nearness. "You think I'm transient, that I'm going to disappear in a puff of smoke somehow, but I'm not going anywhere."

I'm leaning back into him and he feels solid, dependable and strong.

Tate's hand skims the soft skin of my abdomen and then he spins me around and suddenly his fingers snake into my hair. His head swoops down and my mouth involuntary opens to allow his tongue inside. It's frantic but measured, and so carnal it makes my core ache to feel more.

The logical side of my brain screams at me to stop the kiss, now. But the side that is a horny little bitch tells her to shut up.

There's no harm innocently making out for a while.

I'm definitely not sleeping with him.

He tastes like the Pinot that's been sitting in my fridge for the past month, yet on his tongue, it tastes radiant and luminous, expensive and layered like it transcended from the sun-drenched vineyards of France instead of the discount rack at Walmart.

The white-knuckle grip of my control loosens.

It's been a long, emotional day. A little touching and feeling to satiate our latent needs will help reduce the tension in our bodies. It's stress relief, that's all.

I tug his lower lip with my teeth and heat pools in my pelvis. Any restraint I might have had is now long gone and my hands are suddenly pulling his shirt over his head. My mouth is on his pec before the annoying article of clothing is even fully over his head. Ever since he took his shirt off earlier, I've been imagining sinking my teeth into his skin and kicking myself for not doing it last week when I had the chance. He hisses against my neck as I pinch his skin between my teeth and then I'm up in the air as he lifts me and takes two strides to the sofa before lowering me down.

We're a mess of tangled limbs, stripping away the layers that constrict us until we're both gloriously naked.

His skin is so smooth, warm and inviting, that I don't know where to touch first. My hands seem to think it's an all-you-can-eat buffet as they greedily grab and knead. I squeeze his shoulders while he lays kisses on my mouth, then move to his biceps as his lips graze my nipple. He hums an appreciative sound as his tongue circles and I arch my back, letting him know I want more.

My palms skim lower past his naval to scale over the dips of his abs before sliding around his waist so I can dig my nails into his ass. It's smooth and firm and just tense enough that I have to spread out my hand to grab hold.

Tate's mouth returns to mine, his kiss becoming more urgent as I let go of his sweet, sweet ass and pull him closer. "Condom. Nightstand," I hiss and he dashes away, sheathing himself as he returns.

A good girl would have used that time to think about all

the reasons I should stop this, and how I'm going to regret what's about to happen, but I'm a crazy fool who doesn't care right now. I'm hot and horny for him, and a part of me feels like we deserve this. The tension of our revelations has had us both in knots and so I blame it on a much-needed stress release.

His erection is gloriously long and thick as he leans down onto his elbows to hover over me. My body burns with need to feel him inside me. He kisses me chastely, his warm breath fanning my neck and then he retreats.

Panic that he's having second thoughts pulls me apart and I grab his hair and say, "Where the heck do you think you're—"

But I shut up when he parts my knees, licks his lips, and sinks between my thighs.

"Come to daddy," he says and I giggle for just a fraction of a second, until the tip of his tongue licks along my seam and I almost buck off the sofa.

"So fucking sweet," Tate says before going at me again and it takes conscious effort not to rise up and suffocate him. "So fucking wet," he says, widening my legs and sliding one finger in and then two.

He looks up and watches me as his tongue and fingers move deftly through my wetness. Punishing, tantalizing strokes. Gentle then firm, long and sweeping then soft and around. He plays with my arousal and I push my hips toward his pressure as need overtakes pride.

My nerve endings are on fire and threatening to detonate so I warn him, "Fuck. Tate. If you keep doing that I'm going to—" My clit screaming for mercy silences me and then I come right against his mouth with an enormous, earth-shattering groan that I have to muffle by putting my hand over my own mouth to keep from waking Macy in the next room.

My vision blurs and I flake out on the sofa for a moment,

while Tate continues to ride out every last shudder of my climax. The world goes a little fuzzy and I feel so warm and safe it makes me want to stay right here forever.

By the time my brain has rebooted and I'm back in the room, Tate is kissing a trail right up my thigh, across my abdomen up to my breasts. He kisses each one, paying attention to each of my buds, before locking eyes with me and whispering, "Jessie. My Jessie. You're fucking beautiful when you come for me."

I grip the base of his cock hungrily and reply, "Coming for you is fucking beautiful." Then I tease him along my entrance, moistening his cock. "I want you, Tate. I need you inside me."

He rotates his hips teasingly positioning himself perfectly until I am aching to be filled by him.

Tate's staring in my eyes and there's nowhere to hide. "I've missed you so fucking much." He enters me with purpose and achingly slow. "You feel just like I remember. Perfect. Like you were made for me," he says, almost reverently.

He's right. Our bodies do fit together perfectly.

I fleetingly wonder if maybe we were meant to be. If I hadn't let my pride and temper get the better of me and thrown his telephone number away all those years ago, would we have been together all this time? But then Tate circles his hips and I cry out and grip the firm curve of his ass that is nothing short of perfection.

Our bodies are so attuned that it's not long before a perfect rhythm of skin hitting skin harmonizes and it reminds me of before.

"You ruined me for anyone else, Jessie. All these years I've spent picturing you splayed out before me, remembering every dip and curve of your body. I'm so glad I get to have you again."

I remember us in this exact position, and then us fucking all over the cheap motel we rented for the night. I instantly remember how sexy I felt. How powerful I felt, bringing him to his knees. It was liberating, and the memory and his comments provide me with a renewed burst of lustful energy.

He kisses my shoulder and up my neck then along my jaw. I meet his hips thrust for thrust. I can hear both our hearts thumping in time. As though muscle memory, our bodies pulse together in perfect harmony.

"I remember how you felt too," I admit, breathlessly. "My body knows yours."

Every stroke pulsates against my nub and I feel myself getting hotter.

"Your body's mine, Jessie. And mine is yours."

I'm about to object but Tate's kisses become deeper, his restraint now a thing of the past, and his hips become more frantic. I'm clinging to the cheeks of his ass for dear life, lifting myself up to meet every joining of our bodies and crying out with how good it feels. It's exhilarating to let go of all the stress and confusion and just feel good. So fucking good.

He suddenly lifts me and swivels us until I am straddling him, and his mouth is on my breast. I drive with my knees and ride every inch of him. His mouth retakes mine, and his arms pull me in so close that every part of us is joined, but still, we try to get closer.

Our bodies are slick, his mouth ravenous, entering mine and then backing away to tell me, "I've thought about fucking you so often. I've relived every moment of the times we have but nothing compares to being balls deep in you, Jessie."

"Thank you," I pant, losing my mind as I edge toward

oblivion and forgetting the thread of the conversation. "You have a very big cock."

The deep chuckle he lets out causes a vibration that almost sends me over the edge.

I grip his shoulders, my nails leaving deep indents, and I thrust down on him, knowing I am moments from falling. Tate's hands are around my waist, driving me up and down harder, faster, and he growls into my shoulder, letting me know just how close he is.

"Tate—"

"Jessie—"

"I'm—"

He pulls me so close my heart thumps against his and tremors rock through my body. Pulsating at first, then so powerful the explosion rips through me and all I can see is Tate watching me. All I can hear is his heart beat. And all I can feel is the utter bliss of this moment.

Tate let's out a growl of satisfaction and then his expression has a look of tormented ecstasy. My core greedily reacts by clenching around him and I revel in hearing him call my name as he releases his orgasm.

I cling to his warm, broad chest as the aftershocks vibrate through us. I'm a giddy mess incapable of rational thought, so I concentrate on our connection rather than trying to piece together how we navigate what happens next.

Our breaths remain ragged.

We're satiated.

Spent.

I don't realize he's kissing my shoulder until feeling returns to my body and then I feel Tate tense inside me.

"You're ready again, already?" I lean back to check, surprised but not disappointed.

His fingers thread through mine and he lifts my wrist to

kiss its inner side. "Baby, I've been jacking off to the memory of you for three years. I'm just getting started."

"Oh." Pressure builds between my thighs and the slick bundle of nerves there pulsates. "Then we should thoroughly get this out of our systems."

Seemingly agreeing, Tate lifts me and he carries me into the bedroom.

CHAPTER 12

TATE

*J*essie's jaw drops. "What do you mean the condom broke?" She stops midway through putting her bra back on. She's one breast in one breast out and looking at me like she wants to hurt me.

"When I took it off, it had a split." I approach her with caution, hands out ready to hold her if she needs me to. "Babe, it's no big deal. If it comes to it, we can have another kid. I'll take care of all of you. You won't need to do it alone this time." The more I think about it, the more I like the idea. "We can get a little house. Or a massive house with a pool. You can have a nanny if you want one."

"You've lost your fucking mind," she snarls, her mouth twisting like she wishes it was my neck. "How did it split? Show me it. It couldn't have split. No one has that bad of luck twice! You're fucking with me."

I reach out and wrap my arms around her, waiting for the boil of her shock to cool to a simmer.

"It's going to be okay. No matter what happens, it's going to be fine."

I hold her for one, two, maybe three minutes. She's frozen but I know Jessie and inside that beautiful head of hers, her thoughts are racing.

"We'll just wait and see. I bet Macy will love a little brother or sister." My palm unconsciously travels to her abdomen and rubs a circle. I'm imagining her swollen with my child and feeling elated and proud. "It'd be cool if there were twins," I say absent-mindedly and Jessie stiffens in my arms.

She breaks free of my embrace and throws her arms up in the air. "Ooohh. You've really lost your fucking mind. One day. ONE DAY you've been a father." She's pacing the room, her arms flailing around as she emphasizes her point. "You show up here, with your Hollywood hair, spreading your seed, fertilizing my ovaries, not caring about what I want or what Macy needs! She doesn't even know she has a father! And here you are, waltzing around like Genghis Khan at the Playboy Mansion."

"I've never even been to the Playboy Mansion," I defend.

"You need to go," she orders.

"Babe, I can take you to the mansion if you like, but I'm not really sure how that's going to help—"

"No. You. Need. To. Leave. Now."

"What? I know you're shocked; I am too but you can't be serious. We need to talk about this—"

"Oh, I am deadly serious," she retorts. "Get out. I need some space to process this and I don't want to say something that I'll regret. Space. Leave. Now. I'll call you when I'm less convinced I won't castrate you."

I instinctively grab my junk right as Jessie fires my T-shirt at it. I dress like she asked me to and then say, "Don't make me go. I don't want to leave you like this. You're clearly upset. I want you to know, I'm standing by you."

She looks me dead in the eyes and replies, "Like you did last time?" and it hits like a physical blow.

My voice is a whisper. "Jessie, that wasn't my fault. You know—" She's shoving me out the door and I don't resist.

"Put on your hat and your scarf. I'll call you when I... I'll call you."

The door slams in my face and I pause for a moment then turn and walk down the steps.

"Hey, aren't you..."

I pull my hat over my head and storm in the direction of the penthouse.

* * *

"Are you okay, Tate?" Mom asks the next day. She's wearing the T-shirt Callie and I found on a shopping trip that says: *Pugs Not Drugs*.

"I'm fine. What makes you think I'm not?" We are in the penthouse. Mom dropped by right as Jason and Gaynor showed up for an emergency meeting and I'm supposed to be paying attention to their plan, but all I'm doing is thinking about Jessie.

In normal circumstances I'd see Jason and Gaynor over at their offices in Hollywood, but since I'm in hiding up here in Santa Barbara, clandestine meetings with a concerned matriarch popping by unannounced is the best we can do.

I haven't told Mom about Macy but she's a hound dog for information, so I turn away from her and pretend to be invested in the screen of my phone so she can't measure my expression.

It's not that I want to keep the news from her; I can't wait to tell Mom, but I can't tell her before Macy knows I'm her father and has accepted me. Besides, Jessie is annoyed enough at the moment and I don't want to do something else and add to the list of Tate's most irritating qualities.

My cell phone is empty of new messages. Jessie hasn't answered any of my calls but I'm expecting her here at any moment. It's 11 a.m and typically the time she comes to the penthouse to clean. Part of me dreads that she's not going to turn up; that she'll run because she doesn't trust me and if that happens, I don't know how I'll fix it.

Mom's hand lands on my shoulder like she's worried about me. She's been my rock and the one person, outside my siblings, I've been able to trust since I got my big break. While Jason and Gaynor have treated me well, they aren't family and they rely on me for a paycheck. "Jason and Gaynor have been talking for about twenty minutes and you haven't replied once. I'm not even sure you're listening to what they're saying or if you'd be onboard if you were."

I glance at Jason in his pinstripe suit and then Gaynor with her fluorescent yellow stilettos and shake my head. "What were you two saying?"

At that moment, the elevator doors slide open and I see my girl. She looks tired from lack of sleep so I guess that makes two of us.

Jason, Gaynor, and my mom thankfully stay seated around the kitchen island. I leap up to help pull her cart into the penthouse and hopefully get a chance to check she's okay, while holding myself back from pulling her into my arms like I've been thinking about doing since I left her place last night.

"It's fine. I can do it," she hisses, eyeing the others while shoving the cart away from me. I can't tell if she's still angry at me or if she's just making a show of independence.

I lower my voice so the others can't hear. "I don't want you to overdo it."

Jessie rolls her eyes and I let go of the cart. My arms dangle by my sides and it takes every ounce of my restraint not to pull her close and kiss her.

"I'm glad you came," I say and her lips lift by a fraction.

"So am I." She surprises me by winking playfully and I remember watching her come undone for me. Then her expression turns apologetic and she sighs. There's a heavy weight to her gaze, a million things unsaid. "I don't stay mad forever. Last night wasn't your fault. Sometimes, I just need time to process."

"Jessie, it's so good to see you," Mom says, approaching us and smiling so widely I can see every tooth.

"Hi, Mrs. Blingwood," Jessie replies, taking a small step back. She seems shy all of a sudden, self-conscious, and I get the impression she wants my mom to like her.

"Jessie, you've known me two years. I'm Cassandra to you, silly. Are you okay? You seem a little... shaken." Mom looks from Jessie to me and back to Jessie and adds, "Is Tate treating you well?"

"Oh, he's been very... accommodating." Jessie's cheeks flush.

"Good," Mom replies nodding, "I'm glad it's you who is taking care of Tate. You've been so good to my family, Jessie." Mom glances to the corner of the room where one of her rescue dogs is sniffing the carpet like he's about to go potty. "I better get that." She dashes across the room, scooping up the dog before making her way to the elevator, telling me she'll come back tomorrow.

"Accommodating?" I smirk.

Jessie ignores my teasing and instead narrows her perfect blue eyes. "There was a Bentley outside my place this morning, waiting to take me and Macy to day care and then it brought me here. The driver is still waiting outside now." She glares at me accusingly, hands on her hips, but it looks like it's all for show. "Know anything about that?"

"That's Mitch. He was bored with me being stuck in here so he asked if there was anything he could do to make himself useful." I shrug, needing her to not only hear but see that it's of no consequence to me, that she's not putting me out in any way. "He's your driver now, and to be perfectly honest, Jess, I need to be sure my girls get where they're going safely. Was the car seat installed properly?"

Her shoulders drop and I can practically hear her expelled breath, as if she's put up the white flag for this battle. "Yes. Top of the line with its own airbag and cupholder."

I nod, resisting the urge to grin. "Did Macy like it?"

Jessie's annoyed scowl relaxes. "She loved it."

"Yes!" I turn my back so Gaynor and Jason don't see me punch the air. It feels good to have done something as a father that makes Jessie and Macy's lives easier, so good in fact, it could become addictive. "Mitch will be at your disposal. You don't need to get the bus anymore. Did you find your bank details so I can deposit the money?" I've asked Jessie a dozen times now for her account details so I can pay her child support, but apparently there's some issue with the app on her phone and she can't access them.

"No. I'll call the bank soon."

"Make sure you do. You don't need to struggle. And you definitely don't need to work as a maid anymore. I probably owe a million in back pay for child support and then there's the monthly amounts we should set up."

"I'm a maid manager and what's wrong with working as a maid?"

Her brow furrows and before we go back to battling, I backtrack as quickly as I can. "There is absolutely nothing wrong with working as a maid and no one, I repeat, no one

121

looks as good in that uniform as you do, but you don't need to. I'm going to take care of you. I want to."

"Tate, when you've finished with the maid, can we have you over here," Jason asks and I immediately correct him.

"This is Jessie. She's my…" Jessie throws me a warning, so I end the sentence with, "She's *my* Jessie."

Jason looks Jessie up and down and nods his head, impressed. "*She's* your Jessie?"

"Actually, I'm just Jessie," she says, taking a step forward and standing taller.

"Well, *just Jessie*, we need to have a chat about you're histo—"

I interrupt Gaynor. If she starts hitting Jessie for every detail of her past, I'm afraid it'll scare her away. "All of that can wait. Now, what did you both want to talk to me about. You can say anything in front of Jess. She's cool." I smile at her and feel a renewed sense of hope when she smiles back.

"Take a seat, Jessie." I gesture to the counter for her to sit with my team and I like how she looks when she joins us.

I stand behind her and rest my hand on her shoulder.

Jessie needed time to calm down after the broken condom, which is understandable. She's used to doing everything alone so I guess it'd be normal for her to revert to that coping strategy. Another baby is a big deal and I didn't show her I'm scared too. She's a passionate woman who wears her heart on her sleeve, and she's been through some stuff, that much is obvious. She'll confide in me when I prove to her that I'm worthy, and then we can start working as a team.

Jason begins, "Dinky contacted me, they're shelving the deal, *for now*. They haven't said they're recasting, but I suspect that's one of the options they're considering. There's been no good press about you in—"

"I've been doing my job," Gaynor interrupts with a hiss, pinning Jason with a stare that warns him not to fuck with her—not that Jason will be concerned about that. Jason and Gaynor, while generally known for being the best in the business, haven't learned to play nice together.

"You'd be doing your job better if Tate's image was intact," Jason replies, his tone sharp.

"I've been working my ass to the bone for him, what have you been doing? Tate's opening a new ward at a children's hospital and making an appearance at Cali Pride. What exactly have you got planned for him? The Dinky deal was supposed to fill his schedule for the next two years. If there's no Dinky deal, there's no work for him, is there?"

Jason's face tells me everything I need to know.

"The Dinky deal isn't over until they cast someone else. Meanwhile, I'm courting scripts from FilmOnDemand, RomanceFlix—"

"They're online streaming services, aren't they?" I check, and my movie career feels like it's suddenly on rewind.

"That's the way the industry is moving, Tate. I know you want movie theaters, but some of these companies are offering big bucks. If only you'd go public with Stella, your popularity would soar and you'd create the wholesome image—"

"No. Not doing it."

I feel Jessie side-eye me.

"It would give you the image Dinky wants to see, Tate. Or you could—" Gaynor looks from me to Jessie and then to Jason whose eyes light up.

"It could work," Jason says to Gaynor.

Gaynor grins her most shit-eating smile. "It'd be perfect. Newfound family. A father. A long-lost love."

"What would be perfect?" Jessie asks Gaynor pointedly.

"You. You and Tate. America's newest family. We could get a reality TV deal, or we could cover it in an interview on *E*. Ooh, your own *TikTok* channel. The Blingwoods! I love it."

Gaynor and Jason are so excited that it takes me a moment to rein them in.

"You think Jessie is who I should fake date to improve my image?" I shake my head. The world has officially gone mad.

"What would it entail?" Jessie asks.

Gaynor lists a bunch of publicity events I have coming up for the Galactic film release by Tripod. "The world is going to find out that Macy is his daughter whether you want them to or not. At least this way, you have the protection and guidance of the brand."

"What do you want, Tate?" Jessie asks and the first word that comes to mind is *you*. "Honestly, I won't be offended if you say it's not me."

"No. Like, you're perfect but I don't want you to do anything you're not comfortable with. I screwed up the Dinky deal—that's on me. I just want to get back to credible acting parts. The commercials are fine, but I want to act in film. I want to inspire people." I check Jessie's reaction, wondering if I sound like a big-headed schmuck saying such things, but she nods approvingly and it spurs me on. "I've dreamed of working with Dinky. They're the best. The franchise is set to have the biggest budget of any movie to date, and the special effects are going to be ground-breaking. It's the stuff dreams are made of, but I screwed it up and it's not your job to save me." I turn to Jason and ask, "If the deal can't be saved, what are my other options?" Since it's my fault and no one else's that I've screwed up my reputation and the Dinky deal, now that I have a family to support, I have to figure out the next step. It's no longer about my goals; I'll do whatever work I have to in order to be the man my parents raised. I want Jessie to believe in me and I'm desperate to have a real relationship with my daughter.

"Why can't it be saved?" Jessie asks. "Where are the negotiations at?"

Jason glances from me to Jessie and I tell him, "She's with me, you can answer her questions honestly."

"Okay, young lady. Well, the—"

"I'm not *young lady*. My name is Jessie, and I'm with Tate. I'm on his side," she informs him and I hide my smirk.

"Jessie," Jason says respectfully. "I'm sure you've heard of Dinky Entertainment. They specifically cater to the family market. Lately Tate's image has taken a hit. He's been pictured indulging in alcohol, has had a wardrobe malfunction with a model whose job it was to escort him on stage, he's been coined with the nickname Triptastic Tate—which makes him appear unreliable—and last but certainly not least, his bare behind was pictured worldwide running through the streets of LA. The trolls are stirring up hate and he's a lick away from getting canceled if we don't do something."

Feeling like a fool, I watch Jessie's reaction. Her teeth clamp down on her bottom lip and her hand comes up to cup mine as it rests on her shoulder.

"I had no idea those types of things could be career ending. Most celebrities seem to endure a certain amount of bad press," Jessie says.

"Most celebrities, but not A-list celebrities with franchise careers. Usually the good press outweighs the bad. Unfortunately Tate's bad press has come at a time when he's between jobs and the Dinky deal wasn't signed when the majority of the bad images hit the press." Gaynor looks at Jason pointedly like she blames him.

"I wanted to wait to sign the Dinky deal. I thought it was in the bag and I needed a break. So when the charity approached me to put my face to a coral reef clean-up campaign, I couldn't resist. This is all my fault," I say, but from Jessie's expression it's like she feels responsible.

Maybe Jessie's worried that when the press finds out I'm a

father from a one-night stand, my reputation will be further ruined, but she needn't worry about that. What concerns me most is what my daughter will see when she one day googles me. How I'm going to keep Macy and Jessie safe from the fallout when the news breaks?

"So how do we fix it?" Jessie says. "And I'm not talking about Stella-freaking-Brimworth. What do we need to do to make Dinky see that there is no better leading actor?"

"Good press and lots of it," Gaynor says.

"A family-man image could save it. If it doesn't save the Dinky deal, it'll promote Tate at his best for future castings. He has a lovable rogue image at the moment. But if he was seen in a steady relationship, he could throw in an engagement, perhaps a wedding. The news would go worldwide. Interviews. Photographs. It'd be huge and not something to enter into lightly, because one foot wrong, and the whole castle of cards would come tumbling down." I know what Jason is getting at, and he's talking directly to me. He's suggesting Jessie, and he's warning me that I need to be sure, because if my relationship with her sours and she goes public with how things really went down with us, she'd have the power to end my career once and for all.

"We'll need to spin a slightly different story. Maybe you say you weren't sure Tate was the father, or else they'll wonder why he wasn't involved sooner and that could make him look bad," Gaynor says, listing out the options like she often does.

"Jessie's not telling people she didn't know I was the father. It implies she slept around and the trolls will come for her. No, she's not throwing herself to the wolves to save my ass," I insist.

"The alternative is that you look bad," Gaynor says. "Which negates the whole point of you two fake dating."

"There must be another option. How about the truth?

That she tried to get in contact with me to tell me about Macy and she couldn't get to me," I suggest, knowing that when it comes to Hollywood, the truth is often the least obvious option.

"And then you'll seem more removed from your fans than ever. A superstar who never reads his own fan mail?"

"Gaynor's right," Jessie says, her eyes wide and pure. "You can't risk your reputation, not after the bad press. I'll do it."

We all gawk at her.

"I mean, if you want me to do it, I'll do it," she says, looking directly at me. "I feel guilty anyway. Some of this is my fault and honestly, if people don't like me then fuck them..."

"How is this your fault? You tried to reach me to tell me about Macy. It's not your fault certain members of my team need to learn to share information—even if they don't believe the information."

Jason clears his throat and announces, "Wonderful! Gaynor, I want to be a part of your plan to scale this. Nothing goes ahead without my say-so. We can't afford for this to fail."

"You mean you can't afford to lose your 15 percent from your biggest star," Gaynor replies and Jason looks pissed.

His tone is biting as he replies, "No. I mean Tate is my brightest star and he deserves the career that awaits him. It's our duty to make sure that is as prosperous as possible. And, we'll take care of Jessie too. She'll require her own security detail to keep her and the child safe. State of the art accommodation, a stylist. She's beautiful already and the press will eat her up, but she's going to need to look the part too. We can spin it like a Cinderella story."

"Wait." I hold up my hand. "Jessie, you don't know what you're getting yourself into. Once you tell people that we're together and they find out about Macy, the press will be rabid. They'll dredge up every piece of your history. Your family. You and Macy won't be able to go anywhere for a straight six months without there being a camera in your face. It'll change both your lives and not necessarily for the better. I signed up for this life, but you don't have to."

"Will you take care of us if I do it?" she asks, and the rare vulnerability in her voice almost knocks me on my ass.

"Always."

"Then I'll do whatever you need."

CHAPTER 13

JESSIE

*B*efore the news breaks, Tate insists we go somewhere while I'm still anonymous to talk everything through. He spends five straight minutes checking my helmet is on correctly and then he sits me on his motorcycle. "I can get a car if you'd rather?"

"Tate, I'm fine. I love riding motorcycles."

"I know but you might be…"

He doesn't say the word pregnant but we're both thinking it.

"How long until you can take the test?"

"About a month."

He smiles. "About a month and we'll know. Perhaps I should call the driver."

"Tate, it's been one day. Stop fussing. If I am, I'm less than one day pregnant."

He nods and jumps in front of me on the motorcycle. "I'll go slow," he says. "Are you ready?"

The engine roars as Tate revs the motorcycle, the vibrations thrilling me. I cling to him, the wind tousling our hair as we speed through the city lights. I let out a squeal as he pushes the bike to go faster and I tighten my grip around him, loving the scent of his leather jacket mixed with his woody cologne. It's exhilarating.

The cool breeze and the temporary freedom of the ride is comforting until I remember what is ahead of me. My mom has Macy overnight and tomorrow, I am putting in a leave at the job I have loved for the past two years to step into my new, temporary life. I had a quick conversation with Skyla and she and Logan are allowing me to take a temporary leave of absence while I help out Tate. Our fake dating would impose too much unwanted media to the resort, so we all agreed that me taking a step back for a while or until the Dinky deal goes through is the best option for everyone. Logan actually thanked me for helping out his brother. My daughter is a lucky girl to be a part of this family.

The rational part of my brain is telling me that I should scream no and run for the hills, but the other part of me feels like I have to help him. I may have had no part in whipping Tate's clothes away and filming his very naked, very lovely butt, but I did construct some questionable memes over the years, and now I feel incredibly guilty having been his number one social media troll and adversary. My guilt is so massive that last night I got in a fight with a troll on a fan site. They said Tate was washed up and I got so angry and threatened to hunt them down, make "merchandise" with their profile picture and send it viral—which actually garnered a lot of support from Tate's real fans.

I owe him my help.

Love him or hate him, he's Macy's father.

And it's just a matter of time before the press gets word of him being her father and then Macy and I will be fair game to the paps anyway—at least by posing as his girlfriend for a while, I'll have Tate's protection until the media loses interest in us. But I won't have control how they present me as a woman and a mother and that scares me too. Thank God, I'll still have a job to go back to when this charade is done.

With the city behind us, the road stretches out before us like an open invitation. The night is dark and peaceful with only the stars for company, and when we arrive at a secluded clifftop spot, Tate skids the motorcycle to a stop and we both clamber off.

Tate lays out his leather jacket on the dirt and gestures for me to sit. Beyond us the view of Seven Falls is expansive, with the sound of the rushing water in the background.

"It's beautiful," I gesture my hand then murmur, "so peaceful." I close my eyes and ignore the chatter in my head. When I open them, Tate is watching me closely, a small grin toying on his lips.

"You're beautiful, Jessie, inside and out. What you've offered to do for me, it's more than I deserve. I'm not sure you should do it."

"Why? If you're serious about being Macy's father—"

"Hey. I'm serious. Don't doubt that. There are no take backs on Macy, I'm all in."

I nod. "Then the press will find out anyway, and they'll want to know who her mother is. There will be speculation."

"Yeah, there will. But what Jason is proposing is quite different. It's a spectacle. It's not living our lives and letting the chips fall. It's an official statement, an interview and photographs. I know Logan and Skyla said you can go back to your job at the hotel, but I'm doubtful. The press will intrude in every area of your life and then some. Trust me, I know."

"What's it like?" I ask. "Fame and fortune. It's what everyone dreams about but you don't seem happy."

He frowns but then his eyes light up my soul. "I love my job. Like, I fucking love it. The set, the lights, the rush of getting cast for a part that I set my heart on and feeling the emotion of the character. It's like nothing else. And then, when the movie comes out and I've put my heart and soul into it, and the fans go crazy for it—that's when I feel like I did good."

"But it's not always like that?" I guess.

"No. There's a dark side. There are the negative reviews for one. I'm thick-skinned. I can take it. I'm probably my own worst critic anyway, no troll has ever said anything worse than the things I tell myself when I'm feeling low. Mostly, I try not to read the worst critics. Jason tells me what I need to know so I can improve, but sometimes late at night I go through them all and just sit in the darkness. Does that make me a masochist?"

"No. It makes you human," I reply. "I watched you in *Denver's Surprise*."

"You did?" He smiles. "Dare I ask what you thought about it?"

I remember writing a review and being a bitch. "Honestly, your performance was captivating. When Deedee died and you put the flowers on her grave, I fucking cried."

"I made the ice queen melt?" he asks, grinning. "Now there's something I never thought possible." His fingers reach to my abdomen and he tickles me until I laugh out.

"Stop!" I insist and he pauses, staring into my eyes like they're about to reveal all my secrets.

Tate's body is half perched over mine, and my lips seem to be puckering for a kiss, but I put the flat of my hand against his chest and push him away so I can sit up.

"So, what happened? When I left you in the motel three years ago you were a college student studying media and you were living on campus because your sisters drove you crazy."

"Macy happened," I admit. "I was twenty. I finished that year at college while I was pregnant and then I moved in with my mom. I planned to go back once Macy was older but it never happened. By the time I work to pay for day care and the stuff Macy needs, there's no money or energy left for study."

His gaze is sympathetic, guilty even. "I'm sorry. I should have been there to help."

"It's not your fault," I tell him. "I've been blaming you but only because it's been hard, and I've needed an outlet. I should have tried harder to find you. Hell, I work for your family and I refused to tell even them. I let my pride get in the way, but I also don't think we can move forward dwelling on that."

He slides my hand into his. It's intimate but also comforting. "I like the idea of moving forward. So, what happened with your mom? You don't live with her now."

"No. I needed my own space, so I found a job that came with housing. My mom's great, but I have five sisters, and most of us have different dads. She falls in love easily, and the men she chooses fall out of love with her and our chaotic household just as quickly. Mom held my hand while I had Macy, and she has her for me when she's not working, but she's spread pretty thin so there's only so much help she can give me."

"Oh, what does she do?"

I bite down on my lip and feel warmth spread through my cheeks.

"You're embarrassed. Why?" Tate shakes his head.

"I'm not embarrassed *about* her. She's a great woman who raised six pretty darn awesome young women. Mom has two jobs actually." Tate nods like he's impressed and then gestures for me to continue. "She cleans at the bingo hall five shifts a week and then she…" He cocks a quizzical

EMILY JAMES

brow as he waits. "She sells adult toys at parties and online."

His mouth pops open but then he quickly tucks away any shock.

I smile anyway. "She's actually pretty good at the second job. Mom has more social media channels than I do and when she can put the time in, she gets pretty good commission. She gets a decent discount so you can imagine what I get for Christmas."

Tate's eyes light up. "You own…"

"Got one of everything in every color."

"Oh, you are going to have to introduce me to your collection."

I laugh. "We need to keep things simple. This chemistry we have on top of a fake relationship… there's too much potential for things to go wrong. We can't date officially. We barely know each other, and I don't want our fake-dating job to get confused with us being the best parents to Macy."

"We are always going to be the best parents to Macy, but we were getting to know each other pretty intimately," he replies.

"Superficially. The sex has been great but I'm not under any illusion that this chemistry between us is going anywhere. I've seen people get caught up in the lust of the moment and I've also seen that spark fizzle out just as quickly. No, it's better that we proceed with our eyes open, that way no one gets hurt."

"The sex has been great. But you know, there's more to me than just a big cock." Tate smirks and I giggle-snort and reply, "I can't believe I said that! Guess I was caught up in the lust." Tate laughs too but there's a heat in his eyes that penetrates my skin. After looking at me a beat too long, he says, "It was more than just lust. You've got it bad for me."

"Oh yeah, well I think Hollywood's soon-to-be golden boy has a big head."

He makes a show of peering at me. "You, Jessie Yates, are my number one fan," he teases and I bat his arm with my hand to stop him, too afraid to admit that I have actually become a fan—and even more petrified of him ever finding out that according to him, Jason, and Gaynor, I'm enemy #1. He's melting my walls and it's scaring the hell out of me, so I change the subject. "Tell me, what do I need to know so we can pull this off?"

Tate studies me so deeply, it warms my cheeks. Like he's fascinated, or maybe I just have food on my face from earlier.

"Tell me everything about you."

"Me? Oh, I'm pretty boring. You already know all about Macy, my mom and sisters, my friends, and my job. That's pretty much all there is to know."

He shakes his head. "There is so much more to you than being a mother, friend, and maid manager, Jessie. You're strong, but you're vulnerable. You've been hurt."

"What? No, I haven't."

"Tell me about your dad?"

I screw my face, feeling the familiar sense of shame and abandonment. "Why?"

"Because if we're going to pull this off, the media will expect us to know certain things about each other." He waits for a beat and when I don't reply he adds, "But mostly, I want to *know* the mother of my daughter and I want to be able to support and protect her if I need to."

I take a deep breath. Talking about my father has never come easily. "He's a cop," I start and Tate nods. "Who never wanted a child." His hand tightens in mine. "When I was old enough to start asking questions about him, my mom would blow me off and say that maybe he didn't get the letter telling him he had a daughter or that he was probably just busy

135

down at the station, solving crimes. In my head he was a hero who didn't get the memo. So, I rode the bus down to the station and I walked in there, cocky as can be, and announced that I was Chuck Peters's daughter and that he'd probably want to know about me. Can you imagine their faces? I was completely blindsided. I was expecting some kind of magical reunion like you see on Hallmark and what I got was something very different."

I chance a glance at Tate and see his jaw tick. He looks angered on my behalf. "What did he say?" he asks, his voice more neutral than his expression.

I look away, unable to bear his pity when I reveal the rest of my story.

"He said my mother was a two-bit whore who could've been knocked up by any guy at the station. Then he gave me fifty cents and told me to never come back."

"He said what?! Fucking asshole! I'll kill him."

"It's okay. I got revenge. I took one of those quarters and scratched *dik* onto the hood of his car."

Tate chuckles and pulls me into a hug. "That's my little firecracker! No one messes with my girl." He musses my hair and I shove his arm. We both fall quiet as the information I just revealed sits uncomfortably between us and then he says, "It makes sense now. You were scared I'd react the same way when you told me about Macy."

"No. I—" My throat starts to ache and I turn to him. "I could've handled it," I reply but he looks at me like he doesn't believe me and so I reframe my answer. "When your people told me I was deluded, I swallowed it down and emailed them back with a big photograph of fuck-you fingers." He smiles and his fingers slide across the ground until they're entwined in mine. "If you'd told me face-to-face you weren't interested, I would have sucked it up and protected Macy. I'd have told her you had to move countries because you were in witness protection or you were a scientist on a top-secret mission—"

"I prefer superhero on an intergalactic quest." His arm rises up and loops around my shoulders, pulling me further into him. "But I'm here and I'm going to be the best damn father I can to the most amazing child on earth."

I nod and smile fondly. "She is amazing. And stubborn."

"I wonder who she gets that from?" He nudges me and I laugh. "Let's not have secrets anymore. Jessie, I swear I am the one person you can always be honest with."

"Tate, there's something I need to tell—"

His cell starts to ring and Tate gestures apologetically as he reaches into his back pocket to retrieve it. "Tate," he answers. The person on the other end speaks and then Tate asks me, "Jason wants to know if you've thought it through. If you're in?"

I nod. "I'm in."

"Are you certain? The media are going to ask a lot of uncomfortable questions. We can rehearse our answers before the shoot, but they'll want to know everything and they don't always print exactly what you say. They'll dredge up every event in your history and contort and twist it like a Rubik's Cube."

"You underestimate me, Tate." I smile through my nerves. "I'm thick-skinned and I have grit. There's nothing I can't handle and I don't care what people think." At least, that's what I have been telling myself most of my adult life after getting knocked up at twenty, and it's almost working.

I just hope I can protect our daughter and Tate through all this.

"She's in." He pauses, listening to Jason on the other end of the phone, and then Tate repeats, "A media interview, day after tomorrow. Is that okay with you, Jessie?"

I nod.

"Okay. We have a plan," Tate says as though to me and Jason. "Let's hope I don't screw it up this time."

He hangs up and then I say, "You know what this means?"

Tate looks at me curiously.

"We've got to tell Macy and our families before the news breaks."

His hands rake through his hair, revealing his ripped abs and I sit on my hands so I'm not tempted to reach out and touch them. "Is your mom going to punch me for knocking you up?"

"Honestly, she might," I reply. "What about your mom? I've met her a hundred times and never once mentioned she has a granddaughter. Do you think she'll punch me?"

Tate laughs. "No. She'll probably force you to adopt a rescue dog and demand she babysit weekly."

"Hmm. I knew I loved your mom," I say and we both chuckle.

CHAPTER 14

TATE

I grab Jessie's hand as we walk past a broken refrigerator in the front yard and pull my baseball cap down. "You sure she won't punch me?" I ask Jessie as we ascend the steps to her mom's duplex.

The place is worn-in in the way a house looks when it's seen its day, with the yellow paint peeling and a bicycle thrown down on the porch.

"She might. But you're a big guy, you can take it." She smiles and I suddenly feel nauseous.

"Jasmine, Jade, Jenna, Jamie, Josie," I mutter as I try and recite Jessie's sisters names.

"Jamie and Josie are away at college. Jasmine and Jade, the twins, should be in bed. Jenna will probably be at her boyfriend's. It's just my mom you'll have to worry about," she says, as if that will make me feel better.

"Who's worrying." I shrug like I'm carefree even though I'm shitting my pants.

"Stop twitching. You're going to be fine," she hisses but I don't feel reassured.

"Jade! You better pick up all your crap from down here or else I'm gonna open a can whoop ass on you!" a woman, who I'm guessing is Jessie's mom, hollers as she pads toward the front door.

Beside me, it's Jessie's turn to fidget as she throws me a nervous stare and then she flicks a piece of flaking paint away from the doorframe. "With my mom's dating history, you'd think she'd have found a handyman by now."

The door flies open and a full-figured woman with blonde hair just like my Jessie opens the door holding a rolling pin. She's in her mid-forties and wearing an apron covered in flour like she's been baking up a storm. Beneath her apron is some kind of leopard-print sweat suit and she's barefoot with bright pink jewels on each of her toenails.

"Jessie, baby. I wasn't expecting you until tomorrow. Macy is sound asleep," she says with a warm smile, opening her arms for a hug. "Come on in." Then she casts her gaze my way and I freeze.

"Hello, Mrs. Yates," I greet her, quickly removing my cap, and it's like I've reverted to a fifteen years old and I've got to tell the lady next door that I broke her window—except this time it's worse. I've got to tell her that I impregnated her daughter—possibly twice.

"Well don't just stand there, get your butts inside," she says.

Jessie ushers me through to the living room with its worn leather couch that's occupied by two identical, disinterested teen girls on their phones.

"You two, out. Now!" Jessie orders and they look up like they have no intention of going anywhere.

I take off my hat and smile a greeting.

"No fucking way!" one of them screeches and the other one seems to wake up.

"Fuck off!" girl number two screams and they both get up and jump up and down like they're at a Harry Styles concert.

"It's him!" Left One says to right one.

"I know!" Right One sings to left and they do some kind of elaborate high five. It's like Dr. Seuss and Thing One and Thing Two.

"Quiet, Jazzy and Jade, or you'll wake Macy and then you'll both be staying home this weekend." Jessie's mom points at the teenagers. "You two, homework, NOW!" Then she looks at me and Jessie. "You two better take a seat and tell me what's going on."

It takes ten minutes, a lot of yelling, and Jessie eventually strong arming her sisters up to their room before we are left alone with Mrs. Yates.

"Sorry. They've never seen a celebrity before," she says.

"Truly, it's fine Mrs. Yates," I reply and Jessie pulls a sickened face at me.

"Brown nose," she hisses beneath her breath and I grin. At home in her natural habitat, there's a feisty, playful side to her that makes her seem younger, like she doesn't have to be the independent grown-up here. I like seeing her relaxed.

"Can I get you a coffee? I just made some snickerdoodles," Jessie's mom says and I smile and say no thank you. I love snickerdoodles, but I'm so nervous there's no way I could eat a thing.

"It's a pleasure to meet you, Mrs. Yates," I start, noticing that she's still holding the rolling pin.

"Call me Selena, sweetheart. None of that Mrs. nonsense. I'm not as fancy as these Hollywood types." She grins at Jessie and asks, "Is Tate your new boyfriend, Jessie?"

"Yes," I say, right as Jessie says, "No."

"Well, not yet but I'm hoping—"

"He's the man that knocked me up, Momma. He's Macy's father," Jessie says and my mouth pops open at how she just threw me under the bus.

"I didn't mean to." I hold my hands up in defense in case Mrs. Yates decides to start swinging the bat in her hands. "It was accidental."

"And how exactly did your penis *accidentally* fall into my daughter, Mr. Blingwood?" Selena's tone softens as she looks at Jessie and asks, "Jessie, did this man hurt you?"

"No, Momma. He was very gentle."

"Good. So, what are you going to do about it, Tate?"

Her stare has my measure and so I answer as honestly as I can, while fearing that she might batter me. "I'm going to take care of them," I announce.

"He's going to get to know Macy and I'm going to fake-date him to try to help him get his career back on track," Jessie replies and I frown at her; I like my version better.

"Fake date?"

"Yeah, he needs a wholesome reputation. I'm not exactly wholesome, but I can pretend to be."

Her mother nods and then asks, "And what exactly do my daughter and granddaughter get out of this?"

"Anything. Everything they want," I say, meaning it.

She stares at Jessie. "And what have you asked for?"

"Nothing, Momma. I don't want anything."

"So, you'll still work at the resort?" her mom says, right-eously confused. Behind her the door moves by about an inch and Jessie yells at her sisters to go back upstairs or they're dead meat.

"No. I'm going to have to quit working at the resort for the time being. Once the press finds out, it'll send them crazy and I don't want it affecting the experience of the guests. I'm hoping that once everything settles down and Tate gets the deal he's hoping for, I can go back to the resort—"

"Jason," I interrupt her, "my agent is finding us a house. Jessie'll be paid, of course, but if we marry, she'll be entitled to half of everything—"

"We're not getting married."

"We might be. I mean, we could," I reply.

"We're not getting married, Momma," she tells her while I say, "We actually might get married." The more I think about it, the more it makes sense—that way if anything happens to me, she and Macy will be protected financially.

Selena smirks. "So, you're not in love with each other?"

I watch Jessie shake her head slowly and it hits like a punch.

"We'll live together temporarily and it'll give him the chance to bond with Macy but after he signs his next deal, the arrangement will end."

"It could take months," I say, suddenly feeling like we don't have enough time. I'm not ready to think about the end yet. "Possibly a year, maybe longer," I add, and Selena's grin widens. "There's nothing stopping us from getting married. Jessie and Macy can both become Blingwoods." The very idea of us sharing the same name causes a warm stirring in my chest.

"A marriage sounds like a wonderful idea. I can just see Macy all dressed up as a bridesmaid. You'll need a lot of bridesmaids dresses. Jessie has five sisters, and there'll be carnage if anyone is left out."

"Absolutely, Mrs. Yates—"

"Please, call me Selena." She smiles and I grin right back.

"Momma, there is no wedding. We're just here to tell you that Macy is Tate's biological daughter and it will probably be in all the papers soon, and there might be journalists on your doorstep."

Selena pulls out her phone and begins texting, basically

ignoring her daughter's protests, which I'm in complete agreement with.

"Mom, what are you doing?"

"Texting Tootsie down at the Cut and Blow. If there'll be photographers, I'll need a fresh blow out."

Jessie nods like she approves and I find myself grinning. The dynamic here is so endearing I don't want to leave. They straight up love each other and I can tell they'd lay down their lives for one another. "Now, tell me everything from the beginning, and Tate, are you sure you don't want some fresh snickerdoodles? They're homemade."

"On second thought, yes please, Selena," I reply and relax into the chair. If I get to choose a mother-in-law, Selena will be a good one.

When it's time to go, Jessie and I check in on Macy and stare at her for a straight ten minutes before kissing her goodbye as she sleeps. Selena has agreed to keep her overnight for us and bring her to day care in the morning.

When we get downstairs, Jessie says, "I'll meet you by the door, I'm just going to use the bathroom."

I do as she says and admire the wall of photographs in the hall when one of Jessie's sisters stops and says, "You better treat my sister right." The other one pops up on my other side and they both cross their arms in warning.

"I will," I reply, hand on heart.

"You know Taylor Swift?" Right asks.

"I could," I say casually.

"Well, we won't beat your ass for knocking up our sister if you can get us concert tickets," Left says.

"I'll see what I can do." I wink and they both start screeching.

"You girls, upstairs and finish your homework, now!" Selena says, popping up behind them and the twins haul ass upstairs. "They share a room and they fight like cats and dogs, but all my girls love each other."

I count how many people live here and guesstimate the bedrooms. They're all cooped up in such a small space no wonder they fight.

"I'm from a big family too," I tell her. "So I totally get it. When the fuss dies down, I want all of you to come over and meet my family. I think you'd really get along with my mother."

"I'd like that. No father?" she asks.

"He passed away," I say and she nods.

"Jessie tell you what happened with her dad?"

"She did. Mrs. Yates, I would never behave—"

She puts her hand up to stop me. "I know you won't, but you need to understand something. Jessie has been older than her years her whole life. She thinks it's her personal responsibility to take care of everyone. Now, I know she's a lot to handle and she'll push you away and punch you in the face before she pulls you close, but that's how she tests your mettle. The question is, are you man enough for the job?"

"I think so," I reply.

"Think or know?" she checks but luckily, I don't have to answer because Jessie walks down the stairs, kisses her mother, and tells her not to say anything stupid to any journalists. Then she pulls some twenties out of her purse and tells her to make sure she paid her electricity bill.

And then the next big revelation… My family.

* * *

I MANAGE to convince Jessie to grab her things from her place and stay with me at the penthouse since my mother, brothers and their wives, and my sister will be coming over first thing tomorrow morning to hear our news.

145

Jessie orders room service and we sit on the couch for a while eating pizza before she announces she's going to turn in. Jessie insists on sleeping in the second bedroom, but I tell her she's sleeping in the primary and there'll be no arguments.

"Fine," she says, and since she seems agreeable and possibly a little horny judging from the way she's been checking me out this past hour, I decide to try something.

"You want to spoon?" I ask, stretching and flashing my abs since I've noticed the way her eyes seem to fix on them whenever they're out.

"Nope," she says, stretching also and pushing up the swell of her breast as she does.

Sweet baby Jesus.

"Do I at least get a kiss goodnight?" I ask, pushing my luck but unable to help myself. She seems to think for a moment and then saunters over willingly and I can't believe my luck. The second she gets close, I wrap my arms around her and pull her in so she can't escape. "You want to kiss me," I say almost gloatingly.

"I do *not* want to kiss you. I'm placating you. You're so needy, you're practically begging for it," she replies, pulling a bored face.

"I'm not kissing you now, you hurt my feelings. If you want me to change my mind, you're going to have to say sorry and beg for my goodnight kiss," I resist, not letting go of her.

"I'll never beg you for anything, Tate Blingwood," she replies and even though it's playful, I realize she's right. She's so stubborn she wouldn't ask me for so much as a dime, too bad I'm going to make sure I give her everything anyway.

She'll never back down, but I decide I'm okay with that. These walls around her, the prickly defense she's built, she struggles to be vulnerable, but she also gives me glimmers that I can break through and for now, that's enough. I'm earning her trust and showing her she can depend on me, so I quickly change tact.

Her gaze is steely.

"Okay," I sigh. "If you're going to give me those puppy-dog eyes, I'll kiss you."

She hesitates. "I didn't—" Before she's finished her sentence, I'm kissing her deeply and loving her taste.

A simple kiss quickly turns passionate and Jessie's arms wrap around me, pulling me in tight as her fingers deftly find their path to knead my ass. I lift her legs and wrap them around my waist, hoisting her into the air so we can be closer and then I perch her on the kitchen counter so we're at the same height.

"I think you love my kisses," I tell her, showering her neck with pecks. She starts unbuttoning my jeans and that's all the encouragement I need to slide the pants she changed into earlier down her waist and off her legs. "I think you love what I do to your body even more." My index finger trails a path up her inner thigh and I tease her entrance.

"This changes nothing," she says between kisses, already pulling off her shirt. "It's just sex. A workout, really, if you consider the calories. We ate a large pizza. We should definitely burn some of those off."

My mouth latches onto the bud of her breast. She can call this whatever she likes, but we both know deep down it's more. I can't keep my hands off her and the way Jessie looks at me, she wants me too. She's just been hurt too much in the past to realize yet, but she will.

Her hand wraps around the base of my cock and I immediately release a bead of pre-cum and her hand becomes slick as she works me.

"Condom," she breathes and I pause.

"Fuck! I haven't got any here."

A whimper escapes her lips.

"I could phone down to reception, get them to send some up?"

"No. You can't do that. They know I'm up here... it'll be..."

"I could pull out?" I say, asking her to trust me, not believing entirely that I can trust myself.

Her gaze fixes on mine and I can see her uncertainty. I rest my forehead against hers. "It's okay, I can still get you off, baby, and I'm going to enjoy every second of it." I lower my head, ready for a feast, but she grips my shoulders and says, "Okay. Pull out. I trust you." And the power of her statement almost knocks me sideways.

"You're sure?" I check.

"Shut up and fuck me, Tate."

"You got it," I reply.

* * *

THE SUN IS BEAMING RIGHT through the open curtains, stinging my eyes, even though they're still shut, but I don't care because I can feel Jessie's naked warmth against my own.

As she gently shifts in my arms, I tuck the comforter around her, turn my head and kiss her temple, "Morning, beautiful."

"How is it morning already?" she sleepily groans.

The sound of a deep throat clearing has both our eyes pinging open and our heads swinging in its direction.

"Morning, sleepyheads. I wish you'd have mentioned you planned to sleep in, I would have arranged to bring *my daughter* over later," Drew's voice is annoyingly cheerful. He's standing beside Callie and flanked by my entire family.

"Fuck!" I hiss, scrambling to cover Jessie's essentials. "We slept in."

"No shit, sherlock," Callie replies and Drew immediately admonishes her. Behind them, Skyla and Layla are grinning their damn faces off, and so I quickly check my junk isn't hanging out. Luckily, it's not so I guess they're just smiling because they're happy to see me and Jessie reconnecting.

"Why don't you two go and get showered, and I'll put on some coffee," Mom says with a grin.

Jessie shrinks beside me and I help her up since our audience seems to have caused her to fall into a deep state of shock. I wrap us both in the blanket, and we hop together in the direction of the bathroom.

When we get there, Jessie's face is an adorable mix of sleepiness and stricken.

"Fuck. Fuck! FUCK!" she says. "This isn't how I wanted to meet your family for the first time."

"Babe, you already met them and they all absolutely adore you." She seems to calm down at my mention of this but then she sags against me. "I didn't want them to know we fucked."

"Newsflash: They're probably going to guess we fucked when we tell them you had my baby," I suggest.

"Yes, but that was ages ago. This is now." She splashes cold water on her face and I hug her from behind before turning her around to face me.

"I'm going to put the shower on for you and grab your stuff from the bedroom. Then we're going to have coffee with my family and they're going to be super happy that I have you by my side, okay?"

She breathes deeply in and out and then responds, "Okay. I can do this." She nods.

"We can do this," I correct then ask, "You want me to make you come first or are you still sore?"

"I..." Her expression is torn. My cock hardens at the

thought of going again but I decide she probably needs to compose herself. I've never seen her so nervous, except maybe the first day I saw her again when she locked herself in the bathroom and cleaned my toilet with oven cleaner.

I kiss the tip of her head and remind her, "It's going to be okay. You're Jessie fucking Yates soon-to-be Blingwood, and you're not afraid of anything."

She nods, not even realizing she's basically agreeing to being a Blingwood and takes a deep breath while I lean out and turn the nob for the shower. "We've got this."

"Yes, we do." I smile, glad she's coming around to the idea of a "we."

* * *

"So, you had a baby, but you're not together, except for last night which was a one-off because you were tired and you ate too much pizza?" Layla says, checking with Jessie who replies, "And emotional. We'd both had a long day and we'd been to see my mom and—"

"You fell into bed..." Layla is nodding knowingly. I haven't known Layla long, but she's marrying my brother Logan and is one of Jessie's friends.

"I like you, Layla. You seem to be able to read between the lines," I say.

"Thank you," Layla says. "I like you too. I'm glad you're not a fatherhood-shirking asshole."

"Me too." I chuckle.

"But it's a fake relationship?" Skyla checks.

"The family man image will help Tate seal the Dinky deal," Jessie replies.

My mom hangs back, taking everything in. Her eyes are welling with happy tears.

"So, you're not really together?" Callie checks.

"Well… grown-up relationships are complicated sometimes," Jessie replies and I enjoy watching her squirm.

"Jessie's into me. She practically begged me to go official, but I suggested we take things slow," I tell my niece. "I still don't know if I can trust her with the TV remote."

Callie sighs. "Uncle Tate is ridiculously possessive over the TV remote so good luck with that. Hey, you'll still be my aunt though, won't you? Macy's my cousin, so you must be, yes?"

Jessie's throat bobs as she smiles. "I'd love to be your aunt."

"That's so cool. And soon I'll be old enough to babysit," Callie replies. "I'll text you my rates."

Jessie slowly nods, a look of uncertainty on her face.

"Why didn't you tell us sooner?" Logan checks but he doesn't seem pissed, it's more like he's curious. "I know you already explained that Tate's team wasn't convinced you were legit, but we'd have made sure you were taken care of."

I wrap an arm around Jessie, pulling her into me in case she needs reminding that I have her back, always. I'm about to speak when Jessie says, "On hindsight, I wish I had told you all the first day I got here but I was worried I'd look crazy." She looks at my mom. "The first time I saw you—on the day I was moving in and you offered to hold Macy while I tossed my bags into the apartment—you wouldn't take no for an answer since you could see I had a lot on my plate. I wanted to tell you then, but Sally came over and introduced herself and I lost my nerve. After that, it got harder each time I saw you. I wasn't sure I'd be believed. Every time I told anyone, I was ridiculed and made to feel like I was deluded. I'm truly sorry I didn't find the courage."

"Hey." Mom pushes me out the way so she can hug Jessie. "Our family has learned the hard way that life doesn't always go as we'd like. So we're not going to dwell on what might have been. We move forward with love in our hearts, and I can't wait to get to know my new grandbaby." Mom's face lights up like Christmas. "I can't wait to meet her as her Nanna. Ooh. Does she like kittens? I just had a gorgeous batch come in that I think she'll love."

"And me, I want to meet her too," my sister Tab's says. "I'm a super cool auntie, she's going to love me."

"She'll need some good financial advice," Logan says. "I'll speak with my team; see what investments we need to put in place for her."

Layla's mouth twists into a grin.

"Ooh. Fun Uncle Logan and his financial investments!" I tease.

"Hey, business can be fun. We can teach Macy when she's older," Layla defends.

"I'll hold your job open for as long as you need," Logan tells Jessie and she thanks him. I want to tell him not to bother, she's not going to need that job but I don't. I stay quiet because it's Jessie's decision and if she ever decides she wants to go back to her job, I'll move heaven and earth to make it happen.

Drew gets into a whole speech about property portfolios and I remind him that I'm going to need a bigger house. "I'll clear my calendar," he says.

"Thanks, Drew," I reply. "Jason's found a house for us to rent for now, but I'm putting the penthouses up for sale. It'll free up a decent budget for a new family home."

"Welcome to the family, Jessie," my mom says. "We're going to take such good care of you and Macy."

"Even though I'm an unconventional fake girlfriend?" Jessie jokes, her expression unsure.

Mom's lips tip up to reassure her. "There's no such thing as fake family, my dear. You and Macy became family the moment we met you. And besides, we Blingwoods like to be a little on the unconventional side."

I knew they'd handle the news like pros, but I'm flooded with pride at how immediately accommodating my family have been toward Jessie, who keeps trying to apologize to my mom about the delay in her relationship with Macy. My mom tells her over and over, everything in life happens when it's supposed to and Jessie nods, but I can tell from her eyes she's overwhelmed.

I usher everyone out.

My girl needs some peace before her life drastically changes and I want her to myself a little while longer.

"We'll make plans for a family barbeque so you can all meet Macy and Jessie's family officially, but for today, I want to spend the day with Jessie and my daughter because tomorrow things are going to get crazy," I say before the elevator doors close.

Then I pull Jessie into my arms and say, "How about we collect Macy early from day-care and take her to see her new house?"

Jessie grins. "I'd really like that."

"Just one of my many talents as a father and partner," I tell her. "Figuring out what you both need."

Jessie smiles like she wants to believe me, but I guess the test will be once she enters my world and I lose control over how shit goes down.

CHAPTER 15

JESSIE

"**Y**ou're early," Lisa says, calling out to one of her colleagues to collect Macy's things.

"We wanted to have a special afternoon with Macy," I say, gesturing to Tate and watching as her eyes bug out of her head.

"You're... You're... umm..."

"Tate Blingwood. Macy's father. Nice to meet you." He holds out his hand to shake and Lisa looks at it like she doesn't know whether to lick it or purr against it.

"You're Macy's.... um... you..."

He grins and nods. "Jessie normally brings Macy to day care but today I decided I'd like to see the place."

"We're in a hurry. If you could get Macy, please," I say, unsure if Miss Dreamy Eyes can even hear me.

"You were in that movie..."

Tate's mouth crinkles up politely and suddenly every inch of him looks like a Hollywood star, instead of just my Tate.

"I've been in a few." He shrugs but he doesn't sound smug, he sounds humble.

"Lisa. Macy, please," I repeat and she puts her hand up to pause me, earning her my instant ire.

"The one with the dog that died," Lisa explains.

Tate smiles politely. "*Ten Owners*," he supplies and she nods. "My mom was pretty cross about that dog dying."

Lisa laughs like he's told a straight-up, piss-your-pants joke, and I scowl at her for being a massive flirt.

"Lisa. Macy. Now. Please."

Lisa turns to me, the flirty smile slipping from her face the second her eyes land on mine. "Sure, Jessie. Oh, before I get her, can I get that check? You have *sooo* many fees outstanding, are you able to clear them up now?"

I shrink a little inside, then stand taller. I will not be made to feel small by the woman flirting with my boyfriend… baby daddy… fake whatever he is. The matter is so muddy now, even I'm confused what territory we have arrived at.

"Sure, I'll pay them just as soon as I receive the invoice." I glare right at her stupid face and she glares back.

"I already sent you the invoice."

"I didn't receive it," I reply with a forced smile, knowing I am damn sure I'm correct. Even though I couldn't have paid them if I had, Lisa is lying and trying to make me look small in front of Tate.

"The fees are well overdue." Her eyes flick to Tate as she smiles for him out of the corner of her mouth.

"I can settle those now," Tate says, pulling out his wallet and I hold my palm up to him.

"That's not necessary. I'll straighten up just as soon as I get the bill in my inbox."

"Honestly, it's no—"

I throw Tate a stare that has him putting his wallet straight back in his pocket.

"Well, I'm sure you can tell we're good for it." Tate chuckles and takes my hand while Lisa looks over his shoulder at the Bentley, complete with suited driver that's waiting for us.

When Macy is finally brought out, she runs right into Tate's arms. "Tate bunny," she says, pointing at the bunny in her left hand.

"That's right, my clever girl," he says, scooping Macy up in a giant hug.

"Does Macy want to go look at our new house?" I say, and she shrieks with joy.

* * *

"She is adorable!" Jason says, giving Macy the once-over. "Your fans are going to love her!"

"The stylist ordered the new fall line from Baby Designer Boutique," Gaynor says and I swing my head her way.

"Macy has her own stylist now?"

"She's part of the brand." Gaynor makes a face at Macy that I think is intended to be funny, but it's like she has never interacted with a child in her life before. "Play your cards right, little squidge, and you could get a sponsorship deal."

I hug Macy tighter, not sure how I feel about her being part of a brand or getting a sponsorship deal.

"The new wardrobe should arrive in time for tomorrow's shoot." Gaynor squares her eyes at Macy like she's a designer handbag and not an actual person. "Do you think we should have hair and makeup take a look at her? Perhaps she should get bangs?"

"Macy doesn't need bangs or makeup. She's perfect already," Tate says adoringly.

We just had the grand tour of the new house Jason

arranged for us and Macy is already eyeing up the pool that is giving me anxiety.

"Your clothes are making their way through customs as we speak." Gaynor holds out her hand to me while she speaks into the earpiece she's wearing and then she glances back at me and says, "They'll be here first thing. They should arrive at the same time as your makeup artist and hair stylist. I booked the full works for you."

I nod, hoping the full works isn't a pixie cut and some kind of lip-plumping vacuum procedure.

Jason leads Tate to a huge glossy white dining table that seats about twelve people to look over and sign the house lease. They chat as they go through all the legal stuff and also the arrangements for tomorrow, while I hang out in the kitchen with Gaynor and try to convince myself that I fit in here.

In the corner of the open plan living area there is already a space set up for tomorrow's photo shoot and magazine interview. There are cameras on tripods with huge lenses, reflectors and diffusers and a green screen behind the three thrones.

"Don't let the kid touch any of that with her sticky fingers," Gaynor says, pointing at Macy who is snacking on a piece of cake from the huge welcome basket that was here when we arrived.

I gaze around in wonder, trying to figure out which parts of the house are actually kid friendly.

"It's impressive, right?" Gaynor says, her eyes gleaming with avarice. She knows the house is a big jump from any kind of house I've lived in before.

"It's a lot to take in," I reply.

"Right?!" Gaynor grins. "The sales value alone is forty-five million bucks. If you threw in the furniture and art it'd be more like fifty. Of course, Tate's just renting it for now. It will look great as a backdrop for the Blingwood's at-home piece the magazine is writing but still, if Tate gets the Dinky Deal he'll be able to easily afford this place." Gaynor checks her phone and then without even looking up she says, "You should make the most of it while you're here. There's a spa, an infinity pool, and of course the sensational view." She glances over the screen of her phone at me and then her mouth tips down like she feels sorry for me. "I don't suppose you have access to much of that stuff at your resort accommodation. No. I imagine, once this is all over, going back to your old life is really going to suck."

"I like my old life," I mutter back, but then it dawns on me, once I've played my part and Tate's career is back on track, he'll go back to his old life and I will have to get used to only seeing him when Macy's needs demand it, and suddenly I start to feel nauseous.

Gaynor's right. Post fake relationship *is* really going to suck.

* * *

AFTER GAYNOR AND JASON LEAVE, Tate fixes us some lunch from the pre-filled refrigerator. Macy and I head to the family room with the huge sectional sofa that overlooks the Pacific Ocean, and Macy runs over to play with a bunch of toys that I could never afford in a million years, and I try to feel happy.

"You want a glass of wine?" Tate asks.

"It's only 2 p.m.," I reply.

"To celebrate our new home," he counters.

Even though it doesn't feel like my new home, I try to get into the mood and reply, "I'll take a beer."

I get a text in the group message I share with Layla and Skyla:

> Skyla: Jessie! How is the life of a movie star wife?

I reply as enthusiastically as I can:

> Jessie: Amazing! You should see the size of the bath tub. This place is insane!

> Layla: You're living the dream!

> Jessie: Hell, yeah I am.

Except it doesn't feel like my life or my dream.

> Skyla: Let's meet up soon. I need details and I have some news to share.

We hold off on setting dates to meet up since my calendar is now managed by Jason and Gaynor, but I immediately wonder if Skyla is going to announce a pregnancy. Skyla and Drew have been trying to get pregnant since their honeymoon. I glance down at my tummy and notice my hand is absentmindedly stroking it. If Tate and I are expecting another baby, then it'd be a cousin to Skyla and Drew's baby. It would be comforting to go through a pregnancy journey with one of my best friends, but also scary because my and Tate's relationship isn't conventional like Drew and Skyla's is. I decide not to think about it until I know, then I can make a plan.

Tate makes some kind of organic, superfood, fresh-boxed meal where all you need to do is throw the ingredients together over some heat and the quality is as good as any fine dining restaurant.

"So... tomorrow...," I say to Tate as I watch Macy spooning some food into her mouth and missing half of it.

My anxiety ratchets up a notch as I worry about the mess my daughter could make in this multi-million dollar estate.

"It's going to be fine," he says, his hand reaching across the table and cupping mine. I stare into his eyes. So warm and friendly, it'd be easy to believe him and not plan for the worst—just in case.

"The interviews aren't so bad. If you feel uncomfortable answering any of their questions, then just squeeze my hand and I'll take over. We have reservations tomorrow night. Gaynor's tipped off the paps, so they'll be there at the restaurant ready to get their shots and then—"

"Wait, tomorrow night?"

"Yeah, Jason mentioned it earlier."

"I didn't hear that. I haven't asked anyone to babysit Macy. Betty goes to book club on Thursdays. It's not fair to ask her to drop her plans at the last minute, and my Mom will be busy taking Jenna to her violin lesson." We could ask Cassandra, but Macy doesn't know her well enough to be left alone with her and I'd feel bad asking for babysitting favors already. My blood pressure is rising and the walls of the vast room feel like they're closing in on me.

Tate gets up and walks around the table, his hands applying the exact right amount of pressure to my shoulders.

"If all of this is too much for you, then just say the word. It's not too late to put on the brakes—"

"No. It's not too much, I just didn't know about it and now I have to find a babysitter—"

"It's already covered. The new nanny starts tomor—"

I immediately stand and swing around to face him. "What?!"

"The new nanny. Gaynor suggested it. She said you'd be okay with it."

I shake my head. I was overwhelmed earlier, but this is the first I've heard of it. I would definitely have remembered any talk of a nanny. "Macy doesn't like strangers," I tell him and I'm certain he's recalling how I said Macy didn't warm to men because she wasn't used to being around them and how she immediately loved him.

"The nanny agency is sending their best person. They're so highly qualified they're practically doctors, Gaynor said."

"I don't care if it's the surgeon general; I'm not leaving my daughter with a stranger."

Tate nods slowly like he's either wrapping his head around my point of view or he's wondering how to persuade me otherwise.

"It's fine. We won't go. No problem," he suggests. Tate's brow is furrowed and I can't tell if he's disappointed or worried.

"No, we can go, perhaps. Let me ask Betty." I hand Tate the spoon to feed Macy so she'll actually fill her belly, and I pull out my cell and walk to the other side of the room to make the call.

We chat for a while, and the whole time Tate makes the spoon every vehicle in the dictionary and meal time takes on a life of its own, meaning that Macy flicks more food around the room than Tate manages to get inside her mouth. And of course, Betty doesn't mind ditching her plans to help me. She's so excited at the possibility of love being in the air that she'd cancel Christmas if that's what it took.

After our late lunch, I tell Tate that I need to unpack while Macy takes her nap, and Tate gives me space to adjust to the new house. Everything is so big and expensive that even the walk-in feels like a separate apartment.

My clothes hang on the rails beside Tate's shirts and an uneasy feeling settles in my solar plexus. We haven't even discussed sleeping arrangements, but I know I want to sleep in this room with him, muddying the waters even more. If I'm only going to be here a short while, I should make the most of it. Immersing myself in this life with Tate feels like the right thing to do. But if it's the right thing to do, why do I feel so uncertain?

By late afternoon Tate knocks on the door to the bedroom and asks to come in. "You okay?" he asks like he knows I'm stressed.

I smile at him and nod. "I—"

"It's a lot," he offers. "I get it. I had time to build up to all of this and you're being asked to adapt in one day."

He steps forward, loosely putting his hands on my waist. "Is there anything I can do to make this easier for you? I canceled the nanny service. I agree, no strangers with our daughter unless we meet and approve of them. You know my mother would be happy to step in as well."

"I know, Cassandra would be thrilled, and thank you," I say. "You're being so kind. I'm not trying to be difficult, but can we just get Macy used to everything a little bit more first?"

Tate takes a half a step back to look me squarely in the eyes. "Jessie, you're not being difficult. I get it. We're in new territory and I'm still learning everything I can about you. I know you need time to process things. But if there's anything you need me to do just ask, okay? I'm worried you're going to push me away."

I nod and Tate's arms pull me closer and I breathe him in. He smells like fresh soap and cologne. His clothes have that brand-new feel and the body beneath them is strong and dependable. He kisses the top of my head and I tilt my chin to look up at him. Sensing my need, his mouth lowers down onto mine and I feel my cortisol drop in response to the flood of serotonin that comes with his touch.

The pressure of his mouth on mine intensifies and I know we're seconds away from getting naked when Macy starts making a babbling sound from her room. "Momomomom."

Tate releases me, his hands sliding to mine. His smile is adoring yet comically disappointed. "Cockblocker!"

I nod and chuckle. "She sure is."

"How do you feel about me teaching her to say Daddy? It seems unfair she only calls for you."

"I think she's more than ready for a new word."

"You sure?"

"Yes."

Tate punches the air and calls out, "Daddy's coming, baby girl!" He takes a step away and then looks back at me. "You're smiling."

I am and so is my heart.

Tate already loves her and for that I feel blessed. I tease, "I'm smiling because at 2 a.m. when she's lost Tate bunny, you're going to be the person she calls out for."

"If my daughter wants her bunny at 2 a.m., then I'll be honored to get it for her," he says grinning. "Put your bathing suit on. Macy and I are going to meet you in the pool."

* * *

BY THE TIME we're ready and Tate has found the swim diapers, the sun is low in the sky and casting a warm glow over Montecito.

Macy splashes Tate as they climb in and I hang back by the sliding wall of doors that open out to the pool and watch. Tate has her securely wrapped in his arms and he keeps checking her floaty suit like he's afraid it'll deflate at any moment. Macy's face is a picture of happiness and I snap a few photos of the two of them together, then come closer and as Tate spins Macy around, he sees me and his mouth pops open like he likes what he sees.

"Hi!" I say, bashfully.

But instead of greeting me, he puts two fingers in his mouth and wolf whistles. And even though it's ridiculously childish, it makes me feel adored.

"Are you ready for some fun, little fishy?" he says to Macy. "Get in, Mommy! The water is fine and Daddy is going to teach Macy to splash!" he coos, adjusting Macy's suit and then sitting her on an enormous pink floaty. He trails her up and down the pool and then puts her on his back and he wades, pretending to be a shark.

Macy kicks her little legs and squeals with delight, her chubby little arms reaching out as though she can grab the glistening ripples of the pool. Water clings to every part of Tate, dripping from his hair and down onto his thick shoulders and I can't help but ogle him.

I watch as they float together, Macy's trust in Tate evident as she relaxes in his embrace. Him repeating dadadada and Macy following his lead with ease, and a flood of contentment threatens to spill from my eyes. Between Macy's toothy grin and Tate's gentle, fun presence, my worries float away. It's like being on an amazing vacation.

"You okay?" Tate asks, paddling over to me with Macy now on his shoulders.

As I stand waist deep in the water, I realize I am okay. How can anything that feels this blissful go wrong? "You're great with her," I tell him. "We're going to be fine tomorrow with the press and I'm going to try really hard to adapt fast."

"I don't feel like I've thanked you enough," he says.

"You thanked me pretty hard last night," I reply, winking and even though he grins, I'm reminded that with how often we're sleeping together, not to mention living together now, it's starting to feel like this is all real.

"I mean it, Jess. Everything you've given up for me, I don't know how I can ever repay you."

"It's fine." I bat my hand in the air flippantly. "You can buy me a Hummer or dedicate your next movie to me," I joke.

"Do days like this make you wonder what it'd be like if we forgot about all the pressure of fake relationships and just continued as we are?"

"I wonder all the time. But then I remember how different our lives are and…" *I worry I won't be enough for you.* "I figure we're better off being realistic. You and me?" I laugh but it sounds forced. "With your ego and my feisty streak? Man, we'd be hating each other before the ink dried on the marriage license."

Tate looks momentarily hurt but he fixes his expression into his cocky smile quickly. "I'm surprised you'd say such a thing, especially as my number one fan."

I swoosh the water at him and Macy laughs. "I think your daughter is your number one fan. I'm just your temporary costar."

"Really? Huh. Maybe I'll have to get her a T-shirt with my face on to match the one you own." He looks positively smug as realization dawns on me.

My voice is so high-pitched, the sound hurts my ears. "You saw the T-shirt?" Not just any T-shirt but the one I received from the Tate Blingwood fan club.

"I might have noticed it while we were packing up your things from your apartment."

Absolute mortification swallows me whole.

He leans into my ear and says, "I really want to see you wearing it."

"That's because you're an egotistical maniac," I immediately reply.

"I want to see you wearing it with nothing else on."

"Never gonna happen, Blingwood. I only kept it in case I needed a rag to clean puke with."

Tate chuckles. "One day you're going to stop fighting this thing between us."

He's right. My defensive wall is crumbling so quickly that right now, it's barely even a pile of bricks. Still, I reply, "You know why we can't get serious. It'll get messy."

"Even if you find out you're…" His eyes dip to my belly and my hand cradles it instinctively.

"I don't know what we'll do if I turn out to be pregnant," I admit and Tate comes closer, pushing a wet kiss onto my lips.

"Maybe there's more than one. But even if the movie turns into a trilogy, it'll have a happy ending," he says, rubbing my tummy.

"If one becomes three, I'm booking you in for the snip."

His enormous grin turns smug. "We're creating a little army of adorable Blingwoods."

"Hmm. In that case, I had better do the procedure myself. Your ego is already out of control. I'm off to find two bricks and a hammer. There's no time to waste."

Tate's free hand that doesn't have a hold of Macy grips the back of my neck and he pulls me in to kiss him again. "You'd hurt little Tate?"

"Babe, if you think I'm feisty now, you wait 'til I've got triple the pregnancy hormones," I say even though mostly, I just remember feeling horny in the early stages of pregnancy. I laugh as the grin partially slips from his face. "Not so funny now, is it?"

"You're not nearly as intimidating as you think," he replies, grinning mischievously. "I can handle you just fine, even with the hormones."

"Really?" I ask, dropping my voice to a conspiratorial whisper even though Macy can't understand. "Last time I was pregnant, I wore out four vibrators."

I'm delighted when shock has his mouth falling open.

"You were… you were…" He steps closer until my breasts are pressed against his chest.

"Horny? Very."

"Sweet baby Jesus. You just cannot rely on technology these days. Fear not, babe. I'm not letting you go through all this alone. I'll be there at your beck and call, attending to *all* your needs." He raises Macy's arms into the air and yells, "Being a dad is the best job on earth!" And Macy squeals in delight, then he tells me, "I think this calls for an early night!"

"Come to mention it, I do feel a little tired," I reply and we all get out of the pool.

CHAPTER 16

TATE

*T*he studio lights are blazing overhead, casting a warm glow on the opulent set arranged for the magazine shoot. The anticipation of my team of stylists, publicists, assistants and such in the room is palpable—a mix of fear that they will no longer have jobs if this fails but also a sense of community and a shared goal.

"Hey, Tate, do you want a vodka?" Lesley, one of the runners from the magazine asks, batting her eyes at me and pushing her chest out as though to remind me she's a woman with breasts.

"No. No thank you," I reply and am immediately surprised. Normally, I'd be three drinks in by now and feeling pretty anxious but with Jessie and Macy beside me, I feel mostly calm yet alert. I won't drink around my daughter and I want to be switched on enough to intervene if the interviewer asks any questions that make Jessie feel uncomfortable.

"Perhaps a shoulder massage to help you relax before you go on?" Lesley offers.

I can feel Jessie's jealous stare without even looking at her.

"A shoulder massage to help relax. What a great idea," I reply and Lesley's mouth puckers.

Jessie stiffens beside me so I turn to her and say, "Hey, babe. Do you want me to rub your shoulders before we go on?"

Jessie grins and replies, "Thanks baby, you're so sweet." And then she leans around Macy and kisses me, hissing, "The audacity of that woman!"

"Jealous?" I tease, but it's all the confirmation I need that she's into me, and hope starts to take root that I can persuade her that we have a shot at a real future.

"No. Absolutely not. I'm not jealous," she hisses.

"Good," I reply to Jessie then I turn to Lesley and say, "Actually—"

"Don't you dare finish that sentence, Tate Blingwood."

I'm side-smiling Jessie as I continue, "Actually, I'd really appreciate a glass of water, please."

"Coming right up!" Lesley replies.

I bounce Macy on my knee and say to her, "Your Mommy is so cute when she's jealous. But Daddy only wants attention from Mommy. Isn't that right, baby girl?" When I dare to look at Jessie, she's grinning enough that I know she hasn't taken any of what happened to heart.

Shortly later Gaynor is at my side going over everything Jessie and I can and cannot say. I frequently glance at Jessie and squeeze her hand to let her know that I'm here, but she seems calm. Either that or her game face is impenetrable.

"I need to go finalize content with the magazine's editor," Gaynor says. "You two just relax, I'll be back shortly."

She toddles away on too high heels and I pull Jessie's

chair closer to mine and kiss Macy, who is now on her lap. "You feel okay?"

"I'm fine. Talk about how in love we are now and our plans for a happy future, and don't focus too much on our time apart. Got it."

"I love you," I say, gazing in those perfect blue eyes of hers. We've been practicing saying it all morning; it's how we're going to end the interview and then we'll kiss and the photographer won't be able to help himself from getting the money shot. Contrived, yet I quickly realize, when I tell her I love her, it's from the bottom of my fucking soul. "You look beautiful." And she does. She's wearing a Dior pant suit and the silk of her shirt has me imagining it sliding off her shoulders.

"Thank you, and I love you too," she replies robotically.

"We're going to need to work on your acting skills," I tell her and smile.

Her hand cups mine. "I'm sorry. I didn't mean that to sound feelingless. I'm still trying to remember all my lines."

"You're going to do great. And so are you, daddy's big girl!" I say and Macy smiles her big toothy grin that punches me in the heart every single time.

"You're on set in five minutes," Gaynor says, as she pulls up a chair the other side of me. "Tate, I really think you should go put the red shirt on. The fan club ran a poll recently on their best Tate Blingwood movie moment and it was the one where you were wearing the red button-down. We can't afford to leave anything to chance."

I stand, used to putting on and taking off clothes as I am told to but Jessie's hand stops me. "The blue of his shirt makes his eyes pop." She gazes up at me and smiles like she can't help herself. "He looks perfect. Leave him be."

I sit down. I liked this shirt best which is why I chose it

from the rack of about thirty options, and if my Jessie says I look perfect then I'm not changing.

"Tate. You should wear the red. It shows off your glossy dark hair, which *Celebrity Gossip* magazine readers voted in a poll as your best feature."

Jessie shakes her head. "His eyes and his smile are his best features. Leave the shirt. You're gorgeous!"

Macy farts really loudly and I let out a roaring laugh. "That was a good one!" I high-five Macy's little pudgy hand and Jessie sniffs toward her.

"I don't think that was just a fart. If you'll excuse me—"

"I can change her," I offer. Now that I've got the hang of diapers, they're not so bad and I have a lot of catching up to do.

"No. You can do the next one. You need to decide what shirt you feel most comfortable in before we get started."

With Jessie gone, Gaynor comes closer. "Things seem to be going well between you both."

I smile. Last night Jessie introduced me to her special box of toys and I managed to make her come five times. "Right now, I'm probably the happiest I've ever been in my life, period."

"I'm glad," Gaynor replies. Her smile is the feline one she uses when she's tackling tricky subjects and I brace myself that she's probably about to deliver bad news. "But be careful, Tate. I've known you three years now, and I've never seen you in a relationship. You're falling fast, but I can't say I'm getting the same vibe from her."

My heart sinks into the pit of my stomach. Jessie not being into me would explain her reluctance to let her guard down.

"Jessie's cautious," I defend, certain there's something more than a shared child between us. "She holds a lot back but that's because she's been hurt and she's still figuring out if she can trust me." I consider the easy relationship she has with her mom, her sisters and her friends. How close she is to Macy and how utterly protective she is of her. "She loves hard when she allows herself to. She's come a long way since she almost tried to kill me." I chuckle, remembering the laces. "Don't worry about me. Jessie and I will be fine."

"Have you spoken to her about what happens after your career is restored? Like, will she go back to the resort, or maybe you can get her a rental and you go to LA and be a weekend dad?" Gaynor asks.

I spot Jessie and Macy on their way back from the bathroom and throw them both a huge smile.

"We haven't discussed a plan for after. And right now, I wouldn't change a thing. But I guess we'll need to make some decisions soon."

"Right, everyone, if you'd like to take your places, the shoot will get underway."

"Show time, baby. You ready?" I ask Jessie, pulling her into a hug and kissing her then Macy.

"As I'll ever be."

* * *

THE SHOOT TAKES four hours and is a constant cycle of clothes, hair, makeup, smile. Wash. Rinse. Repeat. The photographer, Dan, is amazing with Macy and gets some candid shots of her playing on the mat, just her and her bunny and my heart melts.

"I'll have those printed and send them to you as a thank you for giving us the exclusive," he tells me and Jessie.

I'm not sure Macy has ever done a conventional photo-shoot but she rocked it and the entire room fell in love with her. Except Gaynor, but Gaynor is too focused on ruling

Hollywood to care much about kids—unless they're destined to be the next Miley Cyrus or Macauley Caulkin—and no way my daughter is getting into showbiz before she's eighteen.

"So, you met and fell in love three years ago?" Lola, the magazine journalist, asks.

"It certainly was a whirlwind romance," Jessie replies, gripping my hand tighter.

"We met, fell in love, and then I was whisked off to film *Ten Owners*."

"So, you both lost contact?"

"Yes. But boy have we loved reconnecting," I say and chuckle, then kiss Jessie's temple. Across the room, Jason has a hold of Macy who is jabbing his car keys at his face—not that Jason seems to mind as he playfully pretends to have an ouchy.

"So why is the public only hearing about the baby now? Did you contact Tate when you found out about Macy?" Lola asks Jessie, and Gaynor coughs loudly to remind her to stick to the script.

"Yes, but...," Jessie starts and I watch her cheeks color. "Well, you see, I didn't know if—"

"She was worried about telling me since my career was just getting started. That's my Jessie, you see. She's the most loving and selfless woman on the planet," I interrupt. Jessie stares at me in disbelief. She was all set to follow the script and throw herself to the mercy of the trolls who would no doubt slut-shame her, but I can't let her do it. "She tried to get in touch with me to tell me about the baby, but I was barely in the country and we'd lost contact. I've spent much of the past three years on set, but I thought about her every day and then we bumped into each other and it was like we'd never been apart. We fell instantly in love."

"So, you didn't meet your daughter until recently?" Lola

asks dubiously, and so I take Jessie's hand and speak directly to her.

"I lost two years with them both because I was young and stupid. But there's no way I'm ever making that mistake again."

"How do you think your fans will react to the news you're in a relationship? Maybe they prefer you single."

"My fans are the best, most understanding people in the world. I know they'll be super happy for us."

Behind Jessie, Gaynor is furiously writing notes, probably planning how to give weight to the claims we have made. I hastily butt-in before Lola can ask us to elaborate with another question. "And now we have big plans, don't we, love? We're building a new house and plan to get married and there will definitely be lots more children. We love being parents, don't we?"

Jessie smiles and nods while I let her know how proud I am of her by wrapping my arm around her. "It's a dream come true."

At the end of the interview, Lola gushes, "You two can't keep your hands off each other. It's adorable!"

"So, what's in store for Jate now?"

"Jate?" I ask, laughing.

"Do you prefer Tessie?"

Jessie starts laughing and Lola does too. "Our love-star name. You decide, babe," Jessie says. "Jate or Tessie?"

"Definitely Jate. Jessie comes first now, always."

"Jate it is." Lola types that into her device. "So, what's next. When will there be wedding bells?"

"Soon," I reply. "You'll have to watch this space."

Jessie shakes her head but her smile is genuine. "We're going to enjoy being a family for a while and keep Tate's naked butt out of the news."

Lola chuckles and takes out her phone. "Any chance of a flash for your fans?"

I laugh, too; the interview is going well and I'm so relaxed that I feel tempted but I shake my head. "I'm afraid my ass is the private property of one very special, very beautiful woman. My Jessie."

"I'm ending with that," Lola says, standing. "You two make a great couple. It's good to see, Tate. I'm not going to lie, there were rumors circulating that you'd never settle down. I'm pleased we had it wrong. Jessie, you did great for a first interview. I'll send your team my information. It'd be great to do a catch-up piece. Our readers would love to hear all about what it's like to settle into Hollywood. Think it over, maybe try journaling your experiences. I'll be in touch."

I grin at Jessie and she looks happy. We're both on an exuberant high that so far, things are going great.

"I think you made the right decision," Jason says, clapping me on the back. "Now, put on a perfect show at the restaurant tonight. Have fun, but not too much fun," he warns. "And absolutely NO juggling."

I laugh. "You got it, Jase."

* * *

"Do I look okay?" Jessie asks, descending the stairs in a dress that can only be described as WOW.

"You look sensational," I say right as Betty says, "You'll blow the doors off the place."

"Thank you," Jessie replies, seemingly pleased with our reactions. "Macy's down in her bed sleeping. The baby monitor is switched to loud so you'll hear her if she calls out. The TV remote is here, and I already set the channel to *Dancing with the Stars*, and there's sherry in the fridge—I know you like it cold."

"Me and Macy will be fine. You two go and have a lovely, romantic dinner." She pulls Jessie to one side and lowers her voice so I pull out my phone and pretend I'm not listening. "Sometimes, the only way to break free from the past is to take a leap of faith. Dig deep and find your courage to leap with Tate. You two are perfect for each other."

I glance up and measure Jessie's reaction as she slowly nods and flicks her eyes my way, then back to Betty. "I'm trying," she murmurs and then she grabs her purse and I put my phone back in my pocket and hold out my hand for her to take.

When she slides her hand in mine, I decide Betty's right, we are perfect for one another and it's time I made it clear I want more.

* * *

"Jessie, over here! Give us a smile," a paparazzi shouts.

"Jate!" another calls, as we get out the car and walk up the lighted pathway to the restaurant and Jessie pulls me to a stop and pauses. She looks so beautiful I barely even notice the flashes on the cameras.

"You were made for this life," I tell her.

"It's easy when you're on my arm," she replies.

"I didn't expect our celebrity love name to catch on so fast," I whisper into Jessie's ear, taking her arm as security open the doors wide for us to enter.

"I think I like it," she replies.

We're seated at the front of the restaurant, right near the windows as per Jason and Gaynor's instruction. We order mocktails and look at the menu.

"I probably shouldn't order the spaghetti," Jessie jokes, gesturing to the photographers outside. "Can you imagine, me on the front page with tomato sauce all over my face."

"You'd still look beautiful," I say. "Though I have to admit, I usually insist I sit at the back of the restaurant. I feel like we're in a reality TV show."

Jessie bats me with her hand and laughs theatrically until a couple of people look over at us.

"Okay. It wasn't that funny."

"I know, but they're watching. Jason said we're supposed to laugh and look like we're having fun."

She's trying so hard to help me, to follow the plan that I can't help but smile. "Or we could go crazy and actually have fun."

She laughs. "I suppose we could do that too." She looks around. "This place is fancy."

I shrug. "Not as fancy as you."

Her eyes meet mine. "You think the newspapers and online gossip columns will be kind to us tomorrow?"

"I think Lola will write a good piece. I've done a few interviews with her and they've been fair and accurate to what was said. That's not always the case, though."

She nods. "I never realized just how much of the stuff put out there was fabricated. I studied media at college, but here, I feel like I'm learning on the job."

"Talking of jobs, I need to deposit some money for you. You found your banking information yet?"

She shakes her head.

"I was worried that'd be your answer so I set up an account. Your Amex card is in your purse, and I downloaded the app onto your phone." Jessie is about to stop me but I interrupt. "You're going to need money. This lifestyle is more expensive than the one you are used to, and I'm not just talking about clothes and dinners at restaurants. I'm talking Macy. If you need to get out of a tight spot, if you're being followed. If anything ever goes wrong, money might make the difference between you both getting out safe."

The server comes over and we both order the filet mignon and then Jessie pulls out her phone and presses her thumb on the banking icon. "A million dollars?"

My lips curl up. "I wanted to put in more but apparently there's a limit on transfers."

"Wow. I'm a millionaire."

"You're priceless."

She laughs. "Thank you." She swipes her phone and is about to put it away when her eyes focus on it. "I have a notification on Tinder. That's weird. I suppose I better delete my profile before the news breaks." Her fingers swipe and move the screen and she peers closer. "My profile picture has changed."

She clicks on the image and I try to look innocent.

"That's odd, my profile image has changed to a Doberman." Jessie glares at me teasingly. "Know anything about that?"

I shake my head and she looks down at the profile description. "Enjoys going for walks." A deep chuckle escapes from my throat. "Like's belly scratches, naps and treats. Looking for a fetching companion who can throw a tennis ball like a pro."

Laughter erupts from my belly and Jessie shakes her head.

"I can't believe you did that." She laughs, too, and she looks so beautiful it makes me want to kiss her.

"I don't feel bad at all." I lean closer. "Jessie, I don't want you to date other people. I don't want this to be fake. I want us to give this a proper shot."

She stops laughing, her gaze fixed on mine and for a second she looks vulnerable and hopeful. "I'm not sure I want a boyfriend."

"Good. I'm not a boy."

"What if it goes wrong?" she whispers.

"What if it goes right?" I reply. "Jessie, whether you like it or not, we have this connection. We have Macy. Both of us have spent three years thinking of the other—"

"I thought you ran out on me and Macy."

"Are you sure that's all it was? Because we have been in each other's pants from the moment we got back together. Tell me it's not more and I won't ever ask again."

I don't realize I'm holding my breath until my lungs start to burn. Jessie is holding her napkin and looking at me like I'm a complex sum. And then she drops the napkin and shakes her head. "I can't fight it much longer."

"Then don't. I know you care about me. And I... Jessie, I want to be with you."

Her throat bobs as she swallows. She's about to reply when the server brings our dinner.

When she's gone, I say, "So what do you say, will you be my forever girl?"

CHAPTER 17

JESSIE

*T*he restaurant buzzes with the hum of conversation and the soft clinks of cutlery as Tate and I sit across from each other. He's looking at me with those warm, sincere eyes that make my heart skip a beat every time.

"Jessie, are you going to answer me or should I write it in a letter? Maybe record a video for you to watch in your own time." His grin is bashful; he looks humble and less sure of himself.

"Sorry, what did you say?" No fake dating. He's asking me to go steady with him?

My nerves take a hold of me.

"I want us to officially be a couple. I want you to be the woman on my arm at every event, and I want us to be a family. Just to clarify, I don't mean for show. I don't mean that we continue to screw here and there and pretend that we're in love by papering over the cracks, I mean a real deal, all in, relationship."

"Oh," I say, letting his words hang in the air. A mixture of excitement and fear swirl inside my belly and when I look at my hands they are back to fidgeting with the napkin. The idea of being Tate's girlfriend for real is thrilling, but an undercurrent of anxiety tugs at my heart.

I can't deny the connection we share, how he makes me laugh every day, how tender he is when he cares for Macy, and the way my heart feels lighter when I am near him. I want to trust him. Yet a part of me is haunted by that day with my father. How the charming exterior he presented in front of his buddies warped when he laughed and turned me away and made me feel like I was nothing.

Tate's not like him, I remind myself.

In the recesses of my mind, I acknowledge it is me who is flawed, not him.

My heart is scarred but that doesn't mean it's broken. Maybe Betty is right, all I need is the courage to say yes, to trust him, and to hope for something beautiful.

"I'd love to be your girlfriend," I finally reply, looking up to meet Tate's eyes. A grin spreads across his face, and he reaches across the table to hold my hand.

Outside the paparazzi's camera flashes turn into a strobe. I blink and focus hard on Tate's smile.

"I propose a toast," Tate says, standing and lifting his glass. "To my girlfriend, who'll one day be my wife." He pulls me to standing and kisses me breathless and I melt into him.

"One day at a time," I remind him. "Let's get used to me being your girlfriend before we think about me being your wife."

"Okay. Two weeks long enough?" he whispers in my ear and shivers run down my spine.

"How about two years?" I say having no idea where that time frame came from.

"Let's meet halfway and say six weeks."

I laugh and shake my head, enjoying that even when I am vague and unsure, he understands and doesn't give up on me. "Do you want to get out of here?" I ask. Now that we've clarified our situation, I can't wait to consummate our agreement.

"I thought you'd never ask," he replies, pulling me by my hand toward the exit while simultaneously calling his driver and telling the server to charge the meal to his account.

* * *

LATER THAT NIGHT I get an email.

To: Jessie Yates

From: Pablo Benger

Subject: Lucrative offer

Dear Miss Yates,

We'd like to meet in person to discuss a deal we have for you. As Tate Blingwood's girlfriend, we could offer you fifty thousand dollars for private photographs of the two of you. This figure IS negotiable. Please call me on...

I instantly reply:

You're a piece of shit, and if you think I would sell out Tate then you are strongly mistaken. Never email me again. My answer will NEVER change.

OVER THE COMING DAYS, I get a dozen such emails and calls. A member of the paparazzi from down by our gate shouts out a similar offer, and when I am parked outside Betty's house one day, one even puts an offer under my windshield wiper.

I'm amazed and disgusted at the lengths they will go to but I don't tell Tate. A part of me doesn't want him to question if I am capable of such things. In reality, I am still feeling so much guilt that I never told him about BabyMomma4You. He'd have every right to not trust me when I've been less than honest.

Last time I logged in, I got into an argument with someone and got so fired up defending Tate that I forgot to hit the delete button on the account. They said Tate's acting is like a bad soap opera—overdone and cringe-worthy. I probably shouldn't have replied, but I couldn't help myself as I wrote: *Tate Blingwood won an Oscar, but your trolling is like a bad reality show—nobody asked for it and everyone's already wishing you'd just get canceled already.*

I'M BAREFOOT and still in my robe when the door chimes and Gaynor and Jason walk in. Gaynor's bright yellow high heels click-clack on the tiled floor while Jason's back hunches as he carries a briefcase filled with documents. I guess he didn't get the memo about going paperless yet.

"Where's Tate?" Gaynor asks, cutting straight to the chase and asking for the organ grinder not the monkey.

"He left me to sleep in this morning while he took Macy to day care," I reply.

Tate and I discussed whether Macy still needs day care with me no longer working at the resort but we decided for now to keep her routine. It makes sense since one day I'd like to go back and finish my degree.

"Tate Blingwood's first time doing the school run. Had I known, we could have had a team of photographers and staged a story." Gaynor shakes her head, disappointed.

I scrunch my nose disgustedly. "No, Gaynor, you won't arrange anything like that. EVER. I don't want the press and general public knowing what day care facility my daughter attends."

At that moment Tate walks in wearing sweats and a creased T. His dark hair is messy like he just got out of bed and it reminds me why we all got up so late this morning. "What did I miss?" he says, grabbing an apple from the bowl on the island and kissing my cheek before he bites into it.

"Gaynor wishes she knew you were taking Macy to day care this morning so she could have arranged a media story."

"What? Gaynor. No!" He squares her in the eyes. "Keep my daughter out of the papers."

I sidle up beside him and put my arm around his waist, glad we are on the same page about Macy's safety.

"It was just an idea," she replies flippantly. "Now, do I have good news for you!" She pulls her iPad out from her purse and flicks it to life. "Will you just take a look at the photograph printed in today's papers."

I step to the side to see better without the sun glinting off the device, and I see me and Tate kissing on the screen. The journalists have used a picture that was taken right at the moment I agreed to be Tate's girlfriend.

"You like it?" Tate checks with me.

"We look like a real couple," I say, thinking aloud.

Gaynor grabs Tate by the arm. "But look at what's printed below." She proceeds to read the small print: "Last night while dining at the new Michelin Starred Chef and Owner restaurant, Le Rivière, Tate Blingwood, star of *Ten Owners*, was overheard by their waiter asking Jessie Yates, mother of his newly discovered love child, to 'be his forever girl.'"

Gaynor passes Tate the device and he becomes engrossed in reading the comments while Gaynor pats herself on the back. "See? What did I tell you? The fake relationship is working like a charm. Your ratings are skyrocketing!" Gaynor chuckles. "Having the server hear you want *forever*, Tate, that was a stroke of genius!"

I stare down at the screen, reading his fans who comment how romantic and sweet Tate is and the moment feels sullied, like it was all part of the farce.

"This is amazing!" Tate fist pumps. "I honestly didn't know if this would work, but I'm thankful for both of you. My career will be back on track in no time, I can feel it," Tate says to Jason and Gaynor.

"It's not just last night." Jason pulls *Celebrity Gossip* magazine from his briefcase and opens it to the center. "I got an early print delivered to the office this morning. The interview is perfect. You both come off really well."

"They ran the article online already," Gaynor informs us. "No trolling yet and the fans are eating it up. It's a success," she sings. "Or, at least it would be if Jason here pulled his finger out his ass and secured the Dinky deal."

"While I hate to agree with Gaynor, your popularity is soaring. It's a matter of time," Jason tells Tate as Gaynor throws Jason the finger. "And, even better, the fan club is seeing increased subscriptions. Which means your fans aren't deterred by your relationship status. In fact, it's making them hungry to get to know you both. How many emails have you had inquiring what designer Jessie is wearing?"

Gaynor flicks the iPad screen and reports, "Four thousand US. More than ten thousand international. Keep enticing them, Jessie, and you might have interest for your own fan club. Though, I do worry you come across too strong, like maybe you need a vulnerable side."

I shake my head and laugh. "What's wrong with a strong female role model? And don't worry about sponsorships for me. Concentrate on Tate. I prefer the back end of the business, anyway," I reply. This entire conversation is great for Tate, and ultimately for Macy, but it's leaving me with a queasy feeling.

"I'm surprised BabyMomma4You hasn't popped her head up and written something mean," Jason says, still smiling and I cringe.

"Yes, it is very odd she's gone so quiet recently," Tate agrees. "But, she's just another troll in the line of them. In the end, she's a mean-spirited nobody, even if some of her stuff is pretty funny. Let's hope it's the last of her now that everything seems to be hitting all the marks we've been working for."

How am I ever going to be honest with him now?

Jason closes his briefcase. "Still, small blessings, I suppose. You two should definitely celebrate. Tate's becoming hot property again and even if we don't get the Dinky deal back on, offers will be coming in."

"That's great news," Tate says, one arm wraps around me and one hand rests on my belly. "Get the work rolling in, Jason. I have a family to support." Tate's grip tightens around me and it's like he's so happy he needs to squeeze something. "So, it's the film premiere tomorrow. What time are we booked in with the stylists?"

"They'll arrive at midday," Jason confirms. "Jessie, the designer will be here with your dresses later today. Choose whatever you like."

He looks at me like he's checking that's okay with me and

I smile, the pit of my stomach getting larger by the minute. Last night I felt like I was on Cloud 9, and now I just don't know what to think.

Tate's phone beeps with a message and he lets go of me to check it out. "It's Drew about building us a house. I'm going to take this outside."

As he walks from the room, Jason looks me over. "Jessie, I want to thank you for your help with Tate. He, Gaynor and I had so many conversations about reviving his career to get this Dinky deal done, and you agreeing to stand in as his girl-friend has really been pinnacle in bolstering his career." He glances at Gaynor and chuckles, "Who knew an out-of-wedlock kid would be just the thing?" Jason's face turns more serious as he tells Gaynor, "But we need to plan her exit strategy carefully. We'll go through the data together and decide whether we do something like a Demi/Bruce co-family breakup to keep things clean or if we just let her fade into obscurity." I leave the two industry experts to discuss my breakup, not knowing which way is up, or even if I should be defending mine and Tate's newly established relationship.

As I head out into the hallway, Tate bounds around the corner and drags me back into the room. "Great news! Drew has space to see us at the end of the week. My brother is a master at design. If we get this Dinky deal, the future is set and my career will be golden. It'll be all we ever wanted." He looks at me with stars in his eyes.

I can't help but mirror his smile even though it feels forced. "I'm so happy for you."

"Time for us to go," Jason says, looking away from our display of affection. "Don't forget the film premiere," he reminds us and then adds, "And Jessie, call your mom and check on her. Last I heard, her entire front lawn had paparazzi camped out on it."

Suddenly my stomach sinks as I imagine my mom in her

leopard print sweat suit and slippers with curlers in her hair, answering all kinds of personal questions with the openness and honesty that only she knows.

CHAPTER 18

TATE

*M*y mouth dries and my hands sweat as I watch Jessie descend the stairs.

"You look... Um... I can't... find.... Words..."

She's gorgeous but I already knew that. After all, gazing at Jessie has become my favorite pastime. She fascinates me. It's like every thought that runs through her head mirrors a different expression, and each expression is another clue to the world's most sophisticated and endearing puzzle. I could look at her all day and still not quite figure her out, which doesn't mean I'm going to stop trying.

Jessie smiles at my reaction, her eyes become curious. "The dress is good?"

My hand rests against my heart. "Oh baby, it's beautiful. Perfect. But what's beneath it is nothing short of exquisite."

"I feel like a dark princess." She twirls around. The dress is jet black silk with sequins and is off the shoulder, revealing soft skin and a subtle swell of her breasts. My Jessie only comes in at a little over five feet but the split of the long dress goes all the way up to reveal the milky skin of her lithe thigh. My dick immediately hardens. She always looks beautiful, even in ratty sweats with her hair piled up on top of her head, but tonight I feel intimidated and undeserving to have such a beauty on my arm.

"Take that look off your face," she says. "We haven't got time to go to the bedroom. Come on. We better rush, we're going to be late."

We dash to the car and the driver takes us into downtown LA to reach Grauman's Chinese Theater where the movie is being premiered.

"Did you manage to get through to your mom?" I check.

"Yes. She's been serving the press her homemade snickerdoodles and sweet tea. She's actually enjoying the company." I shake my head. "My sisters are happy too. They told everyone at school that their big sister got knocked up by Tate Blingwood and apparently now they're high school royalty."

I grin, glad Jessie and her family are taking the infringement on their privacy in their stride. When the car pulls up to the red carpet, the driver opens the door and I climb out of the limo first and hold out my hand for Jessie.

The sequins catch the flashes of the paparazzi cameras, casting a celestial sparkle around her and as she smiles and poses, I realize they are as captivated by her as I am, and I am accompanying the real star of tonight's show.

"Hey Jessie, has Tate proposed yet?" a journalist calls.

"Jessie, smile this way," another calls.

Beyond them, hordes of women scream my name but Jessie smiles at them and then me, like she's proud. Like she's a fan too.

I stand back and grin as I watch her work the carpet.

Moving through the crowds, her grace magnetic, effortlessly capturing the attention of everyone in her vicinity. When I'm asked for short interviews, she stands beside me rapt with interest in my answers, but mostly the camera crews and interviewers want information about our relationship and Jessie politely steers them back to the making of the movie and the role of my co-stars.

"You were made for this life, baby."

"I'm just making sure I fit the part," she replies and smiles at the cameras.

The realization hits me like a cinematic revelation—a sudden, profound understanding that the world around us has faded in a blur, leaving only her in ultra-sharp focus. It's not just her beauty I love, but the way she carries herself with a quiet strength and inner radiance. She outshines everyone to me now and I realize...

I love her.

"We're a great team," I tell her, unable to take my eyes off her.

"We are," she admits, yet it seems as if there is an air of confusion in her voice. But then she grabs my hand in hers and we ascend the stairs up to the theater, turning to give one final wave for the cameras.

* * *

As soon as we arrive home, Jessie thanks Betty, sees her to the car and then changes back into her ratty sweats and piles her hair on her head and I fall in love with her even more.

My cell rings and I accept the call, not taking my eyes off her. "Tate." It's Jason so I put the call on speaker.

"The premiere was a success! The film critics are calling it the movie of the year and a box office must see!"

Jessie's face lights up.

"But better than that, I just got word from Dinky that the deal is back on the table! They want you to sign this week. They love the image of you as a family man and want to hit the market hard with you taking your daughter to the premiere, and since Macy will be older by then, it makes sense. If you're good with that?"

I check with Jessie and she nods a slow yes. "Of course. She deserves to go with you and see the premier."

When I hang up with Jason, I lift Jessie high into the air and spin her around. "Since you and Macy arrived in my life, it has got better and better. You're my lucky charms."

"Things really are going great for you, aren't they?" she replies.

I stop twirling and set her down. "Are you happy, Jessie?"

Her eyes mist while she thinks for a moment. "Yes. I'm happy."

"Yet, you're worried about something?"

"Good things don't always last," she replies. "I wanted us to be different."

"We are different. We're going to be the exception to the rule that good things don't last. Jessie…" I hesitate. It feels like the right time to tell her how in love with her I am, but I'm also afraid I'll scare her off. "Now that we have this deal done, our future is set." I don't know if she's ready to hear that I'm in it for the long haul. My Jessie still has doubt; I see it in her eyes, but what she doesn't know is I'm never leaving her side. A little more time and she'll come to trust me completely.

Jessie suddenly springs up and drapes her arms around my neck. "How about a little fun to celebrate?" She's got that dark twinkling in her eyes that has my knees weakening and my balls aching, so I don't waste a second overthinking and lift her up onto my shoulder, carrying her up the stairs two at a time.

The moment we cross the threshold to our suite, our hands are everywhere, peeling each other out of the clothes that constrict us and my mouth comes down onto hers. Jessie's hands go to my shoulders and her fingernails drive into my skin, letting me know she wants more. I barely have to push her thighs aside before she raises one leg up to my waist and my fingers slip inside her and my mouth drops to her bare breast.

It's a fast and frantic choreography, her mewling when I hit her sweet spots and my ego going crazy that I have come to know her body so well that I can reduce her to a quivering puddle in seconds.

Jessie works me with her hand, pumping up and down, making me feel sure I'm about to lose my mind, as I work her, bringing her close to the edge and then slowing and restarting the torment.

Jessie warns, "Tate. I'm close." She lets out a rasping gasp against my neck and a surge of need pulsates all the way through me. We are pushed up against the dresser, and all I can think of is throwing her down on the bed and fucking her until I'm satiated, but more than that, I want to hold back. Get closer to Jessie. Become one.

This dance of ours, fast and furious, and animalistic is a stress release that allows us to connect without either of us having to commit to saying the words and making ourselves vulnerable, but tonight I don't want to fuck her. I want slow intimacy as I look in her eyes.

Fuck! I want to make love to her.

I'd light candles if we had any, anything to let her know that I want more.

"I want you inside me so bad right now." Her voice is husky, desperate.

I pull her wrists up above her head, my eyes on hers as I settle my hips between her thighs. She blinks a few times at

193

first as though adjusting to the intimacy and then I kiss her mouth, slow and deep then trail a line of kisses down her neck. I can hear her heart beat hammering beneath her chest as she arches her back while I position myself over her, teasing her entrance.

We've fallen into a pattern of using condoms sometimes, and other times her trusting me to pull out. Jessie's not on the pill but neither of us have been with anyone else since Macy was born so we know we're clean and she nods to indicate that I should enter her bare. This small act of trust that she's given me the past two weeks means more to me than she'll ever know and I enter her achingly slowly, my eyes never leaving hers.

Spikes of pleasure course up my spine, making me want to blow but I hold on, watching Jessie's mouth fall open, her vision become hazy as she too feels the power between us.

I slide into her, kiss her mouth then retreat, keeping the rhythm slow and measured. She's so fucking tight that it takes every ounce of my restraint not to pump harder, faster.

"You feel so good wrapped around me, Jessie. Like we were made for each other."

Goosebumps spread across her chest and she bites her lip. "Tate, I feel like I'm going to shatter," she says.

I drive forward, burying myself into her and kiss her with feather-light swirls that seem to drive her crazy with need.

"You can shatter for me, baby. I'll just put you back together each time."

She looks down at our joining and the intensity of the moment seems to increase. I close in on her another inch, then slowly retreat and a tiny squeak escapes her lips. She's stretched to oblivion and her hands are gripping mine.

I circle my hips and she pleads, "Do that again."

So I drive into her, dragging out the movements nice and

slow. She's so warm, soft and loving right now, I want the moment to last forever, but when she squeezes her muscles, milking me hard, my cock threatens to explode.

"Yes, right there. I'm so close," she gasps, her thighs tightening around my hips and I leverage the angle to go deeper, matching the buck of her strokes one for one.

I circle then drive forward, feeling my groin rub against her slick little bundle of nerves, basking in the sensation and the way her eyes flutter closed then open to pin me with a gaze that is sheer blissful ecstasy.

The temptation to grind into her faster has me gasping. Every sensation bombards me. How she feels. The way Jessie's mouth opens like she wants to cuss but she's too in the moment to speak. This pace, this perfect closeness is what we both needed tonight. I'm burning up from within and I know she feels it too as her hands push against me to leverage her body to join mine.

"I can't hold on any longer," she says, her eyes blinking closed and then opening to watch my face as I pump her core, faster, harder until I am hovering on the edge of heaven. Her tightness contracts and pulsates around my cock and I'm gripping her fists and holding back as long as I can, riding out every moment of her orgasm. She quivers and calls out my name. And it's my undoing. I pull out and explode right away, my forehead resting against hers, collapsing down onto her, hugging every inch of her perfect body against mine and looking into her perfect crystal blue eyes as every drop of pent-up love I have for her spills over her soft abdomen.

I'm spent and my thoughts are incoherent, but the words are on the tip of my tongue. I want to thank her for trusting me. But most of all I want to confess my undying love. It's all there, dying for me to say the words but instead, I kiss her lips and roll to the side then tell her, "Thank you for being perfect in every way."

"Thank you. That was…" her smile is lazy and satiated, her eyes close in a long blink. "The best." I watch her fall into a spent slumber and then I whisper, "I love you, Jessie Yates. With all that I am, I love you."

CHAPTER 19

JESSIE

*T*he next few days are some of the most exciting and scary of my life. Betty, my Mom, and Cassandra take turns to help out with Macy while Tate and I attend interviews to promote his new film. I'm not actually interviewed, but I'm able to watch Tate at his most confident best, and it's astounding. The way he charms even the most soured-faced movie critic is a sight to behold. It's not like I don't know he is good at turning on the charm, since he's done it more than once with me, but boy, when he is in entertainment mode, he has you hanging on his every word.

On the fifth day of promotions, we've flown across the country to the set of *The Flick Show*, where I met Stella Brimworth. It was the meeting I feared most since on screen together, they were fire. The kissing scenes in their movie had me certain I was going to hate her in person, so I'm surprised when off screen, she turns out to be a normal person.

Stella's tall and blonde and much thinner than I am. Her skin is flawless, her manicure resembling my own and her clothes much edgier than I would choose, yet I don't feel intimidated by her like I thought I would. In fact when I see her and Tate together, I see a couple of friends who lack the spark that makes you believe they're the real deal. She and Tate laugh about inside jokes from the set, but Tate always explains why each joke is funny so I am not left out. After the interview is over, Stella asks for my number so we can get together and have lunch at some point in the near future. I give her my number but doubt we'll ever get together because regardless of how much I have truly fallen in love with Tate Blingwood, I am on edge not knowing if our relationship is still all about boosting his career—let alone what he'll think of me if he ever learns I'm BabyMomma4U.

We're on a red eye back from our 24-hour stint in New York, and our time there has reminded me that I've always been fascinated by film and the whole production around the actors that bring a script to life. I'm interested in every element from the casting choices, wardrobe, special effects, and the way in which the movie is shot and I wonder if my relationship with Tate and the inside knowledge I am becoming party to could open doors for me to establish a career in the field I had only dared to dream of up until now.

One of Tate's assistant's meets us off the plane and pushes a bunch of magazines, newspapers and papers into his hands as we walk across the air field to the car where a driver is waiting.

"Did you check on that special thing I asked you to?" Tate asks his assistant and she smiles.

"It's all in hand."

Tate grins an exuberant smile and, even though I know he is exhausted, I can tell something has made him super happy.

"Trina, you don't need to ride back with us. I'll see you tomorrow."

Trina is delighted with getting the night off and totters in the direction of the parking lot.

Once we are in the car and settled for the long drive back, Tate's eyes become heavy. He's worked so hard and he falls asleep with a smile on his face.

It's lovely to see. Tate is the happiest I have ever seen him. He's attentive and loving with Macy who absolutely adores her daddy. My mother loves him and called me earlier and she sounds more excited than I'd ever heard her. Tate apparently had a team of maintenance guys turn up at her house to completely overhaul the place, and while the work is being done, they're all staying at the Hilton. When I asked him why he did it, Tate just smiled and said, "Your mom raised the mother of my child, and she's helped look after my number one girl. She deserves some comfort."

It's the most anyone has ever done for me or my family, not to mention Macy now has a college fund that will allow her to pick any college or university of her choice. Hell, there's so much money in that account that she can probably afford to raise Stephen Hawking from his grave and book one-on-one tutoring in physics.

I know I should be grateful and just go with whatever this is between us, but I can't stop the nagging in my head that what we have isn't real, that once Tate has signed the Dinky deal, he will no longer need me. I mostly manage to push my doubts aside and chalk them up to the ripple effect of my past trauma but they always seem to reappear, which sucks because when we are together, it feels real. Authentic. Meant to be. My heart thumps inside my chest when I am near him and he's so attentive and caring, it's hard to believe that what we have isn't real. Of course, there is another reason I feel like our relationship is fragile. I'm still holding back a secret, one that may well prove to be unforgiveable.

I watch the city whirl past the window and as we head around a corner, the papers Trina passed to Tate slide under the driver's seat so I reach down and pick them up. But I'm startled to see the picture of me from my resort work ID. I scan the page, careful not to wake Tate who needs the rest. The headline reads: "Working with Tate Blingwood's new love. How Jessie Yates bullied me in the workplace." On the bottom right is a picture of Mike, the jerk who used to work in accounts and who cheated on my best friend and tried to force himself on my other best friend.

Anger spikes up my back and my hands shake. When I look at the magazine title the interview was published in, I see it's a small press that no one gives a shit about and so I try to relax. "She subscribed my work email to an erectile dysfunction service. All the guys in IT thought I had ED!" Mike complains in the interview and I chuckle. Yeah, I did that but he deserved it. The interview has half-assed truths mixed with outright lies. There are plenty of people who could back up my version of events, but I decide it's probably best not to sully myself by defending such nonsense.

The car pulls up through the enormous, wrought-iron electric gates to the house we are renting, and I gently wake Tate who looks just as beautiful sleepy with creases on his cheek from the seatbelt as he does on a photoshoot.

"Babe, let's get you to bed," I say, deciding not to spoil his mood with tales of shitty stories sold to magazines by shitty people.

He looks in on Macy before I order him to bed and then I go downstairs and catch up with my mom who has been minding Macy.

"This place is really something!" Mom raves. "The bathtub fills itself on automatic. I pressed this button," she points at the services remote, "thinking I was closing the curtains, and when I went upstairs the bath was already filled!"

I chuckle to myself, knowing she'd wet her pants if I showed her the button that has the mini bar make Mimosas.

"How's the house looking?"

"Oh, Jessie, it's incredible. He converted the attic so Jasmine doesn't have to share with Jade no more. Can you imagine how quiet the house will be without the girls fighting over whose turn it is to use the hair straighteners. He's installing a state-of-the-art kitchen. I just can't believe how lucky we are that you did that for us." Mom's smile is beaming. Tate's right, she does deserve some comfort.

"It wasn't me, Mom. It was all Tate's idea. He didn't even mention it to me; he probably knew I'd say no. Letting him spend money on us makes me feel uncomfortable."

"Well, yes sweetie. You've always been dead against accepting anything you didn't work for but maybe taking care of people is Tate's love language, like fighting for people is yours."

I consider this for a second and start to think maybe Mom is right. Tate wants to provide for us and make everyone's life easier. He doesn't sweat the small stuff and seems to take comfort in knowing everyone has what they need. I want to protect the people I love. Sometimes it feels like it's my job to make sure no one gets hurt. It's part of the reason I got revenge on Mike after he spread mean rumors about Skyla, though after he sold a story on me, I guess I am going to have to try and do less of that—or get better at it so I don't get caught.

Mom picks up her car keys and gives me a hug. "You seem happy."

"I am happy," I reply. I can't actually think of a time when I've been this happy.

"You look like a woman in love," Mom says rather smugly.

"Oh, no. I..." My voice trails off. Things have moved through the stages from baby daddy I hate, to fake boyfriend, to boyfriend.

Mom stares at me, daring me to deny it.

"We're in a good place. I don't want to spoil things now by rushing into declaring our undying love or whatever this is."

"But it is love. I know love when I see it, and you got the glow."

"I'm happy," I admit. "Everything is going well. It feels like things are slotting into place." I consider my life holistically. My daughter is thriving, I'm in a relationship that makes me feel precious, and my friends and family are close and safe. "Though, I would like to go back to work or perhaps finish college. Tate's career has him on set around the world, so I wonder what our lives might look like once he starts filming the next movie." I've been thinking about it a lot. Will our relationship survive space and distance from each other? "How's the adult toy business?" I ask, changing the subject by referring to her side hustle.

Her mouth turns down. "This is the quiet period before things ramp up in time for Thanksgiving and Christmas. I've asked if I can pick up some extra shifts at the bingo hall to clean."

I walk to my purse and pull out my check book.

"No," Mom says. "I don't need your money. I'm fine."

Still I write her a check for ten grand. "Mom, I want you to take it. When Macy came along, you bought her crib and paid some of my medical bills."

"That's because I'm your mother and I love you."

"Well, I'm your daughter and I love you, so I insist."

We hug and then I see mom out to her car. When I come

back inside, I decide to have a glass of milk and I see she left the check behind.

So stubborn. I shake my head then laugh. Guess that's who I get it from.

I put the check back in my purse, deciding I'll deposit it in her account tomorrow, and then I see Mike's interview again. I pick it up, feeling the familiar instinctual pull urging me to get him back, but then I decide he's not worth it. Tate finally has his career back on track and so I resist the urge to do something crazy.

That's when I see there is another interview beneath it. This time, it's a small interview at the edge of the page of the newspaper. Dana Gee's face is pictured next to the headline: "Why I'm glad Jessie Yates isn't my sister-in-law."

The bitch who lied to Tate's brother Logan and said she was pregnant has sold a story on me and has the audacity to say *she* never trusted *me!* My fists harden into balls and the paper gets scrunched between them. If only the world knew what a lying, backstabbing, piece of work Dana was then they wouldn't believe any of her lies about me. In fact, they'd be clapping me on the back, congratulating me for saving Logan from marrying her.

I take a calming breath and decide these two idiots are not worth spoiling my sleep and then go and snuggle up beside my handsome boyfriend.

It might be foolish to hope Tate meant what he said in the restaurant, that he wants me as well as Macy, but while it feels this good, I can't give him up.

* * *

"She said what?!" I shriek.

"Stay calm, baby. It's all lies." I snatch the phone out of Tate's hands and read the headline: "Day care worker from

EMILY JAMES

Tate Blingwood's daughter's nursery: *How Tate used my love for his daughter to woo me into bed.*"

"What the fuck!" I hiss and Tate gently whispers, "We don't swear in front of Macy, remember?" I glance down behind him to see Macy eating toast with Nutella on the white carpet, but I'm too angry with Lisa to even care that my toddler might leave brown oily sludge stains that I know I'll never get clean.

"It says here you asked her for her phone number and then you had clandestine meetings where you made love all night."

"Baby, I did not ask her for anything except for her to take care of my daughter and her bunny until her Nanna picked her up. Then I got the hell out of dodge before Lisa could flirt with me some more. I swear, baby, I would never go there—"

I clamp my eyes shut and he stops talking. I recall the day when she flirted with Tate right in front of me. He dropped Macy off at day care last week before we left to go do the promo for his new film. Tate hasn't had time to screw her. I've been with him all the time, but aside from that, I'm *sure* he wouldn't do that to me.

"That bitch."

"She is. We'll find a better day care facility."

I give him his phone back and sit on the stool at the counter.

Tate's hands take mine and he pins me with a look of concern. "This is a part of the fanfare—it's all just fantasy on their parts and the drive for a quick buck. The stories, the made-up lies. Nothing you read in those reports are ever fact. I swear, I would never cheat on you or hurt you. Here, in our home, away from the cameras, this is truth. Anything you read or see outside of here is not real."

I nod, wanting to believe him more than I want my next

204

breath. "I guess this is what Betty was talking about when she said to take a leap of faith." It goes against all my instincts not to believe these lies and protect myself just in case.

He pulls the stool I am sitting on closer to him and holds me against his body and presses his palm on my heart. "It's not a leap of faith, baby, not when you know the truth in here." My heart thuds in response to his touch. "It's me, you, and Macy against the world. The best team there ever was and we're tight. Yes?"

I nod, accepting the truth of his words. Everything he's done has shown me and Macy he's in this relationship for us. It's time I put my own daddy issues aside and allow Tate the be the best dad to our girl as well as the man I'm believing he was meant to be for me. Taking a deep breath with new resolution, I lower my voice. "We're filing a lawsuit against that bitch."

He grins. "Yes we are." Then he grabs the baby wipes and goes and cleans Macy up. "Let's go cheer Mommy up," he says.

Macy is a picture of happiness in her daddy's arms as they approach me and he takes my hand.

"Where are we going?" I ask.

"Outside," Tate replies and I allow him to lead me to our winding front drive that probably has thirty paparazzi on the other side of the gate waiting to get there shot of me with my hair piled in a ratty knot on top of my head.

In front of the house is a gleaming, bright blue Hummer. "It's custom. Top of the line. The most secure vehicle on the market. It's even bulletproof," he says, grinning his damn face off. "And the color matches your eyes."

"Wow!" I murmur. It's really impressive, and as he opens the driver's door, it sinks in that he has bought the car for me. "It's mine?"

"Sure is. You can still use our driver whenever you want, but I figured you'd want to stay as independent as possible."

I use the step to clamber up into the driver's seat and look at the dashboard that is sleek and so modern, I can't even figure out how to switch on the engine. I glance around the interior and notice the expertly installed car seat in the back.

"It's... insane, that's what it is. How much was it? No, don't answer that. It'll probably just freak me out." I shake my head, remembering my conversation with Mom about love languages, and so I decide to be gracious and accept his gift without argument. "I love it! Thank you."

Tate leans in and kisses me. "Any chance Macy and I can be your first passengers?"

I grin. "Get in, guys! Momma's got new wheels."

* * *

WE TAKE the 101 and work our way to the PCH, stopping for a drive-through meal and I lose the paparazzi somewhere along the way. Tate was right, I needed this. Every aspect of my life is pictured, documented, and commented on. Tate hasn't just given me a car, he's given me the gift of freedom and that will help keep me sane.

I park up at the isolated cliff top spot where a month ago I agreed to be Tate's fake girlfriend and decide I made the right decision. He's done everything I have asked of him and he hasn't let me down. I'm learning to trust him. But more than that, I've fallen for him. The interviews that are coming out of the woodwork don't seem to have done too much damage, and this is confirmed when Jason calls Tate and tells him we should make our way over to Dinky to sign the contract awarding him the franchise.

"Are you okay?" I ask, noticing his eyes welling up.

"I thought if I ever got a Dinky deal I'd know I'd made it,

but this is different. More. Even better than I thought it'd be. This is for my family."

Tate directs me to the studios and the security guard takes one look at Tate's face and waves us straight through. "Jason and Gaynor are meeting us there," he says.

We're offered drinks including champagne. Macy, who has woken from her nap, plays with the shining awards on display and no one seems to care that she might break them.

"I'm sorry we dragged our feet on this," one of the execs says to Tate. "I know every star gets their fair amount of bad press, but sometimes that snowball can turn into an avalanche."

"I get it. I became complacent but I'm a new man now. A family man. There'll be no further drama," he promises.

We're offered dinner, more champagne and more cocktails, but Tate takes one look at Macy and decides, "If it's okay with you guys, I'd rather celebrate at home with my family."

The top exec. claps him on the back. "I never thought I'd see the day Tate Blingwood turned down a free bar." He laughs. "Keep up the good work, this image suits you."

Tate's eyes are on me, making my heart rate soar. "It's easy when you know what you want and you realize it's too good to lose."

I grin back at him and watch as they all shake hands. Then Macy starts to fuss for her juice cup and since the meeting is almost over, I make my apologies and carry Macy outside to the car while they finish up. The sun blasts me as soon as I get outside the air-conditioned building and I'm ten steps from the car when Gaynor catches up to me.

"I love it when a plan comes together," she says, rubbing her hands gleefully. "Now that's all sorted, I can finally take a vacation."

"It's good to see Tate so happy," I reply and unlock the car so I can open the door and find Macy's backpack. When I turn back around Gaynor is beside me, studying my expression.

"It is good he's back on track. So, now it's just a matter of figuring out the rest."

I have a moment of panic, thinking she's somehow found out about BabyMomma4U, but then I relax and realize she would have told Tate the moment she found out. So instead, I give her a questioning look to prompt her into telling me exactly what she means.

"Once I get back from vacation, we'll sort out the breakup and housing. You don't need to worry," she continues on before I have a moment to explain that Tate, Macy and I are staying together. "Tate had his realtor send him a long list of properties to check out for you and the kid. Tate Blingwood is a lot of things, but he wouldn't just chuck you out on the streets with nowhere to go." Her hand taps my arm in a gesture that I think is supposed to be comforting. "You won't have to go back to working as a maid. Tate'll see you're both okay. He owes you that much."

My stomach flips in on itself.

"He had his realtor source properties for me?"

"He wants you both to have some place nice. Besides, it would look bad, wouldn't it? Tate Blingwood living in a mansion while his kid is slumming it in the free staff accommodation at a hotel resort or worse, living in the run-down house of a sex-toy distributor. No, you'll be set for life now. Bet you can't believe your luck!"

I nod then shake my head. I think I show that I'm agreeing, but honestly the sun is in my eyes and I can feel all the blood rushing to my head. I focus all my concentration on sliding Macy into her car seat, fumbling with the fastenings and double-checking and triple-checking she is secure before remembering that she still wants her juice cup.

"Are you okay? You look really pale," Gaynor asks.

"I'm… tired. It's been a long month. I'm fine," I insist.

"Better than fine I imagine with all that lovely money in your account. Have fun with it," she says. "I know I will!" She hoists her purse over her shoulder and pulls out a vape from her LV bag. "I'll see you around." Then Gaynor struts across the parking lot to her red BMW while I get into the driver's seat on autopilot.

In the seat of this fancy car, I realize I'm richer than I ever thought I could be.

But I feel worthless.

* * *

TATE IS FLOATING on air the whole way back and spends the journey on his phone, updating his followers that he's the new face of Dinky. While I spend the journey considering how to bring up my feelings and also my conversation with Gaynor.

As we pull up outside our rental, my phone pings with a text. Tate is already getting Macy out of the car and so I wave for him to take her inside.

The text is from Jason and it contains a link to a website with the message:

You sure have some cooky friends.

I tap on the link and it takes me straight to a celebrity gossip page. The video opens up with Betty, her hair in curlers, holding a broom like she might hurt someone.

"Ya'll get off my yard before I stick this broom where the sun don't shine!" she warns.

"Ms. Goode, you take care of Jate's daughter? Can you

clarify if Jessie Yates is using Tate Blingwood for his money and fame?" the reporter asks.

"I can confirm you are a piece of crap, who will be losing his teeth if he doesn't back off right now!" Betty hisses and I laugh.

Another text comes through before the video is over.

It's from Jason again:

> Don't concern yourself over this. People will understand that not everyone's job is a conventional one.

It links to an article: "Tate Blingwood's almost mother-in-law sex toy scandal." Beneath the headline is a screenshot from my mother's TikTok page where she reviews the products she is selling. The piece quotes my mom telling her followers that, "An orgasm a day keeps the doctor away."

My palm slaps my face and I let out a puff of air.

Why can't my mother have a conventional job like other people's moms?

I switch the engine off and try to relax. At the end of the driveway, the paparazzi crew are snapping photographs and so I force myself to smile so they don't get a shot of me looking like a crabby cow and headline it with, "What does Tate even see in her?" My mother has done nothing to be ashamed of and I am proud of her. She works her ass off for her family and there is no shame in that.

I hit reply and tell Jason:

> My mom is a big advocate for positive sexual relations.

He sends back a laughing emoji with the message:

> Your mother sounds like a woman I'd love to meet.

I'm considering this when Tate calls out, "Jessie, get your behind in here!"

I'm about to get out the car when I get another alert, but this time it's from an internet search engine I'd set up years ago to notify me if ever his name was mentioned online. The link takes me through to one of the national newspapers and my heart sinks as I see the man that made me feel like I was less than nothing.

My father.

I shouldn't read it.

He doesn't know me and he probably only sold me out for a fast buck, but curiosity wins out and I can't help myself from reading the article. Maybe after seeing my name associated with Tate's he regrets how things went down?

The daughter I tried to love.

She was always whining and after every penny I had.

I gave her what I could. I felt sorry for her.

Last I heard she got knocked up too young just like her mother.

She's looking for her next meal ticket.

If Tate Blingwood's stupid enough to marry her, he had better make sure she signs a prenup.

Tears flood my eyes and I blink them back.

The comments section is filled with trolling.

If her own father says that about her, she must be bad news.

Gold digger!

Don't marry her, Tate. Marry me!

It's crushing.

All those people reading this article, thinking what my father said is true.

Why am I so unlovable to him that he could sell me out and have people decide I'm trash?

I suddenly feel too warm, like I'm about to throw up.

I get out the car and slam the door. Down the driveway the paps call my name. One tries to climb the gate to get closer and I stick up my finger as a warning and give him a death stare, yelling at him to stay the other side of the damn gate or risk a hard kick to the balls and then I storm inside.

"How dare he!" I hiss as I walk inside but then I pause. Tate is rocking Macy in his arms singing her some ad-lib song about loving her forever and my heart stops racing. He's looking at her with such sheer, unadulterated love that it stops me in my tracks. My throat aches and my heart fills with love.

That is what love looks like.

How real fathers behave.

The realization takes me by complete and utter surprise.

"What's wrong?" he asks, walking toward me still intermittently singing his song.

I stare up into Tate's warm brown eyes that are filled with love and shake my head. Dirtying this special moment with my father's trash talk seems wrong so I decide I'll talk to him tonight once Macy is in bed.

"Nothing's wrong. Just a pap trying to climb the gate. I yelled at him to get down."

"Want me to go outside and tell them to back off?"

I shake my head. The problem goes much deeper than a few money-hungry paps.

"Why don't you two have a dip in the pool while I start dinner?"

"You sure? I don't mind making dinner."

"I'm fine. You two have fun. I'll call you once it's done."

Tate kisses my temple and then disappears to go have fun with Macy while I try to put all thoughts of my estranged father out of my head, but I can't. My dad selling a story and hurting me deeply feels like karma, and after all, I've been posting negative stuff online about Tate for years. Okay so lately there has been a lot of good stuff, but still, how would he feel if he found out? And would it matter now that he's found a realtor to find me and Macy our own place? I'm still so confused if he was being truthful and he really does view us as a true couple and Gaynor was wrong, or he just got side-railed by the Dinky deal and our fake dating.

Either way I've got to tell him, try to explain, and I've got to do it before he finds out from someone else.

CHAPTER 20

TATE

"*A*pparently there are cracks in our relationship," I say as Jessie walks out of Macy's bedroom having put her down for the night.

"Oh?" Her eyes are like saucers, but I wave my phone at her and she seems less tense. "That's a really bad photograph of me."

"You don't like it? I love the way you're showing the paparazzi the middle finger of your new manicure." I grin.

"It's a good thing you already signed the Dinky deal," she murmurs. "I'm sorry. I'll try harder to paint you in a better light."

I wrap my arms around her and pull her in, breathing in her sweet scent. "Baby, you don't need to change a thing about yourself."

I can't put my finger on it, but something is off with her. Ever since we left the Dinky studio offices, she's been quiet. Distant. I figure she probably needs some space to process

CATCH A FALLING STAR

the past few days. She's probably hurting because the woman from the nursery sold a story on us, and so did the dick she used to work with, but Jessie's usually more resilient than this. She smiles back at me, but it's a placating smile aimed at making me feel better rather than her normal exuberant smile. She's frowning deep inside, I can feel it, and I feel like it's my fault.

"I'm going to have a soak in the tub. After that, maybe we can have a cozy evening together?" She sounds hesitant. "It feels like we've been so busy lately, we haven't had chance to be us."

I pull her in close. With the promotions for the movie, it has been too long since my girl and I settled on the couch and talked. "We can do whatever you want, baby," I say but then quickly shake my head remembering. "Shit! I have to go meet with Jason. He wants to go through my schedule before he takes some vacation. Both he and Gaynor decided they're taking some time off now that the deal is signed." Her barely there smile slips. "I'll be as quick as I can. You'll hardly notice I'm gone and when I get back, we can do whatever you want."

"Okay," she replies and her smile fades.

* * *

I GET BACK LATER than I anticipated after Jason spent the entire evening trying to get his Wi-Fi working at his home office so he could go through my schedule. Turns out, a fallen tree took out the whole network in his gated community, so the evening was a waste of time and when I creep in Jessie is sleeping. I sent her a text letting her know I'd been delayed and she said it was fine, but I knew I messed up.

We spend the next day visiting new day care centers and then we go for lunch while Macy is with my mom. I sign

215

autographs on the way in and one for the server, and Jessie seems content to chat with fans even if she is a little reserved to how she normally is—probably because there are at least fifteen paparazzi following us and we don't have a moment's privacy.

I wish it helped that I know exactly how she's feeling—let down and like a commodity; she's already seen the story sold on her by that asshole she used to work with, not to mention my brother's ex. I wonder if she's questioning every relationship she has and wondering who she can trust and if I'm worth the stress.

"Babe, don't worry about the stuff that's been printed. The people who matter know it's not true. No one is going to believe Dana Gee, of all people."

"I know." Her smile is watery.

"How about I ask Skyla and Layla what they're doing tonight?" I ask, thinking of something I can do to cheer her up. "I know a restaurant downtown. I can rent the whole place. It's got a secured rear entrance so you can get in and out unseen."

Her finger trails along my hand. "You're really sweet, you know that?"

"I've been called worse by you so I'll take it." I laugh and her smile tips up by a fraction. "So, you want me to go ahead and make the calls?"

She shakes her head. "I think I'd like to stay home tonight."

"Okay. If you change your mind..." But I know she won't. When the first stories were sold on me, I wanted to hide from the world too. It's a feeling you never truly get used to, but you get better at eliminating the journalists' sources by making your inner circle smaller. It's an uncomfortable trade-off and not what I want for my two girls. So I decide on a different course of action and text Skyla to arrange a girls night tonight over at our place as a surprise. I'll make myself scarce by heading over to Logan or Drew's. Maybe some time with her girlfriends will be just what she needs.

"You want me to buy you a private island? Just say the word and I'll do it."

"Tate, are you happy?" she asks and I immediately tell her I am.

"Do you trust me?"

"Of course I do," I reply.

"But how can you? You've only known me a few weeks and there are still things you don't know about me."

I stare deeply into her eyes, sensing that she's starting to doubt everything.

"Don't you dare spiral. I know you and you know me. I was instantly attracted to you, but the more I've gotten to know you, the more I am unreservedly certain I can trust you. You're the mother of my daughter, and the person I trust most in the world. Your intentions are always good and I know you're hurt by the stuff in the papers, but the more crap people make up, the harder we have got to try and trust one another and the stronger we'll get as a result. Agreed?"

"I like the sound of that," she replies, pushing some chicken around her plate.

As we're leaving the restaurant and getting to her new car, a photographer pushes his lens so close to Jessie's face that I shove him out the way.

"What the hell, man?!" I hiss, pushing the guy away then I pull open Jessie's car door and help her inside.

"Tate, is it true you're worried Jessie is a gold digger?" a pap calls out.

"Have you given her any money?" says another.

"How lucrative is it being Tate Blingwood's girlfriend?" another shouts.

I ignore them and walk around the car to get in the

217

passenger side of Jessie's Hummer but another one tugs on my arm and says, "What does Jessie have to say about her father's accusations?"

His comment sends a flood of ice through my veins and I grip his arm. "What did you just say?"

"Her father, he sold a story on Jessie, calling out her gold-digging ways."

My elbow immediately jabs the guy's throat and he makes a choking sound. It's followed by a frenzy of camera flashes and a cacophony of questions.

I turn to all of them and say, "My future wife is loyal and kind! Her heart is pure and she would never do anything to hurt me. Have you all got that?"

"Tate, will she be signing a prenup when you marry?" I'm tempted to reach out and punch the fucker right in the nose but since Jessie is staring out the window, watching and listening to every word, I hold back.

"Anything negative that has been said about Jessie is all lies," I spit and get in the car. One look at Jessie's face tells me everything I need to know.

"Your dad sold a story?"

She nods and I see her throat bob with her swallow.

"Why didn't you tell me?"

"It was bad enough reading it. I couldn't bear to say those things out loud to you, of all people."

The hurt in her eyes is killing me. It all makes sense now. Her distance. I was worried she was having second thoughts about us, but it's because her loser dad was after the fast cash, resulting in my girl's spirit being broken a second time by that douchbag.

"You don't have to worry about my faith in you getting rocked, Jessie. I am the one person who knows what this kind of betrayal feels like and also the one who can help fix it. I'm going to kill him!"

Fury has my fists balling and I'm imagining all the ways I can stop him from talking ever again.

"No, you're not. What was it you said? We take the lies and use them to make our truth stronger." She pulls the car away and says, "There's something I need to tell you."

Whatever it is will need to wait because right now, the only thing I can focus on is making that sorry excuse for a man pay for hurting my girl.

"Baby, we'll talk everything over tonight. I've got a meeting I need to hop on since last night was a fiasco. Can you drop me off at Jason's office?" He won't be there, but I can hitch a ride from one of his team.

"Sure," she replies and my hand goes to her thigh. I try to rub comforting circles, but she's so tense I'm not sure she can feel me beside her, cheering her on and letting her know I have her back.

Her phone pings a text and she ignores it, keeping it on the console charger beside mine. It's like street-racing out here, and she needs all her concentration; the bastard paparazzi follow us the whole way, driving dangerously close.

"I'm going to jump out near the doors to the building, you pull a U-eey and get home. I'll let security know to expect you. And baby," she looks at me, her eyes still filled with stress, "relax. I'm going to take care of all of this. Your father, if you can call him that, is going to get hit with so many lawsuits, he'll be scared to say his own name, never mind yours."

She nods and throws me a watery smile. Her heart is hurting and it makes me sure what I am about to do is the right course of action.

I chastely kiss her, grab my phone, and jump from the car, banging the roof with my hand and yelling for her to, "Go, go, go!" before the paps catch up to her. I'm about to walk into the office, when I see one of the security team arriving behind me on a motorcycle.

"You mind if I borrow that?" I ask him, pointing to his wheels and he replies, "Sure thing, boss."

He hands me his helmet and I pull it onto my head and then speed out of the parking lot.

* * *

I LOSE the paps relatively easily on the motorcycle; it's one of the reasons the bike is my favorite mode of transport. And when I reach a quiet spot in the road, I pull out my phone and get to work.

Except, I don't have my phone. I picked up Jessie's and on the screen is a cute picture of me and my two girls, making me smile and reminding me why what I'm about to do is so important.

I punch in the pin. It's Macy's birthday so not something I'd ever forget, and then I search for the story he sold. By the time I'm at the end, rage is coursing through my veins like fire. Then I type in Chuck Peters and police officer, Santa Barbara. It's amazing what you can find out about a person just using a name and location, and within moments, I have his address and am on my way to his place.

He lives in a sketchy part of town. The homes are a mix of well-kept and tidy, versus rundown with air conditioning units hanging out of windows, overgrown lawns, and broken-down cars. His beat-up Honda is in the driveway but what's stranger is that it's hemmed in by a mountain of manure. It'd take a strong man all day to shovel that amount of shit out the way to release the car.

I park my bike behind it and walk right up to the door. There are things I want to say to this motherfucker, but I keep my profile low by leaving my motorcycle helmet on until I'm shaded inside his porch.

Chuck Peter's has barely registered who he is opening the door to before I force the door open and push him back as I walk right inside.

The guy gawks at me like he's trying to figure out if I'm there to burglarize him.

"You seem surprised to see me," I say and punch him straight in his fucking face. He stumbles back into a dresser and his hand goes to his mouth, wiping at the blood oozing from his split lip.

His place is dark and dingy, the smell of cheap beer hangs in the air like the place is a rundown bar in a nothing town, rather than the home of a supposed pillar of the community.

"What are you doing here?" he stutters. "I never said any of those things they wrote in the newspaper." He's got a three-day scruff on his chin and clothes that look like they were bought down at Goodwill, ten years ago.

Chuck tries to defend his actions but I already read the article before I ran a search on the guy and no way those words came from anyone except him. Besides, I've been in this business long enough to know that no newspaper would risk a libel suit if they didn't have a credible source. The interview would have been recorded to defend themselves in the event of a lawsuit, and the lying bastard would have signed papers to state the information he gave them was true to the best of his knowledge.

"How much did they pay you, Chuck? How much is your daughter's dignity worth?"

"They barely paid me anything. The journalist twisted everything. I told them I want a relationship with Jessie. I asked them to tell her I want to see her and meet my grandbaby but all they were interested in was what I knew of her and you. I didn't know nothing."

"Yet you gave them enough to crush her," I reply, wondering how much they twisted and how much he handed over willingly.

"Mr. Blingwood, you've got to believe me. I love my daughter." His expression is sorrowful, earnest. His cheeks are red and puffy, his nose bulbous through years of too much alcohol. "I want to put all this behind us. Meet her. If you can arrange it, I bet she'd like to get to know her old man. We could be family."

As a father myself, my heart responds to his plea.

"I missed out on Jessie's whole life because of that bitch Selena. She didn't want me to see Jessie, wanted to keep her all to herself," he continues and my shoulders stiffen.

I liked Jessie's mom the instant I met her. Jessie's already told me that some of her sisters see their biological fathers. No way she'd keep Jessie from him if he was worthy of being her dad. I immediately know who to trust and it isn't Chuck Peters. The only reason he wants to know my girl now is that she just became a very rich woman and no way he's getting near her to hurt her again.

I lay my fist straight into his gut and the air expels from his lungs with a hiss.

"Here's what's going to happen, Chuck. You're going to get in touch with the newspapers and retract your statement and issue a public apology." I thump him again in case he didn't hear me and needs help paying attention and then I keep him still by gripping his throat. "You're going to do this today, or my lawyers will be serving you papers. You've made some astounding libelous claims. I know my girl inside out and no way she ever asked you for so much as a dime." I can't be sure we have a legal case until I speak to my team, but if there's a case, my lawyers will take him down. "You're going to stay away from Jessie. You're never going to speak her name again. You hear me?" I pull my fist back like I'm about to punch him again and he flinches like a coward.

"I'll do it," he blurts. "But you got to help me out. I'm desperate. I've got medical bills. I got suspended by the police force. Temporarily probably. They made a big mistake. Just a few thousand to tide me over—"

"Are you for fucking real?"

"I'm Jessie's father," he says. "No matter what y'all think of me, she wouldn't want to see me suffer."

I consider it for a second. Jessie probably wouldn't want to see him suffer. She'd probably hand him over some money and tell him to stay away. And then he'd come back for more, like they always do.

I drop my elbow on his head and spit, "Many years ago, you had the honor of getting to call the most special, loyal woman on earth your daughter, and you didn't just tell her no, you humiliated her and made her feel small, and now you've done it again. This stops now. You'll get nothing from us and if you don't stay away, you'll end up in jail. Can't imagine that working out so well for a police officer who wants to get his job back." I sneer and one look at his face tells me that he knows I'm serious.

I walk out of there pulling my helmet on and filled with disgust that any father could stoop so low. I'm getting back on the motorcycle when the phone in my pocket pings an alert. I take it out and stare at the screen before I even remember that it's not my phone.

Why the hell is Jessie getting alerts from the social media account named BabyMomma4You?

CHAPTER 21

JESSIE

"*W*e've got snacks, we've got tequila, we've got Betty, your momma, and we've also got ten paparazzi outside!" Layla says, walking inside the house with Skyla beside her and my mom and Betty behind.

"What are you all doing here?" I ask, surprised but so grateful to see them and Skyla explains that Tate arranged a surprise visit for me from them.

Mom immediately picks Macy from my arms and Betty showers her face with kisses, while I quickly shut the door behind them before the press can get their shot.

"I don't know why they're so interested in me," I complain.

"Honey, you're dating Tate Blingwood, and your own father just gave an interview where he said you were a gold-digging whore," Betty says and everyone's heads flip her way. "It's caused quite a stir."

"Betty, everyone knows they print trash in those newspapers," Skyla replies, ever the peacekeeper.

"No, she's right. And it's exactly what the people out there'll be saying." I pick up my phone from the counter in order to validate that trash talk will be happening right now and immediately drop it down. "Shoot! Tate took my phone by mistake."

"That's okay, you can use mine," Betty says, holding out her arm.

"No, it's fine. Probably better for my mental health that I don't look. I just wish I could set the record straight. I hate the thought of people believing what he says is true."

"They won't believe Chuck," Mom says. "They'll take one look at him, with his graffitied car, with cow shit all over his driveway and know he's a big fat liar."

I crinkle my nose at my mom. She can't possibly know I graffitied his car all those years ago. Besides, he probably got it repaired by now or got a new car. But the latter part of her sentence has me intrigued.

"Cow shit?"

"Horse manure to be precise," she clarifies.

"What did you do?" I ask.

"Soon as I saw that interview with him saying those things about my baby, I placed a special order. Trent from the farm owed me a favor, and so he poured ten tons of horse shit right behind his car, blocking him in. Let's see how he feels about crap when he spends all day shoveling it off his driveway." She pulls out her phone and shows me a picture. Sure as hell, there's the car I remember from all those years ago surrounded by a mountain of manure.

Skyla laughs loudly and the sound is catching. "Oh my goodness. That's hilarious and now I see where Jessie gets her sassy streak! It's brilliant and so fitting!"

I hug my Mom, taking a second to appreciate how she has

always had my back and then kiss her cheek. "I don't need a dad. Not when I have a mother who is worth a million. Shall I order pizza? Then I'll show you all around. I hope you brought your bathing suits."

* * *

AWHILE LATER AFTER Macy has gone down for the night, Betty is pouring everyone wine and we are sitting at the counter still in our bathing suits, wrapped in towels.

"None for me." I hover my palm above the rim of the wine glass as Betty angles the bottle to pour.

Betty's eyes narrow. "You ain't never turned down wine before." She looks at the label on the bottle and screws her face. "And I know it ain't the wine because this is the good stuff. I found it in your wine cellar and it's older than I am."

I chuckle. "I'm just trying to keep a clear head with all this stuff going on." Tate and I still haven't done a pregnancy test but my period is now officially late by three days. I keep telling myself all the stress I've been through lately is delaying it, but deep in my belly, I am starting to feel like that one split condom might have allowed Tate's best swimmer to make it to my ovaries.

Betty and my mom look at me like they know, while Skyla and Layla argue over which playlist to listen to. When Layla wins out, and there's some kind of rock band playing, she asks, "So what are you going to do about your dad? I bet Tate was furious."

"He seemed pretty angry." I explain how he throat-chopped a member of the paparazzi with his elbow.

"No one messes with the Blingwoods!" Layla says.

"So where is he now?" Skyla asks.

I glance at the clock and shrug. He's been gone hours. "He

had a meeting and then he was supposed to be coming home."

"But he signed the Dinky deal, right?" Skyla checks.

"Yeah. They can't back out now no matter what happens." That fact alone makes me nervous. Tate doesn't need me anymore, and I still have to try and explain that it was me who had a hand in harming his career. What if he decides the betrayal is too much? What would that mean for me and Macy, and can my heart bear the pain if he walks away a second time—though I feel like he'd never abandon Macy. *Me, I'm not so sure about.*

"Where are Jasmine and Jade?" I ask Mom, deducing that Jenna will be at her boyfriend's and Jamie and Josie are still at college.

"Oh, they're at a Taylor Swift concert. Got backstage passes," Mom replies grinning her damn face off. "Tate's driver is bringing them home later. They've got it into their damn heads that now they're the family of Tate Blingwood, the band will want them present at the after-show party. Honestly, these girls of mine."

Mom looks happy, relaxing at the counter with a glass of wine in her hand. It's been so long since I've seen her out of her natural habitat of home, bingo halls and laundromats that she seems like a person in her own right, not just my mom.

"How's it going with what's-his-name?" I ask.

"I had to let Jake go. There was all those paparazzi outside the house and he wanted to come over, but I couldn't take the risk that he'd say something I didn't want him to say, so me and him have gone our separate ways."

My heart swells. "Mom, you broke up with him to protect me?"

"My babies come first always, you know that, hon. Besides, what with you planning to go back to college, Tate getting the house all fixed up for us, and your sisters all in high school and college, I realized something. The pressure is off. For the first time in my life, I can focus on me. So I'm going to focus on my career and make something of myself."

"Good for you, Selena," Skyla says, lifting her glass.

My mom has been dedicated to motherhood for so long now, I can't imagine her attention anywhere else. "So, you're going to focus on the cleaning services? Maybe start your own company? That's great news, Mom."

"Nope. If I never clean another toilet for as long as I live, then I'll be a happy woman! No, I was speaking to your friend, Gaynor. She took a look at my social media channels and she says I've got real potential. She said I'm relatable and according to her, people like me are worth their weight in gold. And then I spoke to that nice Jason fella, and he said my business model is impressive." Mom grins and I start to feel nauseous. "So, I'm going wide with the adult toys."

Layla chokes on her wine and my brows shoot up into my hairline.

"I'm going to advertise. Jason says I could get a late-night spot on the shopping channel. There are women and men, and everybody else—'cuz I'm gonna be inclusive—looking for advice in meeting their sexual needs. The people of America—no the world, actually—deserve to be sexually liberated, and I'm gonna be the one to help 'em."

"Oh my God! My mother wants to liberate the world one sex toy at a time," I grumble. "Have you mentioned it to Tate?" I ask, wondering how he feels about his daughter's nanna being so open about working in the adult market and if it could impact his career.

"It was his idea!" Mom says. "I was telling him about that new range, the three point turn, and I said, 'wouldn't it be great if there was one that could oscillate all four of us ladies' favorite areas'"—she nods her head to her vajajay—"and Tate was real interested and said, you should design one! He'd even invest!"

"He said that?"

"Oh honey, that boy was so interested. I gave him my catalog and he's placing an order." Mom winks at me and Skyla and Layla high five each other.

"We're going to need catalogs too," they both say in unison.

"And me," says Betty. "Bob's got the little blue pills now and everything's working but a little something extra is fine by me."

I desperately search for a topic change, and when Skyla notices my expression, she helps me out. "Do you think you and Tate will marry?"

"Oh. I don't know if…" I'm not even sure that's where this is heading.

"But you love him, don't you?"

"I…" I picture his face. His warm smile and the way he takes my breath away. He's so good with Macy, it's like he's known her all her life, and when I think about bringing another child into the world, there is no one else I'd want beside me. "It's complicated," I say.

"Complicated how?" Layla asks. "You're living together in this great house. You have a child together. You get along, don't you?"

"Yes, we get along. We've actually become really good friends," I reply, remembering how he has my back and encourages me.

"How's the sex?" Betty asks.

"It's good," I reply, avoiding going into too much detail about tender moments and earth-shattering orgasms.

"He's gorgeous, rich, treats you like a princess, and he's stuck around. What else are you looking for?" Mom asks.

"Nothing. There's nothing else I want. I love him," I

admit. "But this all started out as a fake relationship and we haven't said the L word yet. All of this was," I gesture to the house and me, "to get his career back on track and develop his relationship with Macy so they could be a unit outside of me. At least I think that was the plan. We never really hammered it out…"

"Oh, there's been hammering all right," Betty says.

"We've got a lot to sort out. This life, his fame, it's crazy."

"Yet you've taken to it like a duck to water." I scrunch my face but Layla shakes her head to stop me. "I saw the photos of you at the premiere. The interviews. You're built for this life. You're beautiful, articulate, and you can get yourself out of a tight spot better than anyone. Tate would struggle to find anyone better at this stuff than you, and you two were made for one another."

"Well, I'm not sure that's true," I answer.

"I am. And take it from someone that knows love when she sees it, that boy loves you," Betty insists. "You've got better chemistry than he's had with any of the women opposite him in his films, and Tate is the best actor in Hollywood."

"Why don't you tell him how you feel?" Skyla suggests.

It seems obvious. Tell him how I feel and let the chips fall. But I have something else to tell him first. Something bigger. Something that might actually destroy us.

CHAPTER 22

TATE

I find myself parked up outside Drew's house. Logan's car is there, so I guess they're catching up while the girls are over at mine.

"Hey, we've been calling you," Drew says, opening the door. "We're shooting some pool down in the game room if you want to join us?" He stands aside and, as I hesitate at the door, Drew casts a measuring stare my way. "What happened?"

I hold the phone up, still in a state of shock. I don't know what exactly to feel. Outrage, disappointment, humiliation? It's all a jumble. Jessie is my on-line nemesis. The troll who's been out to destroy me. How could she do that? How could she lie right to my face and pretend.

"Come on in, brother," he says, clapping me on the back. He steers me in the direction of the kitchen and then calls Logan to come through. "You want a beer?" Drew asks.

"Yeah," I say sitting at the counter. *Or twenty.* Then I correct myself, "No. I promised I'd cut back and I have a motorcycle out the front. I won't drink and drive." I know myself. In this mood, I could really let the drinking fly, but now that I have Macy, that's no longer an option.

"I'm making Callie some hot cocoa. I'll make us all a cup."

Logan walks in, and sits beside me. "Tate, come to get your ass handed to you in a pool game?"

I don't look up but I feel Logan and Drew exchange glances while I continue staring at the phone, wondering what to do with this new information. I can't even begin to figure out if I'm seething mad or emotionally destroyed.

"What's up with him?" he asks Drew.

"Come on, Tate," Drew says, his voice calm and reassuring. "You're acting weird. What's going on?"

I sigh, raking my hands through my hair. My usual self-assuredness is replaced by a mixture of frustration and vulnerability. I don't know how to say what I am about to, but I force the words out. "Jessie is BabyMomma4You."

"What? That's ridiculous. Jessie is an honest-to-god, tell-it-how-it-is, straight-as-a-die sort. In fact, I'm still pissed off with you for stealing her away from my resort. Hannah stepped up to the job as maid manager, but she's no replacement for Jessie, and with the way you two have been with each other, I doubt highly she's coming back after her leave of absence," Logan says.

Drew slides two cups of steaming hot chocolate in front of me and Logan and then takes a sip of his own. "You better start from the beginning."

I swipe the phone to life and push it into the middle of the counter. "I picked up Jessie's phone by mistake. She's had three alerts for BabyMomma4You in the past hour alone. She's the troll that went viral. The *Triptastic Tate* meme. The reconstructed videos of me with a diaper on. It's all her."

I'm shaking my head, still shocked that she could do something like this.

"Just because she has an account in that name doesn't mean she did that stuff. Maybe she hacked the person who was actually responsible," Logan says, his hands on his hips, staring at the phone. "Have you actually looked through the accounts?"

I cast him with a shitty glare. "No. It's an infringement of Jessie's privacy. I'm not doing that." Besides, do I really want to see it all, then I'd have to actually face the truth: she hates me and she's been lying to me this whole time. Another betrayal.

"Okay, so have you spoken to Jessie and asked her about it?" Drew asks.

"No. She's got her mom and her friends over at our place so I decided to come here and wait it out. I don't even know if I can face her. I thought we were falling in love. What if it's all been a lie?"

Drew's eyebrows shoot up in surprise and then he starts shaking his head. "She wouldn't do what you're accusing her of. Jessie's in love with you. Skyla said she's certain of it, and my wife is never wrong."

I smile even though I'm dying inside. Until an hour ago, hearing that Jessie loved me was all I wanted. Now it means nothing if I can't trust her, knowing she's been lying to me.

"There's only one way you'll know what you're dealing with and that's if you check it out." Logan picks up the phone and presses the icon to one of the apps. While he scrolls, I'm torn between telling him to put it down and pretending like I don't know she's been mocking me online so we can continue our masquerade as a legitimate couple. But I'm also torn because I need to know the truth.

"I know it's her. She even said there was something she

needed to tell me. I brushed it aside, thinking it wouldn't be anything that could hurt us, but maybe it was this."

Logan chuckles and my jaw stiffens. He holds his hands up apologetically then says, "I'm sorry but she's really funny."

"See, I told you it was her."

Logan nods then slides the phone to me. On the screen is the video she adapted of me wearing a diaper and running through LA. As it plays on repeat, the headline she assigned it flashes: *Will Tate Blingwood ever grow up?*

"But what's interesting is the comments. Read them," Logan insists.

I look at the first one and read it aloud. "'What a loser.'" My heart sinks at the thought of Jessie reading comments like that about me. Knowing she instigated them is even worse. I slide the phone away. "Thanks, man. I couldn't have gotten through tonight without reading the outpouring of support."

"You ass, keep reading. And look at the dates," Logan says, pushing the phone back in front of me.

I sip the sweet chocolate as a delay tactic and then continue reading.

JustSleeping: Hahahaha. Good one!

AvocadoLover: Must suck to be famous.

TBFan1: Even in a diaper he's got a peachy ass I'd like to take a bite of.

BabyMomma4You: Best ass in Cali

TBFan1: I thought you hated him?

BabyMomma4You: I love to hate him. There's a difference.

TBObsessed: I think Tom Dordan would be better in the Dinky franchise.

BabyMomma4You: You crazy girl? No way anyone else is going to play that role better.

The comments go on and on and then I swipe to the next

meme, the next video, the next status update. All thinly veiled insults but as soon as anyone else says anything negative, my little kitten gets her claws out.

"See what I mean?" Logan says smugly. "She's defending you more than she's trolling you."

Drew nods. "She's venting her frustration, but dude, that's not trolling. You want to see trolling, you should see the stuff Logan and I post about you." My brothers grin at each other, then high five.

"You love her, don't you?" Logan asks.

"Yes," I reply much too quickly.

"Then talk to her. It's no great surprise she got you good. When I broke up with Layla, Jessie made me a coffee, and when I read the cup she'd written *Dipshit* on it—but she was right, I'd been a dipshit, and yes, when she posted that video of you, you did need to grow up. She's a prankster, but she's not malicious. In fact, what was it you said when BabyMomma4You wrote that you needed to grow up?"

I'm forced to admit, "I agreed."

"Exactly. Go see your girl and tell her you know. Then get down on one knee and make things official. At least if your engaged it'll get Mom off my back as to when the next round of grandbabies are going to arrive."

I immediately imagine Jessie swollen with my child and my throat hurts when I swallow. I already missed that part once, no way I want to miss it again, but can I trust her?

"Whatever you need, we're here for you bro," Drew says.

"Look at you three sitting there drinking your hot cocoa. Did you already eat all the little marshmallows?" Callie says as she walks in the kitchen.

"We're actually very manly men," Logan defends.

"Nah, you're all pussy-whipped." Drew's mouth gapes open and he's about to chastise her but she holds her hand up to pause him. "But I like it. You're all happy and you're setting a good example for me and my baby cousin."

My beloved niece referring to my daughter as her baby cousin has my eyes welling up.

"I've got to go," I say, sliding the mug to Callie. "I need to kiss my baby goodnight and straighten out some stuff."

CHAPTER 23

JESSIE

By the time I've said goodbye to Mom, Betty, Skyla and Layla, it's already ten and I'm starting to worry. Tate has never been out this long. I stare at his phone and feel myself pine for him.

Every scenario runs through my head. Like maybe he got in an accident. Or he got kidnapped by a deranged stalker. Perhaps he went on some kind of bender. Then I wonder if maybe some of his celebrity friends encouraged him to go out and celebrate the Dinky deal, or worse, he's on a call to Gaynor strategically planning our breakup. What if the paparazzi or some of his friends are warning him I'm only after his money and now he's had time to think, he's listening. After what my own dad wrote about me, he'd have every right to at least explore if I'm worth the risk. My stomach lurches as I think about living my life without him, and when I try rehearsing the things I need to tell him, I feel certain I'm going to throw up.

I thought I could handle anything, but I now realize I don't want to be without him.

I once told Tate I'd never beg him for anything, but I'm starting to realize that's not true. I don't care about his money, he can have every cent back, but I do want him. I want him so bad my body aches for him.

Tate's phone starts to ring, and noticing the caller ID, I answer it.

"Jason? Have you seen Tate? He hasn't come home."

"Jessie? Slow down. Where is he? Did you guys have a fight? He's not with me."

My stomach plummets. "He has my phone. I don't know where he is and when I called my phone, he didn't pick up."

What if something happened to him? I shudder. He's only been in my life for just over a month and already I can't imagine my life without him.

"All I know is he took a motorcycle from one of our security guys. Then about a half an hour ago I got a call to say Chuck Peters has retracted his interview. An apology will be printed in the papers tomorrow."

"That's weird. My mom said Chuck was stubborn and pig-headed. You think…"

"I think Tate might have had a word with your father."

The room starts to spin as I imagine all the spiteful things my dad could have said to Tate. What if they got in a fight or my dad had him arrested? What if he's turned him against me? The BabyMomma4You account would be the final nail in our coffin.

"Jason, I'm worried," I say.

"Jessie, it's going to be okay. He's an A-list movie star who doesn't know how to keep a low profile. We'll know where he is soon enough."

"Okay. Can you call me if you hear anything, please?"

"Of course I can, honey. Try not to worry. He probably

got caught up with a load of fans at a gas station and he'll be home soon."

I nod. "Yes. That's probably all. Thanks, Jason."

I'm about to hang up when Jason says, "Before I go, how's your mom?"

"My mom?"

"I sent her some numbers. A few people I know are interested in working with her."

"Oh. Well, she said she has a few options right now. She's super excited."

"Good," Jason replies. "And did she happen to mention anything about... me?"

Despite my unease, a smile at his cuteness tickles my lips. I like Jason, and I think Jason likes my mom. "She mentioned what a nice man you are," I say.

"Nice, huh?" I can hear the smile in his voice. "I'll make some calls and check on Tate. I'll speak to you soon."

I hang up then pour a glass of wine out of frustration and stare at it. My boobs are hurting and I swear there's no sign of my period. What if I'm pregnant and Tate is already done with me? Maybe he's better off without me. When I think of all the things I posted online, I feel sick.

"You going to stare at that glass all night or shall we share it?" Tate says, shrugging out of his jacket as he walks inside.

"You're home!" I say, feeling relieved and rushing to put my arms around him. When his hug is a little stiff, I pull back but pretend like everything is fine between us. He smells like cool night air and cologne and when he kisses the top of my head, I suddenly feel safe.

"Tate, I was worried. I didn't know if you were coming home."

He takes a step back, resting the palms of his hands on my shoulders.

"No way I would stay gone." His warm brown eyes fix on

mine and he says, "Earlier, you said you wanted to tell me something. What is it, Jess?"

The thought of hurting him twists like a knife in my gut. I rest my palm against his cheek and start by saying, "I'm sorry."

"What for?" His voice is almost devoid of emotion and it's scaring the shit out of me.

"I did something bad. Something hurtful and mean and… I thought at the time you deserved it, but really I was just lashing out."

He takes a deep breath and nods his head. "It's okay," he says. "I know. I know all of it."

"You know?" I check, wondering if he knows I trolled him, or if my dad made up some new stuff.

"So, it was you? *Triptastic Tate.* The photoshopped images of me with a diaper and the bus stop sign with the horns and black teeth. It was all you?"

My gut twists and I nod. I'm ashamed of myself. "How did you find out?"

He pulls my phone out of his back pocket and slides it into my hand. It feels like a bomb and I want to throw it against the wall and make anything I ever wrote disappear.

"I was angry," I say, the lump in my throat making it difficult to talk. "I thought you denied me and Macy and my heart was so filled with pain that I unleashed that hurt on you. And I'm so sorry, I should never have acted that way."

"The video of me running through LA with my ass out, was that you too?" he checks.

I shake my head. "That was all you I'm afraid."

"And the model who pulled my shirt off at the awards, did you arrange that?"

I laugh. "No, that wasn't me. I don't have access to models and honestly, seeing her so close to you shirtless, it drove me crazy with jealousy."

His expression is unreadable.

"I get it if you want to get rid of me now and finally end the charade of our fake-dating. I'll agree to whatever terms you, Jason, and Gaynor come up with to break us up. Your deal with Dinky is back on and you have a relationship with Macy. I'd never stop you seeing her. After the stories that have been sold on me, after what my dad said, I'd understand if you want to draw a line under everything. It'd be too hard for you to trust me now anyway. I guess those people selling stories on me is my karma for what I put you through. I'm just sorry I didn't tell you sooner, but I'm glad I managed to make it up to you in a small way by posing as your girlfriend."

Tears well in my eyes.

"Posing as my girlfriend," he repeats. "Is that how it felt, like you were posing?"

"No. When we were alone, every part felt real." Real as any measure of love I have ever felt.

"And that's what you want, is it? For me to walk away?" he asks, tilting my chin so that he can look in my eyes. Tears streak down my cheeks but I don't move. If this is the last time I get to stare into his eyes, I want to drag it out as long as I can.

I shake my head. "No. A breakup is not what I want. I want you. Since the start of all of this, I've been expecting things to go wrong somehow. I even prepared myself for it. It didn't seem right that I could feel so happy, not when deep down I knew that I'd hurt you."

"You've had hundreds of chances to tell me, Jess." He shakes his head, and fear that this is where he tells me it's over grips me.

"To begin with, I told myself you deserved it, but by the time I realized I was wrong it was too late and I had too much to lose by coming clean. I was going to tell you, when you asked me if I was sure I wanted to fake date you, but then Jason phoned and interrupted us and it seemed like it was going to be temporary anyway and so I let it go."

"You let us go, you mean? I've been all in with you but you've been holding back." He takes a step back and he feels further away than ever.

"I've been holding back? You've been planning my exit strategy with your people since the start."

"Exit strategy?"

"Your realtor found you some properties for me. After all, we can't have the baby momma slumming it in staff accommodation when the star of the show is living his best life in a fifty mil mansion—"

"Jess, I asked for advice on listings the night I found out about Macy. I couldn't tell anyone about us, and I needed to feel like I was doing something worthwhile for you both. But I quickly filed them away. No way I was going to plan an exit strategy when everything I wanted was sleeping beside me!"

"What do you mean?" I huff.

"I've been waiting for you to realize you want a life with me."

"But Jason and Gaynor, they said they were planning how to break the news of our breakup. I wondered if when you said you wanted forever at the restaurant that maybe you just got caught up in the moment. The next day, Gaynor said what a stroke of genius it was and I thought maybe it was part of the act."

Tate squeezes his eyes with his finger and thumb as though to make sense of what is going on. "Part of the act? Jessie, there's been no acting on my part, at least." He stares me down and I want to run away and castigate myself for being so spiteful. "I don't share every detail of my private life with my agents. I told you I wanted you forever and I meant it. What part of that sounded like I was making provisions for us parting ways?"

I think through all the conversations and Tate is right. At no part has he ever told them, at least not in my presence, that he wanted me to move out. Jason and Gaynor assumed things hadn't changed. That we still planned to end things once the Dinky deal was back on.

"Why didn't you come to me?"

Tears brew in my eyes. "Because the last time I went to a guy and asked him to commit to me he laughed in my face."

Tate takes a step forward and his palms rest on my shoulders. "I'm not like your father, Jessie."

"I know you're not. I was scared. Scared of hurting you. Scared of losing you. But most of all I'm scared of feeling this way about you and never finding the courage to tell you I love you."

"You love me?"

I nod and another tear trickles down my cheek.

"I knew you did."

A shallow chuckle passes my lips and I can't help from teasing, "Still got the biggest ego in Hollywood, I see."

"You're pretty for a troll, you know?" he counters, and then grabs my phone and scrolls the BabyMomma4You account. "So in this comment here," he angles the phone so I can see it, "someone is saying what a loser I am and you told them to shut the fuck up." I nod. "And here, you told someone if they didn't like my film, they should hold their breath until the next one comes out."

"We're family. I can say you're a big dope but no one else can."

He chuckles, and it's like a lifeline, a hint that he isn't leaving me, but then he says, "So you think I should walk away?"

I nod. "I hurt you."

"You'd let me walk away without a fight?"

The thought of him walking away hurts so much I cling to him like it might stop him. "Tate, I'm begging you not to end this. I love you. But how can you trust me? I betrayed you."

He scrunches his face. "At first I thought it was betrayal, but it's not. This was you trying to get my attention and it worked. Tell me, why, out of all the hotels and businesses in the world, did you choose to go and work at the Blingwood Resort? The same resort that is owned by my brother?"

"The benefits and—"

"And because you had a wild hankering to be a maid?" He cocks a brow at me.

"I don't know," I reply, but he's right. I chose to work at Logan's resort because it gave me the best chance I had of running into Tate.

"You sure you don't know? You claimed to hate me, yet none of the stuff you posted was cruel. You inserted yourself in my life as best you could, and now you're scared. You're offering me an out."

I shrug. "I'm being honest. No more lies."

"And what's the God's honest truth, Jessie?" he asks.

The answer suddenly seems obvious. "That maybe you could love me, that if I could just get your attention, then maybe you'd choose me. You'd choose us."

He nods. "You didn't hate me when you posted that stuff, you loved me."

"Yeah, well you loved me too," I reply and he smiles.

"Yes, I did."

Did.

"I'll see if I can stay with Betty for a while, until I figure something out," I offer and let go of him.

"Why would you do that?"

"The online posts, the betrayal. I let you down."

"You didn't let me down. Jessie, you were using your voice the best way you knew how. I finally know that for all that time we spent apart, you were thinking about me, like I was thinking about you. I don't care if you made some videos and posted some crap online."

Tate bursts into laughter.

"It's not funny! I'm a bad person."

"No, you're not. You're the best woman I know and you're perfect for me."

"How can you be so sure?"

"I knew as soon as I met you that you were the one. I sensed the shift within myself, but I was too blinded by my pursuit of a career in Hollywood. I'd spent so long telling everyone that I, Tate Blingwood, was going to make it, that my pride couldn't take failing. I left you in that motel room three years ago when I should have made sure you came along with me. It's me who betrayed you. I knew the feelings I had for you were big, and I was worried I wouldn't make it if I was distracted. I was scared. These past few weeks with you and Macy have been the most special of my life. The way your eyes light up when you laugh, the cadence in your voice when you're fighting for the people you love, your stubborn streak… you make my heart beat stronger. It's impossible for me to walk away now, Jessie. My heart can't beat without you."

Gratitude radiates through me like a fever.

"I'll never hurt you again," I promise.

Tate pulls me closer, leaning his forehead against mine. "You're the heart and soul of our family. I'll never again leave without kissing you goodbye. I'll make sure I'm never gone long enough for you to miss me too much, and I will never take for granted that I am owed or guaranteed your love. I'm going to work for you and our family and give you all the moon."

"Just a star will do," I reply.

Tate pulls me to sit on the sofa and he kneels between my legs; his expression is nervous like he's gathering all his courage. "Jessie, I'm not just telling you I love you because things are going great with my career and I'm pumped. I mean it. I've been staring at you for weeks and thinking it, now I need you to know. I love you. I am in love with you. I have been in love with you since the very first time I set eyes on you and I have never felt this way about anyone."

He's holding his breath, waiting for my response.

His vulnerability is both heart-breaking and beautiful. And it's like every emotion I've been holding back across years has suddenly surged forward, overwhelming me with its rawness. Tears are streaming down my cheeks but I don't wipe them away. I want him to witness the depth of my feelings, knowing he won't laugh, that he'll appreciate my truth.

"Baby, you got to say something," he urges. "I don't want to make you cry. I only want to make you happy."

I finally let out a sob and say, "I'm crying because I'm happy." My lips are trembling but still I smile. "I love you too. I wasn't expecting us to turn out to be so perfect together. I didn't believe I'd end up so happy, but I am. I'm happy with you and I know you'll never hurt me. I feel it," I say, pulling his hand against my heart.

Tate leans into my kiss and his lips press against mine. Slow and tender, he kisses me then wraps his arms around me.

"And so, the grumpy troll and the dashing prince finally get their happy ending?" he jokes, resting his head against mine.

"I'd prefer we recount the story to Macy as, the lovely princess finally got woken from a deep slumber by the prince with the big… ego," I reply, looking in his eyes and feeling like I have indeed woken up to the feelings that were there all along.

He kisses me tenderly and agrees, "And now we get to rule this town as king and queen of Hollywood."

CHAPTER 24

TATE

*T*he air in the downstairs bathroom of our house is thick with anticipation as Jessie hovers over the pregnancy test like it holds the secrets of the universe. She's done her part, and now we wait. Macy sits on the floor, eyeing the stick with a mixture of curiosity and mischief. If I've learned anything from parenthood so far, it's that nothing is sacred, not even the bathroom.

"We're going to find out if we're getting a baby," I tell Macy, pointing at the test. "I bet you'd love a little brother or sister." The more we talk about it, the more I think if we're not pregnant, we should start trying.

I wrap my arm around Jessie and kiss her temple. "I'm going to take care of you all no matter what."

"We're going to take care of each other. Family, right?" she replies and I fist bump Jessie's waiting hand and then kiss her deeply.

"I'm so excited." I pace. "Is it time to look yet?" I ask and Jessie hands me the stick.

She already explained to me how this went down last time for her. Jessie in a gas station bathroom, on her own, a scared twenty year old. She knows this time is going to be different.

I can't keep from smiling at her as I lift the test and squint at it like it's written in a foreign language. Is that a second line? Or just a smudge? Anticipation sets in and my hands shake with excitement.

Macy, sensing the tension, decides now is the perfect time for a heist. With the stealth of a ninja, she grabs the stick out of my hand and bolts from the bathroom. "Macy, no!" Jessie and I shout simultaneously, chasing after our little escape artist.

She runs right through the living room and out the front door, giggling like it's a fun game of chase. The paparazzi camped outside our gate spot the commotion and immediately put down their donuts and start snapping pictures. Macy, thinking she's the star of the show, waves the test like it's a victory flag.

I catch up to her just in time to see her hand the test to a bewildered paparazzo. "Congratulations, Tate. It seems three are about to become four, or more." He snaps a picture of the test before handing it back to me.

I check the test, turning it around in my hand and then showing it to Jessie.

"That's positive, yes?" I check. Suddenly I don't know which way is up. There are two little red lines and even a word that says "pregnant" but I'm so scared of getting my hopes up, I forget how to read.

Jessie's smile lights up and she nods. "It's positive. I'm pregnant."

I exchange a happy, bewildered glance with Jessie, who

looks just as stunned as I feel. Macy, oblivious to the chaos she's just unleashed, beams proudly. "Baby," she chirps, pointing at the test.

The paparazzi erupt into excited chatter, and suddenly we're the unwitting stars of a parenting sitcom. Jessie and I stand there, dumbfounded, as Macy basks in the attention.

"Well, I guess the secret's out," Jessie says, a mix of laughter and disbelief in her voice.

"Breaking news, courtesy of our daughter," I reply, shaking my head. "I suppose it's cheaper than a two-page announcement in the *New York Times*."

"Do us a favor, guys," Jessie says to the paparazzi. "Can you give us a day's grace so we can tell our families first?"

"You'll pose for a photograph?" one of the guys asks. I think it's the guy I throat-chopped, but thankfully he doesn't seem to hold grudges.

I check with Jessie and she nods and then we open the iron gates and scoop Macy up onto my shoulders so we can pose. I pull Jessie into me and wrap my arm around her and whisper, "I love you."

"I love you too," she replies and we both smile like it's the best God damn day of our lives.

* * *

A FEW DAYS LATER, a visit to our families, and an appointment with the doctor and the news is settling in. And I have never been happier.

"Ladies and gentleman, welcome to *The Now Show* with your host, Emma Dean."

The live audience go crazy as Emma walks onto the set, giving her intro and announcing that I'm today's guest. Then she sits on the couch beneath the studio lights, tells some short anecdotes of today's news, like the single mom from

Santa Barbara who just made her first million selling sex toys on social media after her channels blew up overnight.

I grin at Jessie. She attends most of my interviews now as a part of my social media team. She beams with pride for her mother and then gives me a thumbs up indicating it's time for me to go on stage.

"Welcome to *The Now Show*, Tate."

"It's a pleasure to be here," I reply and smile at camera four.

"So, the big news in Hollywood is that the movie you filmed for Tripod, your latest release, *Galactic Futures* went Box Office number one!"

I grin my damned face off.

"It's been a crazy couple of months," I reply.

"And you just signed a franchise with Dinky," she adds.

"Yes. A dream come true for me. I can't wait to get started."

"But the real news that's trending and what all my viewers are dying to hear, is how is your love life?"

I grin again, knowing that they already heard we're expecting another child. I wonder if I should play it coy and make Emma work for the story, but really I'm too excited to hold back.

"It's better than ever. I'm in love with the woman of my dreams, who keeps me on my toes and makes me feel alive, and we're going to have another baby."

The crowd goes crazy and when I look for Jessie, who is standing behind camera two, my heart fills with love and I throw her a wink.

"So, Tate, how did you know Jessie Yates was the one?" she asks, and I look right across the studio at Jessie as I answer.

"Well, she had my arm bent behind my back. My face was down on the gravel, in a puddle, and she was yelling at me to hurry up and submit already." I chuckle, remembering the mud wrestling match when we first met.

"No, but seriously, Tate, when did you know?"

My eyes are on Jessie. She's still smiling, remembering it too.

"It was the first time she smiled at me."

The audience clap and holler and Emma grins.

"You heard it here first, guys. Tate Blingwood got swept away by a smile. What was your first impression of her?"

"Picture this," I say and Emma leans in. "She walks into a mudwrestling ring and declares herself tribute after none of the guys apparently wanted to take me on. Her golden locks slightly windswept after a day at the beach, wearing mismatched socks, and I'm thinking: 'Wow, she's beautiful, like heart-stopping, don't know if my eyes can survive looking at her, beautiful.' And I'm wondering if she's either crazy or if I'm about to get taken down."

"What happened?"

"She walked right up to me, and I swear my hands were shaking, and she…"

"What did she do?"

"She flung her leg right out in a hooking and decapitating move, taking my legs right out from underneath me until I was facedown on the ground, then she jumped right on my back, pulled my arm behind me and told me straight, 'you're going to admit defeat right now or I'm going to break your arm.'"

"Wow. She really took you out," the host says chuckling. "That's one way to bag a man, ladies."

"Not me though, I'm off the market and also a little terrified."

"I bet you are! It's good to see *Triptastic Tate* has hung up his wrestling gloves. Now, your character in the movie does some pretty epic grand gestures. Are there any you recreated?"

"Just one that I'd like to try, if you don't mind humoring me?" I ask and Emma nods, raising an eyebrow like she's intrigued even though I already gave her the heads up in the green room before we came on stage. "I'm going to need a glamorous assistant. Jessie, get your butt up here."

She gestures to herself, shaking her head.

"Oh yes, baby," I say. "It's time for the world to meet the woman who stole my heart."

A cameraman gives her a little encouragement and she walks on stage to the applause and wolf whistles of the audience.

When she reaches the set of two couches and a coffee table, looking radiant, I grip her hands, and then pull a rose out of the vase on the table and hand it to her. Then I get down on one knee.

Everyone in the audience is screaming, but when I look in her crystal blue eyes, it's like it's just me and Jessie in the room.

"I think we're getting to the good part," Emma says chuckling

I pull the ring box out of my pocket and the audience is suddenly silent. "I thought now might be a good time to show the whole damn world what we have is the *real deal*. I want everything official so there can be no doubt who I love. Who my heart belongs to. Will you make me the happiest guy in the entire world and say yes. Jessie Yates, will you do me the honor of becoming my wife?"

The silence is suddenly deafening. When I planned it, it seemed romantic and I wanted to tell the world how much I love this woman before me, to let everyone know just how much in love we are, to show everyone that no one can hurt us, but as I kneel here waiting for her answer, I suddenly fear that maybe it's too much. Too soon. Too public.

She blinks away tears, and then my heart swells when she begins nodding vigorously. The audience erupts into cheers and she holds out her hand so I can slip the ring onto her finger. I kiss her hand. My legs are shaking but I manage to stand.

"You sure?" I check.

"Yes! Tate Blingwood, I will marry you!" she says loudly enough that the audience must hear because suddenly they are on their feet clapping. Beside us, Emma is unable to contain her happiness as she joins in the applause.

I swoop Jessie up into my arms and say, "Ladies and gentleman, meet the love of my life and my future wife, Mrs. Jessie Blingwood."

I latch my mouth onto hers and seal the deal.

"My family. My wife. She is my life," I announce loudly in case they didn't hear at the back.

EPILOGUE – ONE MONTH LATER

JESSIE

The California sun beats down on us as we gather around the barbecue. The smell of grilled burgers and the rhythmic laughter of children playing in the pool create a soundtrack of a perfect summer day.

Everyone we love is here. My sisters, Drew and Callie, playing on giant inflatables in the pool with Macy. Betty and Bob who bicker as they try to teach Gaynor to play poker. My mom relaxing and chatting with Jason at one of the tables, a glass of champagne in hand. Tate's mom and Skyla who are throwing a ball on the lawn for the dogs, Cindy and Yogi. Logan and Layla are holding hands, laying on the day beds, soaking up the sun. While Tate and I stand by the grill, chatting with his sister Tabitha.

I call the kids in for dinner, and Uncle Drew blows raspberries on Macy as he carries her out, making it a fun game as he wraps her in a plush towel.

We have seating set out for twenty people and enough food for fifty on the oversized grill Tate bought especially for today's family gathering. He and I serve the food on enormous platters and above our heads, the paparazzi's drones fly about—which has taken some getting used to and has meant Tate and I have had to treat outside "fun" like an elaborate game of hide and seek to avoid the press.

With the food laid out, and my sisters complaining that they are starving, while taking selfies and dropping not-so-subtle hints that they'd like to attend Coachella next year, in the VIP section of course, the rest of our gang start loading plates.

Ding. Ding. Ding. Tate knocks a spoon against a beer bottle. "While we're all together, I'd like to make an announcement," he says and everyone stops their chatter. "Me and Jessie," he pulls me up and wraps an arm around my waist, his hand cupping my abdomen, "would like to thank y'all for coming to our barbecue. As you know we're all family now so we'll be hosting these events all the time. Mom, Logan, Drew, Tab's, I know you never thought you'd see the day I'd be a settled man, but my Macy," he points at her and pulls a silly face that makes her smile light up and she giggles, "Daddy!" in response, "my Jessie, and our little bean, have made me the happiest man in the entire world. I just wanted everyone to know that."

Our family and friends around the table all applaud as Tate kisses my temple and whispers, "I love you. And I can't wait to get you alone."

"You got me alone twice this morning," I whisper back.

"I know. Still can't believe my luck that Macy slept in. I'm hoping for a hat trick." He winks and excitement shoots through me. Then he turns back to everyone and announces, "Enjoy the food!"

Everyone immediately starts loading their plates and the noise returns to a rabble. Betty threatens Bob with a fork for the last pork chop and my sisters argue among themselves, and then Callie announces, "Dad, don't you and Skyla have an announcement to make?" She's grinning like a Cheshire cat, while Drew and Skyla share a glance like they're wondering if they should make their announcement. They seem to agree and then Drew pulls Skyla up onto her feet and slips his arm around her waist. "Actually, there is some news we'd like to share. My wife," he kisses Skyla's cheek, "and I are going to be providing Callie with a brother and Macy with a cousin in around five months."

"No way!" I stand and rush Skyla, flinging my arms around her. "I get to go through this with you too." My eyes fill with moisture and I blink away happy tears. Tate high fives Drew and tells him, "Way to go, dude!"

Everyone claps and cheers and little Macy smiles then takes a bite of her chicken.

"Actually, while we're all here," Logan says, standing and pulling Layla up onto her feet. "There's an announcement we'd like to make."

I glance at Tate and then at Layla in a gaze that's one hundred percent, "Holy crap, you're not pregnant too," and then Layla announces, "I'm three months along!"

The feeling at the table is like nothing I've ever felt before. A sense of deeper connection to a family I feel like I've always belonged to.

"Well, this is certainly going to spice up the family tree!" Betty says with a cackling laugh, pulling her wine glass up to clink it against Bob's before taking a sip.

"No way, I get to be an aunty two extra times and a big sister!" Callie adds, her voice taking on a deep, emotional tone. "I'm going to have to start behaving, I guess," she jokes, and Drew squeezes her shoulder and says, "You're already the best role model these kids could wish for. We're all really proud of you."

When I check how Cassandra is reacting, I see big, fat

tears drip from her chin. "I can't believe it. You all made me the happiest mother and nanna alive." My mom leans across the corner of the table and gives her a congratulatory hug and I see Jason check out my mom's butt so I immediately look away.

"I'm so happy for you all," Tate says before adding, "but you all know I'm going to be the coolest dad."

Logan's nose wrinkles. "No chance, buddy. I'm going to be way cooler than you."

Tate shrugs off Logan's suggestion. "I've already got one kid. I've had practice, no way you'll trump me at being a dad."

"Callie's thirteen now. I've had the most practice, and I'm going to be way cooler," Drew argues.

"Okay, boys! Why don't you all sit down and eat your food. You can recommence your urination contests later!" Cassandra says and then wipes her eyes. "I can't believe my sons are all having babies." Her eyes brimming with pride.

As the sun starts to set in the sky, and my sisters ramp up the play system to party proportions, I ask Tate if he wants a beer and he declines, "I could murder for a coffee," he says and offers to make us both one.

"I'll do it," I say and when I come back and hand him the cup, he looks at me surprised.

"Best Dad in the World," he says, reading the words on the cup that all those years ago I took to my biological father.

"This cup finally has a righteous home," I say and he wraps his free arm around me. "I mean it, Tate. You're an amazing father and my perfect partner. I want you to know how much we appreciate you. You're all the daddy we need."

His gaze turns dark. "Oh baby, I think your giving me a new kink. First the mud wrestling, then the maid uniform… now *Daddy*." He winks and my insides warm.

"You're insatiable," I say chuckling.

"You make me insatiable."

Tate puts the coffee down, pulling me close and kissing me tenderly.

"You warm enough?" he checks.

"Toasty," I reply.

"You happy?" he asks.

"Happier than I ever knew I could be," I say, looking into his warm brown eyes and feeling like I have it all.

"Are you disappointed that you decided to put off going back to college for another year?"

"What's another year when I have the life I dreamed of?" I say, wishing I could check that one thing off my list but I know I'll get there eventually.

"Actually, maybe you don't. I spoke with the college. They have a day care facility and my work days will be flexible with the franchise. Between me and you, my mom, your mom, and Betty, not to mention all the aunts and uncles, you could do it. If you feel you want to. You can take only a few classes at a time. You don't need to do full semesters if you don't want. I want you to have everything, Jessie. No corners cut. Anything you want, I want to give it to you."

I think through what he's saying. Can I balance finishing my degree with motherhood? With this kind of support around me, it seems plenty doable.

"Yes. I do want to go back to college. And with everyone's support, I know I can do it."

Tate's eyes shine with emotion as he stares back at me and says, "Jessie Yates-soon-to-be-Blingwood, there is not a thing in this world you can't do if you put your mind to it. I was falling before I met you, and you caught me. And I'm so grateful. You didn't just save my career, you saved me."

"You saved me, too, Tate. I love you. Macy loves you." I cradle my belly. "Little bean loves you. We're a family. And I didn't even need to bend your arm behind your back to force you to submit to me this time."

Tate laughs. "You know, I let you win that day."

I laugh. I took him out fair and square. "Rematch?" I suggest.

"I would…," he starts, "but probably shouldn't… you know… the baby."

I poke my tongue out and reply, "Sure. The baby." Then I wink. "If you're scared…"

"Hey, I'm not scared. We're having that rematch right after you recover from the baby."

I nod, satisfied. "Don't worry, baby. Maybe I'll let you win this time."

He shakes his head. "I already won. I got you and I love you." He tips his chin down and presses his lips against mine, and I realize I won too.

I hope you enjoyed this book.
Most people don't leave reviews, but if you can spare 5 minutes I'd be so grateful. I appreciate your time and I read each and every review!

Check out my other books HERE.

ACKNOWLEDGMENTS

To Randie Creamer, the best editor and friend a girl could wish for! Thank you for your relentless pursuit of perfection and all your encouragement, love and support!

Kari March who designed my fabulous covers for this series. I love them. Thank you!

Ellen Montoya, I'm eternally grateful for your support. We're friends for life now and I can't wait until the next time we meet!

To Sandi, the book loving pole dancer! You're a kind, fun soul and I adore you. Thank you!

To Ana Rita Clemente, my sassy, Portuguese friend! You have a heart of gold and I adore you <3

And to my readers, thank you for buying my books, for every review, share on social media and for telling your friends! I'm so humbled at the love I have been shown and forever grateful that because of this love I get to do the best job in the world.

THANK YOU!
XX

ALSO BY EMILY JAMES

The Blingwood Billionaires series

Book 1—Sorry. Not Sorry

Book 2 – Chasing the Wrong Bride

Book 3 – Catch a Falling Star

The Love in Short series

Book 1—Operation My Fake Girlfriend

Book 2—Sexy With Attitude Too

Book 3—You Only Love Once

Book 4—Leaving Out Love

The Power of Ten series

Book 1—Ten Dates

Book 2—Ten Dares

Book 3—Ten Lies

ABOUT THE AUTHOR

Emily James is a British author who lives on the south coast of England. She loves to travel and enjoys nothing more than a great romance story with a heart-of-gold hero. On the rare occasions that she hasn't got her nose in a book, Emily likes to keep her heart full by spending time with her bonkers yet beautiful family and friends.

Facebook
Goodreads
Amazon
Newsletter

Printed in Great Britain
by Amazon